Indy looked around, tilted his head, listening. Something was wrong. He heard a distant squealing. It was getting louder, closer.

Then he saw the glow of the firelight dancing across the walls of the catacomb. A moment later, he saw the rats. Thousands of them squirmed through the narrow passage, stampeded into the chamber, and headed toward the stone platform.

Within seconds, the rats washed over the platform and caskets, a squirming, squealing tidal wave. Then Indy saw what they were scurrying to escape. An enormous fireball roared around the corner—it was feeding on the oil slick and depleting the oxygen, an elemental monster devouring everything in its path. It was spreading across the chamber and heading toward them. . . .

INDIANA JONES AND THE LAST CRUSADE™

Harrison Ford   Sean Connery
Denholm Elliott   Alison Doody
John Rhys-Davies   Julian Glover
and River Phoenix

Music by
John Williams

Executive Producers
George Lucas and
Frank Marshall

Story by
George Lucas and
Menno Meyjes

Screenplay by
Jeffrey Boam

Produced by
Robert Watts

Directed by
Steven Spielberg

A Lucasfilm Ltd. Production
A Steven Spielberg Film
A Paramount Picture

INDIANA JONES
and the
LAST CRUSADE

Rob MacGregor

BALLANTINE BOOKS ● NEW YORK

All rights reserved under International and Pan-American Copyright Conventions. Published in the United States of America by Ballantine Books, a division of Random House, Inc., New York, and simultaneously in Canada by Random House of Canada Limited, Toronto.

Library of Congress Catalog Card Number: 89-90716

ISBN 0-345-36161-X

Manufactured in the United States of America

First Edition: June 1989

"The problem of the hero going to meet the father is to open his soul beyond terror to such a degree that he will be ripe to understand how the sickening and insane tragedies of his vast and ruthless cosmos are completely validated in the majesty of Being. The hero transcends life with its peculiar blind spot and for a moment rises to a glimpse of the source. He beholds the face of the father, understands—and the two are atoned."

Joseph Campbell
The Hero with a Thousand Faces

"One can easily imagine how I felt: suddenly to see in a modern city, during the noonday rush hour, a crusader coming toward me."

Carl Jung
Memories, Dreams, Reflections

UTAH: 1912

CHAPTER ONE

◄◄　►►

DESERT CHASE

The troop charged across the desert, their horses thundering beneath them, a cloud of dust billowing in their tracks. They rode hard and fast, as if to escape the sun, which had peaked over a barren mountain. It was already casting harsh beams of light across the arid landscape, and soon the desert would be baking.

Just ahead was a rock formation, and under it was a labyrinth of caves. The uniformed riders reined in their horses as they saw their commander raise a hand.

"Dis-mount," he shouted.

A rider with a thatch of straw-colored hair was the first one off his mount. He glanced around at the troop members. From a distance, he thought, they probably looked like a company of army cavalry soldiers. Up close, he conceded, it was another matter. Even his best effort to imagine them as soldiers failed. It was pretty obvious they were just a scout troop. Except for Mr. Havelock, none of them was over thirteen.

He watched as a pudgy kid tottered away from his horse. He knew the kid's name was Herman but didn't know him well. He had heard a couple of the other kids say that Herman had trouble at home. He wasn't sure what kind of trouble, but it was obvious that he was also having problems right here. He bent over, wobbled, and looked as if he was going to pitch forward onto his face. Finally he stopped, braced his hands on his knees, gagged, and vomited.

Everyone around him roared. They elbowed each other and pointed at the pathetic scout.

"Herman's horsesick," one of them yelled.

"Yeah, and he wet his saddle, too," another howled glee-fully.

The blond scout, whose uniform was dressed with a Hopi woven belt, walked up to Herman and asked if he was okay. There was a look of concern and understanding on his face and not a trace of ridicule. It was obvious that he was more mature than the others, and no one dared say a word as he led Herman away.

Mr. Havelock yelled for the boys to follow him with their horses. They led their mounts toward the rocks and left them in the shade of a massive boulder. The boys grouped around the scoutmaster as he explained that the original caves were natural formations and were the home of a primitive people. There was also a legend that Spanish conquistadores explored the caves, and it was well known that during the last century miners had opened new passages in their quest for gold. "Now, don't anybody wander off. Some of the passages in here run on for miles." As the troop fell into step behind their leader, the scouts mumbled under their breath. "This better be good," one said.

"Yeah, the circus arrives today," another murmured. "We could be watching them pitch the tents."

They climbed a trail leading up the rocks. It was hot, dusty, and steep. Everyone was too caught up in the ascent to pay any attention to Herman or the blond kid who brought up the rear of the line.

A minute or so later they stepped inside the mouth of the cave. It was cool and dark, and the boys complained they couldn't see. Mr. Havelock lit his lantern and assured the scouts their eyes would quickly adjust to the dim light. They continued on, following a well-traveled route.

Even though he was at the tail end, the blond scout was the most attentive of the troop. It almost seemed as if he were sensing what the place was like when it was inhabited by an ancient people. As the troop turned a corner, he suddenly gripped Herman by the arm.

"Ssh. Listen."

Herman caught his breath. He glanced around uneasily, wondering what had caught his new friend's attention.

Another trail branched off from the one they were on, and from deep within the dark passage they heard voices. They were faint, but distinct. The blond boy signaled Herman to follow him.

"Come on. Let's take a look."

Herman glanced back in the direction the troop had gone. He seemed uncertain about what he should do, then made up his mind and scrambled ahead.

"Okay, Junior, I'm coming."

Spiderwebs tangled in their hair. The passageway was darker and cooler and obviously not well used. "Where are we going?" Herman called out.

The blond kid—Junior—turned, touched his index finger to his lips. The voices were louder now. The walls ahead were suddenly illuminated, and hulking, ghostly shadows danced across them. The two boys pressed against the wall. They held their breaths as they edged slowly forward.

Then Junior spotted four figures digging with shovels and pickaxes. He knew immediately that these were no ghosts. He was sure they were thieves, and he knew what they were doing. According to legend, the Spanish had buried treasure here.

His father was a medieval scholar who taught at the university. He knew all about the legend, and a lot of other things, too. He had tried to get his father to come along today and tell the scouts about the history of the caves and the ancient people who used to live there. But, as usual, his father was too busy to be bothered with a bunch of kids. Besides, he said, North American archaeology wasn't his field of expertise.

Junior looked over the four men as well as he could. One of the men was smaller than the others, and now he could see that he wasn't a man at all. He was a kid, and he wasn't much older than they were. But he looked pretty tough.

"Roscoe, hold the lantern up," one of the men snapped at him.

The man who had spoken was dressed in a leather jacket with fringes. He wore a hat with the rim turned up on one side, and he looked like a Rough Rider. The man on the other side of Roscoe had thick black hair that cascaded over his shoulders. An Indian. No. A half-breed.

The last man was on the far side of the other three, and in shadows. He wore a leather waist jacket and a brown felt fedora.

Junior moved soundlessly ahead a couple of steps to get a better look. He signaled Herman. He heard him breathing loudly and glanced back to quiet him. Herman's mouth was open, and sweat was pouring down his forehead.

I hope he doesn't puke again. Not here.

Herman's foot slipped on a loose stone. It made a soft, crunching noise, and Herman slapped the wall to regain his footing.

Junior hunkered down low, trying to make himself as small as possible, trying to blend in with the shadows. Herman followed his example.

"Sorry," he whispered.

Junior winced and shushed Herman with a wave of his hand.

The man with the fedora turned slowly, raised a lantern, and looked their way. They could see his face now for the first time. "Thought I heard something," he muttered, then turned his back again.

The boys were frightened, yet mesmerized. They watched with rapt attention as Fedora poured water from his canteen over a mud-shrouded object. In the light of the lantern Junior could see that it was a gold cross encrusted with precious jewels.

Fedora's buddies leaned close. "Look at that! We're rich!" Roscoe shouted.

"Pipe down. Not so loud," Half-breed chastised.

"You wait. Soon enough. That little darling is gonna fetch top dollar," Rough Rider said in a hoarse whisper.

Fedora turned the cross in his hand, silently appraising its beauty and value. He seemed aloof from the others, somehow superior to them.

Junior touched Herman on the shoulder, unable to contain his excitement and concern. "It's the Cross of Coronado!" he whispered. "Hernando Cortés gave it to him in 1520! It proves that Cortés sent Francisco Coronado in search of the Seven Cities of Gold."

Herman looked baffled. "How do you know all this stuff anyhow, Junior?"

Junior shifted his gaze toward the men and watched them a moment longer. "That cross is an important artifact. It belongs in a museum. And, do me a favor, don't call me Junior."

"That's what Mr. Havelock calls you."

"My name's Indy."

He hated being called Junior. It made him sound like a kid in short pants. But his father just ignored him whenever he mentioned the matter of his name.

They watched a minute longer, and Indy's demeanor hardened into a look of resolve as he reached a decision. He turned to Herman. "Listen, run back and find the others. Tell Mr. Havelock that men are looting the Spanish treasure. Have him bring the sheriff."

Herman didn't look as if he was listening. His mouth was moving, but no words came out as he stared wide-eyed and horror-struck at a snake that was slithering across his lap.

"It's only a snake," Indy said as he matter-of-factly picked it up and tossed it aside. "Did you hear what I said, Herman? It's important."

"Right. Run back. Mr. Havelock. The sheriff." He nodded and gazed past Indy toward the men. "What are you going to do, Jun . . . Indy?"

"I don't know. I'll think of something. You better get going."

Herman dashed along the passageway, retracing his steps, as Indy returned his attention to the thieves. They had set the cross aside and were busy searching for more artifacts. Slowly Indy worked his way along the wall until he was within an arm's length of the cross. Even in its tarnished state, its jewels sparkled in the lantern light and captured his attention.

He reached out, grasped it, and as he did, saw a scorpion clinging to the cross. He tried to shake it off, but the deadly creature seemed to be glued to the cross. He cursed under his breath, still shaking his hand. The scorpion dropped off, but he'd given himself away.

The thieves turned as one, spotting him. "Hey, that's our thing," Roscoe shouted. "He's got our thing."

"Get 'im," Half-breed yelled.

Indy hurtled blindly down the passageway, clutching the cross, his heart hammering against his ribs. He glanced back once, to see one of the thieves stumble and fall and two others crash into each other as they tripped over him. He stopped a moment as he reached a chimney the gold miners had cut into the ceiling. Faint rays of light filtered down through it, and a rope hung down to within a couple of feet of his head. He looked back to see if they were going to let him go. But no such luck. He saw Fedora cast a disgusted glance at his companions and bolt down the tunnel after him.

Oh, damn. He tucked the cross under his belt and leaped for the rope. He missed, tried again, and grasped it with one hand, then the other. He worked his way up the chimney, hand over hand along the rope, and from one foothold to the next. He saw Fedora and the others race by, and felt relieved. He could take his time. A moment later, he felt a tug on the rope and looked down. Fedora had backtracked and was deftly scaling the chimney.

If only his father were here, Indy thought as he struggled to reach the top. Dad would take care of those guys. He imagined his father pointing an accusatory finger at the thieves and the men shrinking away. Yeah, he'd do something like that.

The light was getting brighter, and finally Indy reached the top. He gasped for air as he crawled from the chimney into brilliant daylight. He paused, squinted, and shielded his eyes as he caught his breath. He glanced about in every direction. He realized he was standing on a boulder not far from where they had entered the cave.

"Herman! Mr. Havelock! Anybody! Where are you?" He shook his head. "Damn, everybody's lost but me."

"Here we are, kid."

Indy turned and saw Rough Rider, Half-breed, and Roscoe scrambling up a rocky trail toward him. He ran toward the edge of the rock and spotted a ladder sticking up. Instead of climbing down, he quickly calculated the distance to the next boulder. He charged the ladder, pushed off, and vaulted the gap.

The three thieves raced to the edge of the rock and stopped abruptly. They glanced around in confusion, wondering how to catch him.

Indy, meanwhile, had reached the far side of the next boulder and was uncertain what to do. This time there wasn't any ladder, and the ground was twenty feet below him. Then he saw the horses resting in the shade, where the scout troop had left them. He placed two fingers in his mouth and whistled for his steed. The horse shook its mane and trotted over.

Indy glanced back and saw Fedora charge past his companions and leap the chasm. Once he was on the other side, he paused long enough to look back at the others with obvious disdain. Then, shaking his head, he pushed the ladder over to them.

Indy crouched, preparing to drop into the saddle, but the horse wouldn't stand still. He hesitated, but heard footsteps. "Stand still, boy," he yelled. "Don't move. Good boy."

He leapt, and at that moment the horse pranced ahead, and Indy missed the saddle. He landed on his feet and rolled over, breaking his fall. The impact jolted his body, rattling him from his heels to his teeth. The cross dropped from his belt into the dust. He scooped it up, shoved it in the saddlebag, and mounted the horse.

As Indy galloped off, he glanced back to see Fedora standing at the edge of the boulder watching him. He grinned, kicked the side of the horse, urging him on. He had to get to the sheriff as quickly as he could so the thieves wouldn't get away.

Fedora put two fingers in his mouth and whistled. None of the horses moved. Instead, two automobiles roared out from behind the next rock outcropping. One of the autos, a convertible, circled around and skidded to an abrupt stop beneath Fedora, who immediately vaulted from the boulder into a cloud of dust. As the air cleared, the car pulled away with Fedora perched on the top of the backseat.

He adjusted his hat with an expression of satisfaction, and yelled, "Giddyup!"

The driver prodded the gas pedal, and the car surged rapidly ahead. The second car lagged behind, as the driver waited for Roscoe, Rough Rider, and Half-breed to catch up.

Indy raced across the desert, cutting through the dry air as cleanly as a blade through butter. The sun blazed down without sympathy, scorching the earth, baking him into the saddle.

Behind him the two automobiles were rapidly closing the gap.

The desolate mountain in front of him wasn't getting a bit closer. It seemed as if the horse were galloping in place. The only things moving were the cars, which were pulling up on either side of him. He felt like a sandwich, and he and the horse were the meat.

Indy glanced to his right and saw a man in a Panama hat behind the wheel of a cream-colored luxury sedan. He wore an expensive white linen suit, and his face was concealed by the wide brim of his hat. In the window of the backseat Roscoe grimaced and shook his fist at Indy. As the driver reached toward his leg, Indy spurred his mount and for a moment gained a few feet.

His extraordinary effort was useless, though. The autos quickly regained the slight margin he had achieved. They were not only keeping pace with him, but were squeezing in on him like a giant vise on wheels. Only the hot wind and the dust separated him from the speeding vehicles. Indy crouched low and leaned forward in the saddle, intent on escaping. His heart pounded, his adrenaline pumped, and he flew forward.

On his left, Fedora climbed over the side of the convertible and stepped onto the running board. Indy looked down into his face. The man grinned up at him as if to let him know he was enjoying the chase. Then, he sprang gracefully onto Indy's horse.

But Indy was just as quick and equally as daring. Before Fedora could reach him, he hurled himself onto the hood of the sedan to his right. He landed on his knees, braced himself by hanging on to the edge of the roof. Rough Rider and Roscoe crawled out the windows and were reaching for him when Indy suddenly realized that he no longer had the cross. His head snapped toward the horse; he spotted the cross hanging half-out of the saddlebag.

Fedora, however, was unaware that the cross was within inches of his hand. He looked irritated and leapt on top of the sedan. He thrust an arm toward Indy, but Indy bounded back onto the horse, avoiding his grasp and slipping away from Rough Rider and Roscoe, who knocked heads as they lunged for him.

Indy pulled back hard on the reins, slowing the horse as the two automobiles sped past. Inside the shroud of dust, he veered in a new direction and galloped toward the railroad tracks, where a train was quickly approaching. Behind him the autos swung into wide turns and resumed the chase.

As Indy reached the tracks, the train was barreling alongside him. There was something odd about the train, he thought. The railcars were a blur of color rather than the usual brown and gray. But he didn't have time to consider it because the two autos were catching up to him. He had only one choice.

He tucked the cross into his belt, rose up in his saddle, and grabbed on to the ladder of the nearest railcar. He started to climb to the top, but changed his mind when he spotted a nearby window that was open. He clutched the side of the car like a spider and worked his way toward it. He glanced once over his shoulder, to see the autos pulling up to the train.

Indy reached the open window and tumbled through it. He landed on something soft, voluminous, like a bed of marshmallows. But it was a human marshmallow. He sank into rippling, undulating folds of flesh. He pulled away and realized his head had landed in the copious cleavage of an immensely overweight woman.

Startled and embarrassed, Indy jumped up. The massive woman was seated on a wide bench large enough to accommodate her four hundred—plus pounds. He backed away, smiling. He heard someone laughing and spun around. His jaw dropped open.

Gawking at him were a host of the strangest looking people Indy had ever seen in his thirteen years. There were pinheads, a bearded lady, dwarfs, a rubber man, a boy with flipper feet.

Of course. It was the circus train headed for town.

"Ah, hello. I hope you don't mind me dropping in like this." He kept turning around as he spoke. "I couldn't really help it. I had a horse, but ah . . ."

He stopped as a dwarf approached him. "You mean you jumped on the train from a horse—like a circus trick?" The man spoke in a tiny voice that matched his size.

Indy smiled. "Yeah, I did."

"I didn't see any horse."

"He's lying," someone else said.

"I bet you want to join the circus," the dwarf said, poking him in the stomach.

"He's too normal looking," the rubber man groused.

"Leave the kid alone," said the bearded lady, running her fingers through the hair on her face.

The dwarf, who was eye level with Indy's belt, leaned forward and examined the cross.

"What's that?" he asked, frowning a little.

"Oh, nothing."

"Can I have it?"

"No." He said it too quickly, too loudly. "I'm taking it to a museum. That's where it belongs."

"A museum," the dwarf repeated. "Uh-huh. I bet."

Indy sat down on a box so the dwarf would stop eyeing the cross. He figured he would slip off the train when it passed near his home. Once they were in town, the thieves wouldn't dare bother him. They would be too afraid of getting caught. If they tried anything, he would just yell for help. And once he got to the house, he would explain everything to his father.

It was going to be okay, he told himself. His father would be proud of him. He was always complaining about people who looted archaeological sites. And now his son, Junior— Indy, I'm Indy—had caught four of them red-handed.

He felt someone tapping him on the shoulder, and he turned to see the dwarf, who was now nose to nose with him. "I've got another question."

"What's that?" Indy asked.

The dwarf pointed past him. "Did he come on a horse, too?"

Indy jerked around and saw Fedora staring at him through the window.

CHAPTER TWO

◄◄ ►►

CIRCUS TRICKS

"Making new friends?" Fedora asked with a grin.

Indy stood up and started backing away. "Yeah, sure am." He kept his eyes on Fedora but spoke to the others. "Watch out for this man. He's a thief."

Fedora climbed in through the window and tried to squeeze around the fat lady.

"Now just a minute," she said, pushing herself to her feet and blocking Fedora's way. "We don't want your kind on this train."

Indy seized the opportunity and charged for the door at the end of the car. He pushed through it and leapt onto a flatcar. In the center of it was an impressive calliope with rows of shiny steam whistles rising behind a pearly keyboard. He ducked around it and glanced back to see Fedora crashing through the door with the bearded lady clinging to his throat. Fedora threw her off and vaulted onto the flatcar.

Indy grasped a lever on the side of the calliope for support, but the lever moved and the calliope burst into life. Steam and noise blasted from the pipes. Fedora's companions, who had boarded the flatcar from the auto, stopped in their tracks and covered their ears against the horrendous off-key honks and squeaks. They staggered back and were nearly blown from the train by an explosion of steam.

Indy, meanwhile, scrambled to the roof of the next car and clambered along it until he reached a trapdoor. He threw open the lid and lowered himself onto a catwalk suspended from the ceiling of the car. Several feet below were numerous vats that

13

looked as though they contained every species of snake, lizard, alligator, and crocodile. It was a virtual Noah's Ark of the reptile world.

Indy stared into the vats, fascinated and horrified. The last thing he wanted to do was end up down there. His only hope was that the others would somehow miss seeing the trapdoor and would keep going to the next car. But the moment he thought it, the door flew open and Half-breed and Roscoe dropped down onto the catwalk.

Now what?

Indy scurried toward the rear of the car, wondering what he was going to do when he reached the end of the catwalk. No matter how brave and strong he thought he might be, he knew he wouldn't be able to handle both of them. Hell, Roscoe alone could be trouble. He was the sort of kid who would fight dirty, would do things like give up and then jump on you when your back was turned.

He noticed a second trapdoor above him at the end of the catwalk. Great. He'd slip out before they cornered him. Sure. It'd be a cinch. But before he could take another step, a metallic screeching sound pierced the air. The catwalk started shaking. He looked up, and dread filled him like a poison gas. Their combined weight was too much for the structure, and one of the bolts holding it to the ceiling had begun to pull loose. The catwalk was slipping and swaying, threatening to dump them into the vats of slithering reptiles.

The three of them froze in place, fearing that a single step would send them tumbling. Indy glanced up at the trapdoor. It was a step away, and there was a handle next to it. He could grab it, swing up, kick open the door, and swing out onto the top of the car.

And then what, hotshot? The other two thieves are probably waiting up there, Indy said to himself.

He didn't know what he would do, but there wasn't time to think about it.

He crouched and leapt for the door handle. His fingers grazed it, but he couldn't get hold of it. He landed off balance on one foot and grasped the railing. The catwalk swayed beneath him, and he heard a series of loud cracks as several bolts suddenly tore free. Roscoe and Half-breed screamed, but it was Indy's side of the catwalk that dropped. He plunged to the floor of the car, landing with a heavy thud on a raised wooden platform.

For a moment he didn't move. He was afraid he had broken something—his legs, maybe his arms, maybe even his neck. But worse than the fear that he had broken a limb was the darkness. He couldn't see. Panic bubbled in his throat, and a scream slid down his tongue—but then he realized he'd squeezed his eyes shut when he fell. He laughed softly to himself, but as he opened his eyes, his laughter turned weird, desperate, almost a cackle. He was eye to eye with an enormous anaconda.

The head of the snake was so huge that it looked more like Tyrannosaurus Rex than a snake. Its tongue darted out and flicked against his cheek. An icy chill raced down his spine, his eyes widened in horror. He rolled over, bolted to his feet, and edged backward.

He was afraid that if he looked away from the anaconda, it would attack him. He wasn't watching where he was going, and one foot stepped off the edge of the platform. He wobbled a moment, then tumbled backward. He landed softly; he wasn't hurt. But then he realized where he was—he had fallen into a vat of snakes.

Hundreds of writhing reptiles were suddenly sliding under and over him. The roiling mass engulfed him like quicksand. Only it was worse than quicksand, much worse. He was smothering. The snakes were sucking away his breath, his life. Once, when he lifted his head from the wiggling nightmare, he glimpsed Half-breed and Roscoe struggling to stay on the dangling catwalk above him.

Roscoe clung to Half-breed's leg, but the dark-haired thief wanted no part of the kid. He reached for the trapdoor and shook his leg, attempting to rid himself of Roscoe, who cried out, terrified that he would plummet into the jaws of one of the carnivorous crocodiles snapping below them.

Then the snakes covered Indy again, and he lost sight of everything. But he didn't give up. He was fighting for his life. Snakes were piled below him as well as on top of him, and that kept him from regaining his footing. So he did the only thing he could do: he kicked against the wall of the vat.

After several kicks at the same spot, the side of the vat cracked open. With all the energy he had left in him he kicked again. This time the wall gave way, and the wiggling mass of snakes suddenly slid out the side, taking Indy along for the ride.

He leapt up, gasping for breath. He jerked snakes off his shoulders, his legs. He would never feel the same about snakes again. Above him he heard the screech of metal and curses, as the two thieves struggled to get through the trapdoor. But his focus now was on a door in the floor that was probably used when the car was cleaned out.

Indy snapped open the door and was immediately bombarded by the pounding din of the cars speeding over the rails. The tie beams of the tracks blurred below him. He hesitated —his father would kill him if he knew what he was about to attempt. Bad enough that he'd leapt onto a moving train from a horse and had fallen into a vat of snakes, but now he was going to attempt the impossible.

But he wasn't about to stay in the car with snakes and gators. And there was no other way out. Besides, he had to get away from these thieves.

He took a deep breath and lowered his head through the door. A steel bar ran the length of the car. He reached down and touched it with his hand. It was warm but not hot, and it was just high enough above the tracks to accommodate him as long as he kept the bar close to his chest.

Only ten feet. That was all the distance he had to crawl.

And ten feet isn't impossible, is it? I can crawl ten feet. I know I can, Indy told himself.

Carefully he lowered himself through the door, gripping the steel bar first with his hands, then with his arms and legs. He inched forward; the clatter of the train vibrated through his body, threatening to shake him from it.

Oh, shit. What did I do this for?

He told himself to concentrate. He knew that as long as he concentrated and used every ounce of his strength, he could do it.

I'm going to make it. I'm going to make it. He said it over and over again as he pulled himself forward.

Finally he reached the end and realized he hadn't figured

out how he was going to get off the bar. The front of the car extended a foot or so beyond the end of it. Maybe if he just stayed where he was, he'd be okay.

But how long could he hold on before his arms would tire? The vibration was already jolting him to his bones.

He thought a moment about the cross tucked beneath his belt. If it slipped out and smashed on the tracks, all his efforts would be useless. He let go with one hand, and carefully reached forward to the end of the car. His fingers patted the lower edge of the front wall, feeling for something to grasp. But he didn't find anything.

Then he remembered the safety cable that connected the cars below the coupling. Where was it? He extended his arm as far as he could reach. His fingers touched something, then slipped off. He tried again, and this time he grabbed the cable.

Now what?

He was stretched between the cable and the bar and he had to go one way or the other. He was momentarily paralyzed by indecision. Which way? Does it matter? He closed his eyes, let go of the bar with his other hand, and reached blindly for the cable. He grasped it and slid his feet along the last inches of the bar. Then his legs were dangling in midair, and he was pulling himself forward, hand over hand. He opened his eyes and saw the coupling above him. He hooked his arm over it, then swung a leg up as if he were mounting a horse. He had done it! He was riding atop the coupling between two cars.

He pulled himself forward toward the next car. It was virtually a cage on wheels. Inside, behind the bars, was a huge Bengal tiger. He reached up to the nearest bar, stood up on the coupling, balancing himself. Then he climbed to the outside of the cage.

He edged his way along the narrow outer skirt of the car by holding on to the cage. He stopped once as he felt something crawling along his leg. He wriggled his nose as he reached into his pants and pulled out a snake. He readjusted the cross under his belt and moved ahead.

The tiger paced back and forth inside the cage, watching him. Indy stared back. As he neared the front of the cage, the tiger paced closer and closer. He crouched down to rest, hoping the massive cat would ignore him. Even though the bars were between him and the tiger, a swipe from the creature's paw through the space between the bars would be deadly.

What he didn't realize, though, was that another sort of danger was literally around the corner. Rough Rider had worked his way along the opposite side of the cage and was inching across the front now. Like the tiger, the thief had fixed his eye on his prey.

Indy was staring at the tiger, mentally telling it to back off, when a hand clamped on his neck.

"Gotcha!" Rough Rider shouted.

At that moment the tiger lunged at the bars. He thrust his paws out, raking his claws across Rough Rider's shoulder and back, shredding his jacket. The thief yelled out in pain and surprise and grabbed his shoulder. He tottered a moment, then fell from the train.

Indy glanced back, to see Rough Rider rolling along the railroad bed. He turned toward the front of the car, and a fist sank into his stomach knocking the wind out of him. He doubled over, gasping for breath, certain he was dying. He looked up, to see Roscoe hovering over him.

"Girl Scout." The kid sneered and drew back his fist to punch him again.

But Indy slammed the heel of his boot down onto Roscoe's foot. He poked him in the eye and bit his hand. The kid yelped in pain, and Indy scooted past him. He fled to a neighboring stockcar and climbed up a ladder to its roof.

Roscoe quickly recovered and cursed Indy as he climbed behind him. Indy had just reached the top when Roscoe grabbed his ankle. He fell to the roof, and the two boys grappled, rolling perilously close to the edge.

The rattle of the rails pounded in Indy's ears as he saw Roscoe raise a knife in the air. The tip of the blade glinted as Roscoe thrust. Indy rolled over just in time to avoid the plunging blade. He crawled away, but Roscoe scrambled after him, tackling him as he tried to rise to his feet.

Whatever was in the boxcar beneath them must have been huge, Indy thought, because every time he or Roscoe moved, something pounded against the side of the boxcar, shaking it. But he didn't have time to ponder that matter. He was too busy trying to stay alive.

"Gimme that cross!" Roscoe shouted, flashing the blade in the air over Indy. "Right now!"

Indy grabbed Roscoe's wrist, bending it back, trying to get him to drop the knife.

Suddenly a rhino horn slammed through the roof's wooden slats, missing Indy's head by inches. He rolled to one side, and Roscoe's wrist slipped free. Indy pushed him away, but Roscoe lunged for him, stabbing the knife at his throat. Indy jerked his head, and the blade slammed into the wood, just missing his ear.

As Roscoe struggled to loosen it, the rhino struck again and this time his horn went right between Indy's legs. Roscoe pulled out the knife and thrust it at Indy's midsection. Indy saw it coming down, saw the blade gleaming in the light. His legs shot out and slammed into Roscoe's chest, throwing him back. Roscoe faltered a moment, arms pinwheeling for balance, and barely avoided falling off the car.

Indy rolled over onto his stomach and looked back just in time to see Roscoe hurtle the knife at him. It probably would have slammed into his face, but at that instant the rhino horn burst through the roof next to Indy's head and the blade struck it.

Indy stumbled to his feet and saw a water tank alongside the tracks directly ahead. Its spout was facing the tracks and protruded above the train. He suddenly knew how he could get away. He ran to the side of the car, calculated the distance, and timed his leap.

He caught the spout perfectly, but the train's velocity caused the spout to swing rapidly around the water tank. He hung on, closed his eyes, and finally, as the spout slowed, he let go. He only dropped a couple of feet and realized he had spun completely around. He was back on the train! This time he landed on the roof of another stockcar and immediately collided with Half-breed, who was knocked off his feet.

Indy reeled backward, dazed by what had happened. But what happened next confused him even more: he fell through an opening in the roof.

Dust flew up around him as he struck the floor. Rays of sunlight leaked through the cracks in the boards, but it took a moment for his eyes to adjust to the dim light. He smelled a heady animal scent in the air, and his nose twitched. Then he saw the source of the odor. In the opposite end of the car an African lion was slowly rising to its feet. Obviously it was intent on investigating the creature who had dropped into its den.

The lion roared, and the stockcar walls seemed to shudder. Dust swirled in shafts of sunlight around the lion as it stalked him like prey.

"Oh, boy." Indy gulped as he backed away toward the corner of the car.

He saw a glint of light reflect off something on the floor and suddenly realized what it was. The cross had dislodged from his belt when he fell, and now it lay at the lion's feet.

He glanced around and continued stepping back until he felt the rear wall of the car against his spine. He pressed his hands against the wall as the lion continued stalking him, preparing to make a deadly pounce. His right hand struck a nail. Under it he felt something leathery. He snapped his head around, thinking it was another snake. Instead, it was a whip —a lion tamer's whip.

He carefully took it down by its handle. The lion recognized the whip and growled softly. Indy swallowed hard and gave the whip a snap. It unraveled awkwardly, its tip flying back and striking him across the face, cutting his chin.

The lion growled louder.

Indy quickly gathered up the whip, wet his lips, and tried again. This time it cracked sharply, as it was supposed to, as he'd heard it crack at the circus when the lion tamer circled the king of beasts, whip in hand.

The lion bellowed, swatted the air, and snarled, then backed off. He knew from experience what the crack of the whip meant.

Indy grinned, amazed and delighted by his feat. He cracked the whip again, and the lion backed away even more. Indy inched forward until the cross was just in front of him. The lion stood its ground about ten feet away. Slowly, Indy bent over. Never taking his eyes off the lion, he picked up the cross.

Then he stepped back and realized his hands were shaking

and sweat was pouring down his face. He took a deep breath of musty air, exhaled, gathering his wits. Now, how was he going to get out of here?

He looked up at the opening he had fallen through and saw Fedora looking down at him. Fedora nodded to him, smiled, and extended a hand.

That was all it took. Indy decided he would rather face Fedora than remain a minute longer caged with the lion. He tossed one end of the whip toward the hole, and Fedora snagged it.

Fedora slowly reeled him in as Indy walked up the side of the wall. He looked back once, to see the lion crouched and ready to pounce if he fell. He quickly turned back and concentrated on getting out.

When he reached the edge of the hole, Fedora clasped his arm and pulled him out, depositing him on the roof. Indy dropped to his hands and knees. He was breathing hard; he was exhausted. The lion had finally taken the fight out of him.

"You've got heart, kid. I'll say that much," Fedora said. He pointed at the cross. "But that belongs to me."

Indy looked up to see that he had more company. Half-breed and Roscoe were also there. He stared at Fedora. "It belongs to Coronado."

"Coronado is dead. And so are all his grandchildren." Fedora reached out, turning up his palm. "Come on, kid. There's no way out of this."

"Yeah, fork it over," Roscoe barked, then grabbed at the cross. Indy clung to one end of it, refusing to let go. A tug-of-war ensued. In the middle of it, a snake slithered out from Indy's shirtsleeve and wrapped around Roscoe's hand.

"Get it off me," he screamed. He let go of the cross and shook his arm until the snake was flung away. The lion roared beneath them. Indy took advantage of the momentary diversion and darted between Half-breed's legs and bounded onto the next car. Half-breed was about to give chase, but Fedora motioned him to wait.

"Stay put! Don't let him double back." He turned and headed after him.

Indy scurried down the ladder between two cars and entered the caboose. The car was full of costumes and magic equipment. He looked around for a place to hide. He heard Fedora coming down the ladder and slipped out of sight.

Fedora walked calmly into the caboose and surveyed the car. He strolled over to a large black box and casually pulled off the cover. One by one the four sides of the box flopped away, revealing nothing.

He smiled confidently when he saw the top of another smaller box move slightly. "Okay, kid. It's all over. Come on out."

He opened the box, and several pigeons flew out, scattering about the caboose. He was getting fed up with this elusive boy. He pawed his way through the costumes and magic gear. He picked up a cane and prodded into the corners, but the cane wobbled and turned into a handkerchief. "Damn it. Where the hell . . ."

Then he saw a couple of the pigeons fly out the rear door of the caboose, which was swinging in the breeze. Realizing what had happened, he rushed out onto the rear balcony. The train was slowing as it neared its destination, and in the distance he saw Indy disappearing down a street of modest clapboard houses.

CHAPTER THREE

◄◄ ►►

THE HOME FRONT

Out of breath but still carrying the Cross of Coronado, Indy charged into his house. He quickly locked the doors and raced from the kitchen to the living room, peering out windows. The street was clear.

He hurried through the hallway and ducked into another room to check outside again. He squinted into the sunlight. He could still taste dust in his mouth. Water, he thought. He wanted a big, tall glass of ice water. But first things first. His father. He needed to talk to his father.

"Dad?"

There was no answer, but Indy knew his father was in his study. Ever since Indy's mother had died, it seemed his father lived in his study, forever hunched over old books and parchments. The ancient past was more real to him than the present.

Just look at the house, Indy thought. The rooms said it all: no feminine touches, nothing soft, no color, just books and old things everywhere. He was the only one who cleaned the house. Sometimes Indy felt as if his father had abandoned life beyond his study. That was the only place his father's presence was real to him.

He opened the door to the study. Books spilled off shelves and were piled on the floor. The walls were covered with maps of ancient lands and pictures of wonderful old castles and cathedrals. In one corner was a rusting helmet that a knight had once worn. Everything in the room seemed to possess meaning, even if Indy didn't know what it was. All of it reflected a passion for medieval European studies.

Indy cleared his throat. "Dad?"

Behind a heavy, dark mahogany desk, his father, Professor Henry Jones, was absorbed in his work. Papers and books were strewn around him. Indy stared at the curve of his father's back, willing him to speak, to nod, to acknowledge him in some way. He knew his father had heard him, but the fact that he didn't greet Indy, didn't even turn around, meant he didn't want to be disturbed.

He never wanted to be disturbed.

Still, this was important. He neared the desk, glimpsed the ancient parchment his father was working on, and said, "Dad, I've got to talk to you."

"Out!" Henry snapped at his son without even turning to look at him.

"But this is really important!"

Henry continued with his work. "Then wait. Count to twenty."

"No, listen. . . ."

"Junior," Henry warned, his voice low and threatening and stern.

Indy gulped, nodded, and took a deferential step back. He knew his father was annoyed with him. There was little he could do. He started counting in a faint voice and, as he did, looked over his father's shoulder.

He saw that the top page of the parchment revealed an illustration of what looked like a stained glass window containing several Roman numerals. His father was busy copying the drawing in his notebook.

"This is also important . . . and it can't be hurried . . . it's taken nine hundred years to find its way from a forgotten box of parchment in the Sepulchre of Saint Sophia in Constantinople to the desk of the one man left in the world who might make sense of it."

". . . nineteen . . . twenty." *This is really important. Pay attention to me.*

Indy pulled the Cross of Coronado out of his shirt and started talking fast and loud again. "I was in the cave with the scout troop and . . ."

"Now do it in Greek," Henry commanded, still not turning from his work or listening to his son.

He never listens to me.

Indy hated him for that.

In a louder, angry voice, Indy began counting in Greek. He imagined each number was a curse word that he hurled at his obstinate father.

He heard a car stop in front of the house. He backed out of the study, still counting, and spotted a police car.

Now what should I do? He realized that if his father saw the police there, he'd think Indy had gotten into trouble again. He wouldn't even give him a chance to explain. He knew that from experience.

He glanced back into the study at his father, who was still working on his sketch. He listened as his father spoke softly to himself.

"May he who illuminated this, illuminate me."

Indy held his breath as he carefully closed the study door and stepped into the hall. He jammed the cross back under his shirt as the front door swung open, and Herman stumbled, out of breath, into the living room.

"I brought him, Indy! I brought him!"

The door opened again, and the sheriff entered the house and looked around.

"Sheriff, sir! There were five or six of them! They almost got me, but . . ."

"All right, son." The sheriff held up a hand. "Do you still have it?"

"Yes, sir. Right here."

Indy pulled out the cross again and handed it to the sheriff, who casually took it without even bothering to look closely at it. As the cross left his hand, Indy sensed something was wrong about the way the sheriff was acting. If he only knew what he had gone through.

"That's good, boy. That's good . . . because the rightful owner of this cross said he wouldn't press charges against you if you cooperated."

Indy did a double take. His jaw dropped. His fingers curled into fists. "Press charges . . . What are you talking about?"

Fedora walked into the house and removed his hat. He nodded to Indy in a friendly manner and patted Herman on the head.

"Theft," the sheriff said. "He's got witnesses, five or six of them."

The sheriff and Fedora were in cahoots. What else could it be? The lawman wasn't even going to listen to him. He didn't care about what really had happened.

"And we wouldn't want your mama turning in her grave, would we now?"

The sheriff handed the cross to Fedora, who put it into the leather pouch that hung from his hip. As the sheriff walked away, Indy glanced through the screen door and saw a cream-colored sedan, the one that had chased him through the desert. It was parked behind the sheriff's vehicle and was coated with a thin layer of desert dust. Behind the wheel, waiting patiently, was the man in the Panama hat.

Fedora lingered behind after the sheriff was gone. When he spoke, it was in a man-to-man tone that was laced with irony. "Well, you lost today, kid, but that doesn't mean you have to like it."

He took off his fedora, held it a moment by the crown. Then he took a step forward and extended it as if he were about to place it on Indy's head as a show of respect and admiration. But he checked himself as Indy spoke up.

"The Cross of Coronado is four hundred years old, and it still has a long way to go. I aim to be around. You can count on it."

Fedora grinned, dropped the hat on Indy's head, and turned away. "I'll tell the boss," he said, and laughed.

He stopped a moment at the door and looked back at Indy. "You were good with that whip today, kid. I like your spunk."

Indy kicked the door, slamming it behind Fedora.

He heard Fedora chuckling as he walked down the sidewalk.

He ran to the window and saw Fedora slide into the cream-colored sedan, the cross in his hand. He saw him pass the precious artifact to the man behind the wheel and watched them drive away.

He would get that cross back, he swore to himself as he touched the brim of the felt hat. He would do it no matter how long it took.

AT SEA: 1938

CHAPTER FOUR

◄◄ ►►

ATLANTIC CROSSING

Thirty-foot waves crashed across the deck of the old cargo ship, washing away everything that wasn't tied down. Rain whipped it from every side. Wind howled. The old cargo boat's wood shrieked as though it were being yanked apart at the seams. It was a hideous sound, the sound of a thing in pain, and Indy couldn't block it out.

He clung to the edge of his bunk, certain that in the next second, or the one after that, a wave would slam through the wood, crushing it, and sweep him away. He squeezed his eyes shut as the storm hurled the ship to the right, the left, the right again. Now it was slammed down at the stern. Now it was flung backward. Now it rolled, it rocked, it rose and fell.

I'm going to puke.

But when his eyes flew open, the press of the dark against his porthole took his breath away. Then a wall of water crashed against the side of the ship, smeared against the glass, and the impact threw him out of his bunk. He smacked the floor and for a second or two just lay there groaning.

Get up, man. Make your move now.

Right. His plan. He had a plan, didn't he?

He lifted himself up on his hands, shook his head to clear it, and grappled for a hold on anything that wasn't moving. On your feet, mate. Now. Make your move now while the captain's on the bridge.

Yeah, the captain. The captain and the cross. Got it.

He gripped the edge of his bunk and pulled himself to his feet. He buttoned his leather jacket with one hand, tugged his

29

fedora down tightly over his head, made sure his bullwhip was secure at his waist, and reeled toward the door.

Forward, mate.

Right foot, left, right foot again. Good, real good. He was going to make it to the door and then outside onto the deck and then down the deck to the captain's quarters. Where the cross was.

Indy had booked passage on this cargo ship after receiving a tip on the location of the Cross of Coronado. A man had called his office at the university and told him that if he was interested in the cross, he should meet him in Lisbon, Portugal. When he had questioned the caller, he had accurately described the man Indy had seen only once when he was a child—the man who had taken possession of the cross, the man he had pursued for years.

When Indy asked what he wanted for the information, the caller had said he was only after revenge. The man with the cross was his boss, and only recently he had found out the man was having an affair with his wife. The tip—and the justification—seemed reasonable to Indy, and he had a few days available. He had followed leads that were far less substantial, and this one sounded like the break he needed. He had narrowly missed catching the man whose trademark was his Panama hat several times, but he hadn't had a lead for a couple of years.

When he arrived in Lisbon, his informant told him the cross had been moved and that he should wait until further notice. Eight days passed, and he was ready to give up and return to the States. He was already late for the new semester of classes. That day his informant contacted him and told him the cross was being sent on a cargo ship to the United States the next day, and the captain of the vessel had been entrusted with it.

Now Indy was on the ship, and this was the first chance he'd had to search the captain's quarters. With weather like this, he was certain the captain would be on the bridge.

First and maybe the only chance, mate.

He flung the door open, and the wind lashed him. He moved against it, one hand holding the fedora down on his head, the other gripping the doorjamb.

The ship rolled to the left; Indy rolled with it and nearly lost his footing. He had to let go of the fedora to grab on to the other jamb, and the wind whipped up under the hat's brim and swept it off his head, back into his room. He left it. He leaned into the wind, into the thickness of it, and made his way out onto the deck, slamming his door shut behind him.

The ship lifted onto the crest of a wave, its tired wood moaning and screeching, and Indy grabbed on to the railing, waiting for the boat to slam down. When it did, water rushed across the deck, almost jerking his hands from the railing. It was over in seconds, and he thrust himself forward, hand over hand, pulling himself through the violence. The wind howled around him. The taste of salt coated his lips and stung his eyes until they were barely slits.

The captain's on the bridge, and it's now or never.

He kept moving. The storm tossed the ship around like a piece of driftwood. He thought of the cross. The cross burned through his mind, brighter than mercury, hotter than the sun. After a while he no longer felt the wind or the storm or the rolling of the sea. He moved as the ship moved, as though he were a part of it, one with it. His legs seemed sturdier, more certain. He found new strength. The image of the cross in his head burned and burned.

By the time he made it to the captain's quarters, he was soaked to the bone. Water ran in rivulets down the sides of his face. Salt was thick against his lips, his tongue. He took out a long, slender tool, like an ice pick but made of a more malleable metal. It was a tool used by thieves, not archaeologists. He gripped the doorknob and held his hand as steadily as possible. He pushed the tip of the tool toward the lock, but the boat swayed, and his arm lurched about like a symphony conductor waving a baton. He tried again, and this time stabbed himself in the wrist.

Damn it. He shook his hand. Steady. Steady.

He made two more efforts before finally inserting the tool in the keyhole. He eased it into the lock, gingerly prodding and jiggling it until it was fully inserted. He took a deep breath and carefully turned the doorknob. He smiled as it opened.

The moment he was inside, the door slammed shut, blocking the din of the storm. He looked around, making sure he was alone. Then he headed straight for the captain's bunk. The lamp on the wall flickered, blinked out, on, and the ship rolled onto its side. He grabbed on to the edge of the bunk and held on until the vessel righted itself again.

His informant had assured him that the captain would keep the cross in the ship's safe. He had not only told him where the safe was located but had even handed him a scrap of paper with the safe's combination. When Indy asked him how he'd gotten it, the man smiled and told him not to question his good fortune.

He was wary about the guy. He didn't like him. But this was the best lead he'd had in years, and who said you had to like everyone you work with?

Now he would see just how good his fortune was. Maybe the whole thing was a hoax.

He dug his hands under the mattress and lifted it. The safe was there, all right, built into the floor, beneath the bed. He grasped the bed frame and shoved it aside.

So far, so good.

The next question was whether he could open it. If the combination didn't work, he wouldn't be any closer to the cross than if he'd stayed home. He twitched the dial back and forth, getting the feel of it. He had memorized the combination—he turned to the first number, then followed the sequence of five more numbers.

He paused a moment when he was finished, then slowly turned the arm. The safe opened. It was dark inside. He reached blindly into it. He felt a couple of boxes, jewelry boxes no doubt. His fingers ran across a packet of papers. He reached beneath them and felt an object wrapped in cloth—in the shape of a cross.

He pulled it out, growing increasingly excited. He untied the knot in the string that bound it, then unraveled the cloth. It was the Cross of Coronado. He hadn't forgotten its beauty, but the sight of the precious artifact still stunned him.

It felt cool and heavy in his hands. It felt right. He tucked it under his jacket, inside his belt, in almost the exact same spot where he had hidden it twenty-six years ago.

He closed the safe, spun the dial, and pushed the bed back

into place. Once he was outside again, the place where the cross rested against his wet shirt seemed warm, thick, protected. He was giddy with relief and fatigue and a sense of triumph. Twenty-six years, you bastard, he thought. Twenty-six years.

Something gnawed at the back of his mind, something he couldn't focus on, something important. He tried to seize it, to scrutinize it, but he was so tired and the wind was so loud and . . . later, it'll come to you later.

Then he looked up and saw a burly sailor staring sullenly at him from the end of the corridor. He turned and saw another at the other end. Suddenly he understood.

A setup. No wonder it was so damn easy. No wonder the informant had the combination. It was all too easy. That's what had bothered him.

The sailors rushed forward from either side. He was about to throw a punch, but the boat swayed, and he stumbled back right into the arms of the second sailor. They pinned his arms behind him and dragged him to the end of the corridor and onto the deck. Then a third figure stepped out of the wet shadows and punched him in the gut.

Indy gasped. He felt his legs crumpling. One of the sailors held him up and jerked him to the right, under an awning that offered some protection from the storm. And that was when Indy saw him, the bastard who had punched him. It was a man clutching a Panama hat to his head, the same man behind the original theft, and the one no doubt behind the setup. He was older, but even in the dark Indy could see his icy blue eyes glowing like twin moons.

"Small world, Dr. Jones."

"Too small for both of us. I see you haven't changed your style a bit," he commented, glancing up at the Panama hat.

"How observant. I seem to have seen your favorite attire somewhere myself. But let's get down to business."

The man grabbed his jacket with such force that Indy thought the leather would rip. He reached into Indy's belt and removed the cross. "As you know, this is the second time I've had to reclaim my property from you, but it's no coincidence that we meet here tonight."

"I know. You set me up."

"You're the fall guy, Dr. Jones."

He told Indy that he was well aware of his persistent search for the cross, the prize of his collection. Ever since the Depression had weakened his financial base, he had been attempting to sell it. Finally he had been offered a sizable sum that would end his economic woes. The catch: the arrangement included a stipulation that the pesky Dr. Indiana Jones must be disposed of before the transaction was completed.

"So I decided to arrange for you to come to me. I played fair. I even gave you one more chance to steal the cross." He grinned at Indy. "Too bad you were caught again."

"That cross belongs in a museum."

"So do you." He glanced at the sailors. "Throw him over the side."

Indy was propelled across the rolling deck toward the rail. As they passed a bundle of fuel drums, he saw his chance to take advantage of the storm. Using the sailors as leverage, he kicked up his feet and broke the clamp on the metal bands that held the drums together.

Suddenly the drums were loose and careened wildly across the deck. Indy jabbed his elbows into the stomachs of the startled sailors and rushed toward his nemesis.

Panama Hat saw him coming and lurched toward a ladder that led up to the bridge. But before he could reach it, a huge fuel drum crashed against the ladder, blocking his path. The drum started to roll back toward him. He leaped to the side, and as he did, the cross flew out of his grasp and skittered across the deck.

Indy pitched forward toward the cross, but one of the sailors blocked his way, then swung a crowbar at his head. He ducked just in time, then let loose a powerful uppercut that caught the sailor under the jaw. The man reeled backward just as a wave slammed against the deck.

Indy looked around frantically for the cross, and spotted it several feet away. He threw himself at it and slid across the deck on his stomach, arms extended like wings. He snatched up the cross just as another wave crashed against the deck, burying him in water.

He slid a few more feet and saw a giant fuel drum rolling toward him. He pushed off from the deck, but lost his footing.

An instant before he would have been crushed, he dived and rolled, and the drum thundered past.

He looked up to see several more drums rolling his way. He leapt to his feet and sidestepped them all. That was close. Just then, he turned and saw another sailor brandishing a stevedore's hook and moving his way.

He unhitched the bullwhip from his hip and flung his arm forward. The whip cracked. It struck its mark, wrapping around the sailor's ankle. He jerked on the whip, and the rolling ship did the rest: the sailor crashed to the deck.

Indy paused to admire his nifty work. At that moment a net dropped over his head, and Panama Hat pummeled him with his fists. The man took pleasure in his work, beating him hard and fast, again and again. Indy tried to dodge the punches, to ward them off with his arms, and to escape the net, but it was no use.

All the drums that Indy had dodged when they rolled from port to starboard changed direction as the ship began to list the other way. Now they trundled back in his direction, and this time they were also headed for a large stack of crates near him marked TNT—DANGEROUS.

Indy shouted as one of the drums bore down on him. Panama Hat turned, saw the drum, and tumbled across the deck. Indy jerked away in the other direction, barely avoiding the drum.

He struggled to pull the net away from him, but the cross was tangled in it. The only way to escape it would be to drop the cross, and he wasn't about to do that. He looked up just in time to see another fuel drum rolling directly toward the explosives.

There was only one thing to do, and he did it. He hurtled himself over the side into the stormy seas.

The moment he hit the water, the ship split apart in a fiery blast. Bits of debris rained from the sky as if they were part of the storm, and what remained of the ship quickly sank beneath the waves.

The concussion of the water and the blast tore the net away from him. He tumbled about in the water and finally bobbed to the surface like a piece of cork, still clutching the cross. His legs kicked frantically as he tried to keep his head above water.

He grabbed for something to hold on to, went under, surfaced again, coughing and spitting out water. His hand found something—a preserver, one of the ship's doughnut-shaped life preservers. He hooked one arm, then the other, through it.

Then he saw something else floating by that looked familiar. He reached out and snatched it and held it up to his face. He recognized it as the shredded remains of a Panama hat.

In the distance an American freighter sounded its horn. Indy waved his arm, hoping to get the ship's attention, and realized he was waving the cross in the air. He wondered how the hell he would explain it. I'm a priest. I saved the cross. The cross saved me.

What the hell did it matter? He wanted to laugh and to cry at the same time. He knew, damn it, that he was going to make it. And, hey, he had the cross.

NEW YORK : A
FEW DAYS LATER

CHAPTER FIVE

◄◄ ►►

ON CAMPUS

The warm spring afternoon had drawn students outside in droves. Young women in calf-length dresses and men in ties strolled along the tree-shrouded brick paths that twisted through the campus, past ivy-covered brick buildings. Books were bundled under their arms, pencils rested behind their ears, and none of the young people seemed to be in any hurry.

A black raven soared silently above the students and landed on a window ledge on the second floor of one of the ivy-covered buildings. Inside, a professor wearing a tweed jacket and wire-rim glasses glanced toward the window, momentarily distracted by the bird, then turned back to his class. The students stared attentively, waiting for him to continue.

Despite his professorial attire, there was an underlying ruggedness about him, a sense that when he took off his coat and tie and ventured out into the field in search of ancient artifacts, anything could happen and probably did. It was this mysterious air about him—as well as a certain shyness—that appealed to the coeds who seemed to dominate his classes. For his part he never complained about the profusion of attractive young women who showed up for his lectures.

Those who knew him well were aware that he tended to understate his own experiences. Maybe it was because he felt he lived in the shadow of his famous father, the renowned medieval scholar, Dr. Henry Jones. Whatever the reason, he tended to say one thing about himself and his career but at the same time told you in other ways—gestures, sly looks, and hidden smiles—that what he was saying was only part of the story.

He looked out over his class, hands jammed in the pockets of his pants. ". . . So, forget any ideas about lost cities, exotic travel, and digging up the world. Seventy percent of all archaeology is done in the local library. Research and reading— that's the key. We don't take mythology at face value, nor do we follow maps to buried treasure and *never* does X mark the spot! The Lost Continent of Atlantis! Knights of the Round Table! Nothing more than charming, romantic nonsense."

He paused a moment, feeling the weight of the jewel-encrusted gold cross that was resting in his coat pocket. He looked down, scratched behind his ear, and continued. "Archaeology is our search for *fact* . . . not *truth*. If it's truth you're interested in, ladies and gentlemen, Dr. Peterman's philosophy classes are a good start."

The class laughed, and Professor Indiana Jones glanced at a pretty coed seated in the front row and smiled. He cleared his throat. "Next week: Egyptology. Beginning with the excavation of Naukratis by Flinders Petrie in 1885. Irene, my secretary, has the list of assigned reading for the semester." Expecting a rush of students to the podium, he added: "If you have any questions, please see me in my office."

As the students filed out, Indy gazed toward the back of the lecture hall, where Marcus Brody, director of a prestigious archaeological museum and longtime friend of his father, waited for him. He stepped around the podium and headed down the aisle.

Brody, who was discernibly English, was about sixty, a man who was incessantly caught between the tallies of the museum's accountants and the whims of wealthy contributors. He had told Indy more than once that he saw him as a light in the darkness, a man with conviction who was willing to stand toe-to-toe with those who only saw quick profit in ancient artifacts.

He had an expressive face that was filled with deep furrows and lines, each of which told a story. He nearly always looked worried, too, and Indy felt his usual compulsion to pat Brody on the back and assure him things were going to turn out just fine, really.

"Marcus!" Indy slapped his pocket. "I did it."

Brody's eyes lit up. "I want to hear all about it."

"Come on."

As they left the room and headed down the hall, Indy slipped the Cross of Coronado out of his jacket pocket and held it out for Brody to see.

"You've really got it. Bravo. I'm elated. I'm more than elated. I'm overjoyed."

"How do you think I feel? Do you know how long I've been after this?"

"All your life."

"All my life."

They had spoken at the same time, and both of them laughed. "Well done, Indy. Very well done, indeed. Now tell me how you did it."

Indy shrugged. "It wasn't much. It just took a little friendly persuasion, that's all."

"That's all?" Brody asked skeptically.

"Well, when the cordialities wore out, it took a bit of diplomatic arm twisting."

"I see." Brody nodded. It was obvious he was interested in hearing more. But he was also worried that he would hear something that wasn't up to the standards of the museum he represented.

Before Indy could even begin his story, though, two of his colleagues approached them in the hallway. "Where you been, Jones?" asked the taller man. "Semester break ended a week ago."

The second colleague shoved a ceramic fertility goddess toward Indy. "Have a look at this, Jonesy. I picked it up on a trip down to Mexico. Possibly you could date it for me. What do you say?"

Indy turned the piece of pottery over in his hands. A wry smile crossed his lips. "Date it?"

The man adjusted his tie and looked uneasily at Indy. Then, with a false tone of self-assurance, he added: "I paid almost two hundred dollars for it. The man assured me it was pre-Columbian."

"Pre-October or November. Hard to say. But let's take a look." Before the startled professor could say a word, Indy snapped the figurine in two. "See, you can tell by the cross section. It's worthless."

"Worthless?"

"You got it." He handed both pieces of the figurine back to the professor and walked off with Brody.

"I should have showed them what a real artifact looks like," Brody said, holding up the cross.

Indy shrugged. "Why bother?"

A moment later they stopped in front of Indy's office. "This piece will find a place of honor among our Spanish acquisitions," Brody assured him.

"Good. We can discuss my honorarium later on over champagne."

"When can I expect you?"

Indy thought a moment. He hadn't been to his office yet and wasn't looking forward to the stack of paperwork that was probably awaiting him as a result of missing the first week of the semester. "Let's make it in half an hour."

Brody smiled, slipped the cross into his briefcase, and was still beaming as he walked off.

Indy opened the door of his office and winced. The outer office was bursting with students, who immediately surrounded him.

"Professor Jones, could you . . ."

"Dr. Jones, I need . . ."

"Hey, I was here first. Professor. . ."

Indy shouldered his way to his secretary's desk. The woman, a teaching assistant named Irene, looked as if she was suffering from shell shock. She sat transfixed, ignoring the bombardment of students. Then she saw Indy and was suddenly reactivated.

"Dr. Jones! For God's sake, I'm so glad you're back. Your mail is on your desk. Here are your phone messages. This is your appointment schedule. And these term papers still haven't been graded."

Indy nodded and took the papers, then turned to enter his private office. The students were still clamoring for his attention.

"Dr. Jones."

"Wait, Dr. Jones. My grade."

"Sign my registration card."

"Listen, Dr. Jones. If I could just have . . ."

Indy held up a hand, and suddenly the mob was silent and attentive. "Irene . . . put everyone's name down on a list in the order they arrived. I'll see each and every one of them in turn."

Irene glanced from Indy to the students. The horde immediately descended on her like a swarm of mosquitos. "Well, I'll try," she muttered.

"I was first. . . ."

"No, I was here before you. . . ."

"I'm sure I was second. . . ."

"Hey, watch where you're stepping there."

Indy slipped into his office and impatiently sorted through his mail: an assortment of college bulletins, archaeological newsletters, the current issues of *Esquire* and *Collier's,* and a thick envelope with a foreign postmark on it.

He stared at it a moment. "Hmm . . . Venice." He tried to think of whom he knew in Venice and came up with a blank. Before he had a chance to open the envelope, Irene's distraught voice squawked over the intercom.

"Dr. Jones . . . there seems to be some disagreement out here about who arrived first, and I—"

"Fine, fine," Indy cut in. "Do the best you can. I'll be ready in a moment."

Like hell I will.

Indy stuffed his mail into his coat pockets, took a quick look around, then opened his window and crawled through it. He took a deep breath of the late-afternoon spring air as he stepped out into the adjoining garden. Roses, gardenias, grass. It was marvelous.

"A fine day," he said to himself, and headed across the garden away from his office. He walked swiftly and confidently. He was smiling, enjoying his freedom, and ignoring any thoughts about responsibilities. After what he had been through to recover the cross, he deserved a little break.

If anyone complained, well, he never said he was as conscientious as his father. He was well aware that his father's reputation was a double-edged blade. When it cut one way, it served to secure his position at the university. When it cut the other way, it made him feel like a second-rate scholar who never would measure up to the old man.

Maybe that was why he was irresponsible and why he took chances. In his own way he wanted attention. What he couldn't equal in scholarship, he could master in the field. And the field was forever a wide-open space full of adventure.

As he reached the curb outside the building on the edge of campus, a long, black Packard sedan pulled up to him. Indy glanced inside and was about to continue on his way when the back door swung open and a man stepped out. He was dressed in a dark three-piece suit, with the brim of his hat pulled low enough so that his eyes were in shadow. There was a no-nonsense look about him. Everything he saw told Indy that he was a G-man.

"Dr. Jones?"

Indy met his gaze. "Yes? Is there something I can help you with?"

"We have something rather important to talk to you about. We'd like you to come with us."

Indy hesitated, looking the man over closely. A bulge in the coat. *Terrific. I need this.* As if to justify his suspicion, the man let his coat fall open, revealing a shoulder holster. Indy eyed the gun, then the three men in the car. Each of them was cut from the same mold as the guy in front of him.

He didn't know what they wanted, and he didn't care to find out. "I'm not sure I have the time at the moment," he said in a halting voice as he tried to think of an easy way out.

"There's nothing to think over, Dr. Jones. I'm afraid we insist you come with us."

For the next half hour Indy was ensconced in the backseat of the Packard between two of his burly escorts. A couple of times he attempted to find out what was going on, but they said he'd find out soon enough. When he commented about the spring weather, the man to his left grunted. The one on his right just looked ahead.

Real friendly bunch.

It occurred to him that none of them had shown him any identification. He turned to the guy next to him and asked for his ID. The man acted as if he hadn't heard him.

"You guys are feds, right?"

"We're delivery boys," one of them said, and all of them laughed.

Indy laughed, too, and squirmed uncomfortably. Things were getting very funny.

CHAPTER SIX

◄◄ ►►

THE CRUSADER TABLET

It was nearly dusk when the Packard pulled up to an exclusive Fifth Avenue building overlooking Central Park. Indy climbed out and was accompanied into the building by two of the men. He was whisked through the lobby and into a private elevator. When the door opened to a penthouse, he stepped out and looked around, impressed by the luxurious surroundings.

"Come on," one of the men muttered. "You can do your sight-seeing inside."

They ushered him into a plush art deco penthouse and disappeared, leaving him in a room furnished with numerous museum-quality artifacts on display. Indy walked around, examining one after another. Whoever owned this place had money and taste, with a considerable amount of the former. He picked up a ceramic pot with a painting of a peacock on one side. He recognized it as Greek in origin, and even though it was over twenty-five hundred years old, the luster of its colors was incredibly well preserved.

Indy's inspection was interrupted when a door opened in front of him. He heard soft piano music and voices, and momentarily glimpsed a cocktail party inside before the doorway was filled by a tall, broad-shouldered man in a tuxedo. His jaw was square, his blond hair thinning. Even though he appeared to be well into his fifties, his physique was trim and muscular, like that of a much younger man. There was something regal about him as he strode across the room, and Indy had no doubt that he was about to meet the owner of the penthouse.

He looked familiar, but why? Then he knew. He was one of the major contributors to the archaeology museum. He'd seen him a couple of times at social events associated with the museum, and he had heard Brody fussing about him more than once. His name was Walter . . . Walter Donovan. That was it.

"Notice the eyes in the tail feathers," Donovan said, nodding to the pot that Indy was still holding.

He carefully set the precious artifact back in place. "Yeah. Nice eyes."

"You know whose eyes they are?"

Indy smiled. "Sure. They're Argus's eyes. He was a giant with a hundred eyes. Hermes killed him, and Hera put his eyes in the peacock's tail."

Donovan regarded him a moment. "I should have guessed you knew a bit about Greek mythology."

Indy shrugged. "A bit."

The study of Greek myths was an aberration of his childhood, one that he had undertaken at the insistence of his father. He had grudgingly enjoyed some of the tales, especially the ones about Heracles and his feats, but all the while he had despised his father for forcing him to read and learn them. Now, however, he was amazed that thirty years later the heroes and their stories returned so easily to him; it was as if he'd read them last week.

"I trust your trip down was comfortable, Dr. Jones." Donovan smiled, exuding confidence and power. "My assistants didn't alarm you, I hope."

Indy was about to make a crack about the fascinating discussions en route, but Donovan extended a hand and introduced himself.

"I know who you are, Mr. Donovan," Indy said as Donovan released the firm grip on his hand. "Your contributions to the Old World Museum over the years have been extremely generous."

"Why, thank you."

"Some of the pieces in your collection here are very impressive," Indy added, looking around.

Now what the hell do you want with me?

"I'm glad you noticed."

Donovan walked over to a table where an object was cov-ered by a cloth shroud. It was one of the pieces Indy hadn't examined. Donovan pulled back the cloth, revealing a flat stone tablet about two feet square. "I'd like you to take a look at this one in particular, Dr. Jones."

Indy moved closer and saw letters and symbols inscribed on the tablet. He removed his wire-framed glasses from his pocket, slipped them on, and leaned over for a closer exami-nation of the ancient artifact.

"Early Christian symbols. Gothic characters. Byzantine carvings. Middle twelfth century, I'd say."

Donovan crossed his arms. "That was our assessment as well."

"Where did you find this?"

"My engineers unearthed it in the mountain regions north of Ankara while excavating for copper." He paused a beat, studying Indy out of the corner of his eye. "Can you translate the inscription, Dr. Jones?"

Indy took a step back. His eyes were still fixed on the tablet. He explained that translating the inscriptions wouldn't be easy, even for someone like himself, who was knowledge-able of the period and languages.

"Why don't you try, anyhow?" Donovan said in his most persuasive voice.

Why the hell should I?

"I'd appreciate it," Donovan added.

Yeah, I bet you would.

Indy frowned as he stared at the inscription. Finally he cleared his throat and spoke in a slow, halting voice, like a child who was just learning to read.

". . . drinks the water that I shall give him, says the Lord, will have a spring inside him . . . welling up for eternal life. Let them bring me to your holy mountain . . . in the place where you dwell. Across the desert and through the mountain . . . to the Canyon of the Crescent Moon, broad enough only for one man. To the Temple of the Sun, holy enough for all men. . . ."

Indy stopped, looked up at Donovan with a startled expression, saw no reaction on the other man's face, and continued with the final line. ". . . Where the cup that holds the blood of Jesus Christ our Lord resides forever."

"The Holy Grail, Dr. Jones." Donovan's voice was hushed, reverent. He was obviously impressed by what Indy had read. "The chalice used by Christ during the Last Supper. The cup that caught His blood at the Crucifixion and was entrusted to Joseph of Arimathaea. A cup of great power to the one who finds it."

Indy rubbed his chin and looked dubiously at Donovan. "I've heard that bedtime story before."

"Eternal life, Dr. Jones." He emphasized the words, as if Indy hadn't heard him. "The gift of youth to whoever drinks from the Grail."

Donovan, it seemed, was taking the inscription at face value rather than considering it in a mythological context. Indy nodded but didn't say anything, not wanting to encourage the man in a pursuit that had consumed countless lives. He was too well aware how the search for the Grail Cup had become an obsession for even the most rational scholars.

"Now, that's a bedtime story that I'd like to wake up to," Donovan continued.

"An old man's dream."

"*Every* man's dream," Donovan countered. "Including your father's, I believe."

Indy stiffened slightly at the mention of his father. "Grail lore is his hobby." He spoke evenly, covering the discomfort he always felt when the Grail and his father were mentioned in tandem, like parts of a rhyme or a riddle.

"More than simply a hobby," Donovan persisted. "He's occupied the chair of medieval literature at Princeton for nearly two decades."

"He's a professor of medieval literature. The one students hope they don't get."

"Give the man his due. He's the foremost Grail scholar in the world."

Indy gave Donovan a sour look and was about to say something when the door opened. The music and sound of chatter suddenly pumped into the room, and both men turned as a matronly woman in an expensive evening gown stepped through the door.

"Walter, you're neglecting your guests," the woman said in a tone that didn't hide her annoyance. Her eyes shifted from her husband to Indy and back again.

"Be along in a moment, dear."

Indy turned his attention to the tablet once more when it became evident that Donovan wasn't going to introduce him to his wife.

Mrs. Donovan sighed, a sigh that said she was accustomed to this, and returned to the party, her gown rustling as she walked away.

In spite of his skeptical comments, Indy was fascinated by the Grail tablet. He wouldn't swear to it, but he was almost certain the tablet was what it appeared to be. The fact that it existed was an important discovery. What it could lead to was something he didn't even want to consider right now.

He had forgotten all about the way he had been picked off the street. It was inconsequential. The tablet, and what it said, was what mattered.

"Hard to resist, isn't it?" Donovan commented, acutely aware of Indy's interest. "The Holy Grail's final resting place described in detail. Simply astounding."

Indy shrugged and recovered his skeptical, scientific attitude, the one that dominated his classroom persona. "What good is it? The tablet speaks of desert and mountains and canyons. There are a lot of deserts in the world—the Sahara, the Arabian, the Kalahari. And the mountain ranges—the Urals, Alps, Atlas . . . Where do you start looking?"

Then he pointed out the obvious flaw in the discovery. "Maybe if this tablet was completely intact, you'd have more to go on. But the entire top portion is missing."

Donovan wasn't about to be easily discouraged. He acted, Indy thought, like a man who knew something he wasn't telling—a *big* something.

"Just the same, Dr. Jones, an attempt to recover the Grail is currently under way."

Indy frowned and shook his head. "Are you saying the tablet has already been translated?"

Donovan nodded.

"Then why drag me here, just for a second opinion? I could charge you with kidnapping." His tone was deliberately gruff.

Donovan held up a hand. "You could, but I don't think you will. I'm getting to the reason. But first let me tell you another 'bedtime story,' Dr. Jones. After the Grail was entrusted to Joseph of Arimathaea, it disappeared and was lost for a thousand years before being found again by three knights of the First Crusade. Three brothers, to be exact."

"I've heard this one, too," Indy interrupted, and finished the story himself. "One hundred and fifty years *after* finding the Grail, two of these brothers walked out of the desert and began their long journey home. But only one made it back, and before dying of *extreme* old age, he imparted his tale to a Franciscan friar."

Donovan nodded, clearly pleased that Indy knew the story. "Good. Now, let me show you something." He walked across the room and returned with an ancient leather-bound volume. He opened it carefully. It was obvious that the pages were extremely brittle.

"This is the manuscript of the Franciscan friar." He paused a moment, letting that fact fully register. "It doesn't reveal the location of the Grail, but the knight promised that two 'markers' had been left behind that would lead the way."

Donovan pointed at the stone tablet. "This, Dr. Jones, is one of those 'markers.' This tablet proves the story is true. But as you pointed out—it's incomplete."

Seconds passed. Indy could almost feel them filling the room and felt his own body tense, waiting for Donovan to continue. "The second 'marker' is entombed with the remains of the knight's brother. Our project leader—who has brought years of study to this search—believes that tomb is located within the city of Venice, Italy."

"What about the third brother, the one who was left behind in the desert? Does the friar say anything about him in his manuscript?"

"The third brother stayed behind to become the keeper of the Grail." Donovan carefully closed the ancient manuscript. "As you can now see, Dr. Jones, we're about to complete a great quest that began almost two thousand years ago. We're only one step away from actually finding the Grail."

Indy smiled. "And that's usually when the ground disappears from under your feet."

Donovan sucked air in through his teeth and expelled it, a sigh that spoke of some minor inconvenience that had somehow become a burden. "You may be more right than you know."

"How so?"

"We've hit a snag. Our project leader has vanished. So has his research. We received a cable from Dr. Schneider, his colleague. Schneider has no idea of his whereabouts or what's become of him."

Donovan looked down at the ancient manuscript, then back at Indy. His eyes seemed distant now, almost glazed, as though a part of him were as lost as Schneider's colleague. "I want you to pick up the trail where he left off. Find the man and you will find the Grail. Can you think of any greater challenge?"

Indy held up both his hands, patting the air and shaking his head. He gave a small, uncertain laugh. Challenges were one thing; stupidity was quite another. Besides, he rationalized, he had a commitment to the university to fulfill. He couldn't just run off, especially since he had just returned late from another little field trip.

"You've got the wrong Jones, Mr. Donovan. Why don't you try my father? I'm sure he'd be fascinated by the tablet and ready to help out in any way."

"We already have. Your father is the man who's disappeared."

CHAPTER SEVEN

◄◄ ►►

THE GRAIL DIARY

Indy sped along a tree-lined boulevard through an old neighborhood. He cranked the wheel of his Ford coupe, skidded around the corner, and almost hit a man who had stepped into the street.

"Indy, for the Lord's sake and my poor heart, slow down," Brody yelled, from the passenger seat.

A block later Indy pulled over, screeching to a halt at the curb. He gazed for a moment through the windshield toward the house partially hidden by a hedge and trees.

It was two stories, with numerous windows and a nicely landscaped front yard. It might have belonged to an ordinary family with kids and pets, the sort of family that had barbecues on weekends, the family Indy had never had. It didn't look anything like the place where he and his father had lived when he was younger. But it elicited the same feelings of unease, of awkwardness, even though he hadn't set foot here in at least two years.

But none of what had happened between him and his father mattered now.

He hopped out of the Ford and was halfway to the front door when Brody caught up to him. He was breathing hard from the burst of exertion; a frown creased his forehead.

"Your father and I have been friends since time began. I've watched you grow up, Indy. And I've watched the two of you grow apart." He climbed the stairs to the porch a step behind Indy. "I've never seen you this concerned about him before."

Indy strode across the porch. "He's an academic. A bookworm, not a field man, Marcus. Of course I'm concerned about . . ."

The front door was ajar, and it silenced him. He and Brody glanced at each other, and Indy stepped cautiously closer, muscles tight, expectant. He touched his hand to the door and nudged it open. It creaked. The air that struck his face was cool—and empty.

"Dad?"

"Henry?" Brody called out as he followed Indy inside.

Their voices echoed hollowly. Indy's dread bit more deeply. He called for his father again and moved quickly down the hall, peering into empty rooms, rooms that hadn't changed all that much since they moved here from Utah when he was fifteen. The furniture was nicer, there was *more* of everything, but the air here was just as barren and devoid of character as it had been in the other house after his mother had died.

A clock ticked in the silence. The refrigerator hummed. The quiet mocked him. Gone, Indy thought, and flung back the curtain that separated the hall from the sitting room.

He grimaced, and Brody whispered, "Dear God."

The room hadn't just been ransacked; it had been decimated. Drawers had been pulled out and dumped on the floor. Shelves had been swept clean. The couch cushions had been torn away and hurled across the room. Books, letters, and envelopes were strewn through the mess.

For several long moments Indy just stood there, his eyes flicking this way and that, seeking something, anything, that would provide a clue.

He bent down and picked up a photo album that had been cast aside. Several pictures fell out, and he plucked them from the ruin and stared at the top photograph. A young boy stood with an unsmiling older man whose beard had not yet turned completely gray. Both the man and the boy were stiff, obviously uncomfortable, and they both looked as though they wanted to be anywhere other than where they were. And that, he thought, had always been the point with him and his father, even as far back as when this picture had been taken. They had never felt comfortable around each other, and now, as all the old feelings flooded back, something hitched in Indy's chest.

The picture had been taken the year after his mother's death. His father had been sullen that year, and Indy knew he thought a lot about the woman who had formed a bridge between father and son. When she died, the bridge vanished. His father had never talked to Indy about her. If he mentioned his mother or anything related to her, his father would cast a frigid glance at him and change the subject or give him a chore to do.

Then there was the intimidation. He remembered the constant reminders that he would never measure up to the old man. He didn't have the discipline, the determination, the intellect. Sure, he had a sense of curiosity, his father had conceded. But what good did it do him? All he did was get into trouble.

As Indy grew older, all the anger and resentment he felt only grew worse. One day, he told his father that he would show him. He would be an archaeologist, too, and a good one. His determination to be as knowledgeable as his father seemed to have grown in direct proportion to his old man's stubbornness and insistence that he would never amount to anything.

The sound of Brody's footfalls on the stairs snapped him back to the present. His misgivings about his father were quickly replaced by a huge and terrible guilt for the times he had wished he would never have to see him again. And for the times he had wished him dead. In spite of his father's toughness and unwillingness to grant him an inch, the texture of everything was different now that he was missing. Right this second there was no one in the world whom Indy wanted to see more desperately.

"He isn't anywhere in the house," Brody said.

"I didn't think he would be."

Brody's face skewed with concern and worry. "What's that old fool gotten himself into, anyway?"

"I don't know. But whatever it is, he's in over his head."

"I just can't imagine Henry getting involved with people he couldn't trust. Look, they've even gone through his mail."

Indy stared at the clutter of torn papers and envelopes and suddenly realized he had forgotten about his own mail.

"The mail. That's it, Marcus!"

He immediately rifled through his pockets and pulled out the overstuffed envelope he had been carrying around since he left his office. He looked at the foreign postmark again and shook his head.

"Venice, Italy. How could I be so stupid?"

Brody looked baffled. "What are you talking about, Indy?"

He tore open the envelope and pulled out a small notebook. He quickly flipped through several pages. It looked like a journal or diary. Page after page was covered with handwritten notes and drawings.

Brody glanced over Indy's shoulder at it. "Is it from Henry?"

"That's right. It's Dad's Grail diary."

"But why did he send it to you?"

"I don't know." He looked around at the room again and back to the diary. "I've got the feeling this is what they were after. It looks like somebody wanted it pretty badly, too."

He lightly stroked the leather cover of the diary. He trusted me. He finally did something to show that he trusted and believed in me.

"Can I see it?" Brody asked.

"Of course. It's all in there. A lifetime's worth of research and knowledge."

As Brody paged through the diary, the lines on his face deepened by the second. "The search was his passion, Indy."

"I know. But do you believe in that fairy tale, Marcus? Do you believe the Grail actually exists?"

Brody stopped turning pages as he came to a picture pasted into the diary. It was a depiction of Christ on the cross, his blood being captured in a golden chalice by Joseph of Arimathaea.

He glanced up and spoke with conviction. "The search for the cup of Christ is the search for the divine in all of us."

Indy nodded and tried to disguise his skepticism. But his indulgent smile wasn't lost on Brody.

"I know. You want facts. But I don't have any for you, Indy. At my age, I'm willing to accept a few things on faith. I can feel it more than I can prove it."

Indy didn't say anything. His gaze flicked to a painting on the wall. It portrayed eleventh-century crusaders plummeting to their deaths over a high cliff. One crusader, however, floated safely in midair because he was holding the Grail in his hands.

He remembered how his father had forced him to read Wolfram von Eschenbach's *Parzival*—the Grail story. He was only thirteen and couldn't think of a drearier way of spending his summer afternoons. At least not until the next year, when Dad made him read it again, this time in the early German version. That was followed by Richard Wagner's opera, *Parsifal*, based on Eschenbach's work.

Each day his father would ask him about the story, to make sure that he was understanding it. If he didn't know the answer to one of the questions, he was required to go back and reread the related section. As an incentive his father promised him that he would be rewarded when he had satisfactorily completed Wagner's work.

He had thought about what kind of reward his father might give him and hoped it would be a trip to Egypt to see the pyramids, or maybe to Athens to see the Parthenon, or Mexico to the Yucatan to see the Mayan ruins. At the very least he figured he deserved a trip to the museum in the state capitol to see the mummies.

As it turned out, his reward was the Arthurian Grail legends. First, came *Le Morte d'Arthur* by Sir Thomas Malory, and he had to read it in French first, then English. After that was Lord Tennyson's *Idylls of the King*. Some reward, he glumly thought. In spite of his hatred of the difficult books and his silent anger about his reward, he had never forgotten the adventures of the knights Parzival, Gawain, and Feirifs— the heroes of *Parzival*—or Arthur, Lancelot, and Merlin from the Arthurian legends. In fact, now that he thought of it, those books probably had considerable bearing on how he lived his life.

When Indy didn't speak, Brody cleared his throat, and continued: "If your father believes the Grail is real, so do I."

Indy wasn't sure what to believe, except that he needed to act, to do something, to begin searching. "Call Donovan, Marcus. Tell him I'll take that ticket to Venice now. I'm going to find Dad."

"Good. I'll tell him we want two tickets. I'm going with you."

They motored to the airport in style, seated in the rear of an opulent limousine, accompanied by its owner, Walter Donovan. Indy had taken an emergency leave of absence from the university. At first, when he had made the request, the dean had stared at him askance. How could he even think about petitioning for a leave when he'd just missed the first week of the semester? Then Indy had informed him of the details, and the dean's attitude immediately changed at the mention of his father's name.

He had nodded solemnly, glanced out the window, and told Indy a story about his father. Indy had heard it before, but this time the story had a different twist at the end. It dealt with an incident in which a particularly arrogant colleague of Dr. Jones held an exhibition of his latest archaeological finds. Because of his prominence and his power in academic circles, the reception was attended by scholars and archaeologists from several eastern universities. They had attended not because they admired the man but because they feared him.

When the moment came to unveil the most significant find of the collection, Dr. Jones had stridden to the front of the room, ripped the covering from a piece of pottery that supposedly predated anything ever discovered in the New World. He then smashed it on the podium and declared it fraudulent. He had been quickly ushered away by guards, but the evidence left behind proved him right, and the professor's reign of terror ended.

The dean had turned from the window and looked Indy in the eye. "That professor had been my adviser and had been on the verge of having me expelled because I'd disagreed with him on the dating of an artifact. What your father did inadvertently saved my career. Yes, by all means, go and find Dr. Jones. The world needs men like him."

Indy spent the trip to the airport quietly mulling over what he knew about his father's disappearance. The problem was that there were still too few facts. What he suspected was that the man's passionate interest in the Grail Cup could very well have led him to undertake an uncharacteristic expedition.

Considering his age, he had probably felt this would be his one and only opportunity to find the Grail and to complete his life's quest.

Damn that old man and his obsession.

If only they had been on better terms, this never would have happened. He blamed himself. He always had a bad attitude about anything that dealt with his father. But now, somehow, he was going to make up for his past shortcomings and rectify things.

As the limo pulled over to the curb outside the airport entrance, Donovan shook Brody's hand. "Well, Marcus. Good luck."

Like luck's got anything to do with it, Indy thought.

"Thank you, Walter." Brody nodded nervously. "Now, when we arrive in Venice . . ."

"Don't worry," Donovan assured him. "Dr. Schneider will be there to meet you. I maintain an apartment in Venice. It's at your disposal."

"I appreciate that, Walter."

Brody climbed out of the car, and Indy was about to follow, when Donovan touched his shoulder. "Be careful, Dr. Jones. Don't trust *anybody*. You understand?"

Indy met his gaze. "I'm going to do whatever is necessary in order to find my father."

The plane soared through bright sunlight, past clouds that clung to the sky like tiny white commas. The Atlantic stretched below them, an endless stretch of blue, a desert of blue, brilliant and blinding. But Indy saw none of it. For most of the trip he was preoccupied with his father's Grail diary.

He went through it, carefully reading each entry, each page, seeking clues. "'The word *Grail* is derived from *graduale,* which means step-by-step, degree by degree,'" he read on a page near the beginning. "'There are six degrees or levels of awareness in the Grail quest, and each one is represented by an animal.'"

The raven was the symbol of the first degree and represented the messenger of the Grail and "the finger of fate" that initiated the quest.

The peacock signified the second degree and symbolized

the search for immortality. It also suggested the colorful and imaginative nature of the quest.

The sign for the third degree was the swan, because the one who took up the Grail quest sang a swan song to selfish and indulgent ways. In order to succeed in the quest, one must overcome weaknesses of the mind and heart and move beyond petty likes and dislikes.

The fourth degree was signified by the pelican, a bird willing to nurture its young by wounding its own breast. It symbolized the quality of self-sacrifice and the willingness to endanger self for the sake of saving one's own people.

The lion was the sign of the fifth degree. It stood for leadership, conquest, and the attainment of high goals.

The sixth and highest level, represented by the eagle, was achieved at the end of the quest. At that time the seeker of the Grail would have gained the power and knowledge necessary to understand fully the significance of the search.

Indy looked up from the book and shifted his position in the tight quarters of his seat. It was typical of his father to couch things in symbols and metaphors. As a scholar, he worked in the abstract. He suspected that the Grail diary was almost as mystifying as the Grail Cup itself.

The mention of the animals reminded him of something he hadn't thought about for a while. When he was eighteen, he had returned to the Southwest and undertaken a vision quest under the guidance of an old Navajo Indian. He had climbed a mesa in New Mexico alone and without food. There he had built a shelter and waited.

The Indian had told him that he must wait until an animal approached him, and from that time on it would be his protector, his spiritual guardian. Two days passed, and his stomach was empty, his throat dry. He wanted more than anything to climb down and find water. He stood up and walked to the edge of the mesa and stared down. Whatever had possessed him to do something so crazy?

He was about to start his descent when he thought he heard the voice of the old Indian telling him to wait. Startled, he turned around. No one was there. His hunger and thirst were causing him to hear voices, he thought. But instead of climbing down the mesa, he headed back to his shelter.

He had taken no more than a dozen steps when suddenly an eagle swooped out of the sky, skimming low over the flat, rocky surface. The majestic creature landed on the wall of his shelter. He had found his protector. When he had told his story, the old Navajo nodded and said that the eagle would always guide him on his journeys.

Indy snapped out of his reverie as the steward tapped him on the shoulder and asked if he'd like a drink. He nodded, and as he adjusted himself in the seat, a folded piece of paper fell from the diary into the aisle. The steward picked it up and handed it to him along with a drink. He set the glass down on the tray in front of him and unfolded the paper.

It was a rubbing that he immediately recognized as an impression of Donovan's Grail tablet. The top part of it was blank, as if space had been left for the missing section of the tablet.

"Look at this, Marcus."

He held it out to Brody, then realized his traveling partner was fast asleep.

He refolded the paper and was about to slip it into the diary when he noticed the drawing on the page that had fallen open.

It was a sketch of what appeared to be a stained glass window of a knight. Below it was one word: Venice. He wondered about its significance.

It wouldn't be long before he would find out.

VENICE

CHAPTER EIGHT

◄◄ ►►

ROMAN NUMERALS

"Ah, Venice." Indy sighed, looking around, nodding to himself, drawing a kind of sustenance from his surroundings. Venice was like no other city on earth and was a perfect balm for his dark mood. As he and Brody traversed the city by water bus, the gloom that had hovered over him ever since he found out about his father's disappearance lifted.

The air smelled sweetly of water, the sky overhead was a soft cushion of blue, and Indy's spirit soared. It's going to be all right, he told himself. He would find his father. He had to believe that.

"Think of it," Brody said, "a city built in a lagoon on a hundred and eighteen islands."

Indy nodded. "And look what they built."

Venice's heritage was visible along virtually every street and waterway. The city was a harbor of culture and knowledge, of history and romance, and no doubt intrigue and adventure as well.

As he and Brody disembarked from the water bus at a boat landing, Indy's sense of euphoria abruptly evaporated. A band of Fascist militiamen passed by with a civilian suspect in tow. At the sight of the boat, the civilian started struggling to escape. The militiamen reacted swiftly and harshly. They struck the man with their clubs, kicked him with their heavy boots, and the man whimpered and cried out and tried to get away. He finally collapsed against the cobblestones, his face bloody, his body as still as a dead man's.

It disturbed Indy at a level too deep for words. He sensed a

65

vengefulness in the militiamen's attitude that far exceeded military code. They obviously enjoyed their work, and reminded him of the sailors he had tangled with on the cargo ship.

"Ah, Venice," he said again. But this time his voice was heavier, thicker, reflecting his concern for what was taking place in Italy and throughout Europe. Fascists and Nazis had thrown the continent into havoc. Who the hell knew where it would all end? Or when? Or how? Or if?

Some of his earlier gloom returned.

"I find that sort of thing very disturbing," Brody remarked as they made their way across the dock. "I hope we don't encounter any more violence on this trip."

Indy glanced at him; Brody wore his fretful expression again. "Yeah, me, too." But he had the feeling that wouldn't be the case.

As they looked around, Indy wondered aloud how they would recognize Dr. Schneider when they saw him. Donovan hadn't given them any description of his father's colleague. He just said he'd be there waiting.

"Maybe he'll be holding a sign," Brody suggested hopefully.

A woman suddenly approached them from the crowd, and smiled. She was an attractive blond with high cheekbones and a slender figure. Her lapis-colored eyes were bright and intelligent.

"Dr. Jones?"

"Yes." Indy smiled. Schneider must have sent his secretary to pick them up, and he didn't mind one bit.

"I knew it was you." Her manner was brazenly flirtatious. "You have your father's eyes."

Indy was instantly attracted to her. "And my mother's ears. But the rest belongs to you."

He expected her to be flustered. Instead, she laughed. It was a light, beautiful sound, full of life, and for a second, he thought she was laughing at him. What the hell, he thought. So it wasn't the most original line. Who cared? He would have said it again just to hear her laugh once more.

"Looks like the best parts have already been spoken for," she said.

Indy grinned, enjoying the repartee.

The woman turned to Brody. "Marcus Brody?"

"That's right."

"My name is Elsa Schneider."

Indy's grin faded.

Brody tried to cover his surprise but without success. "Ah, Dr. Schneider. I see."

He shook her hand as she extended it. He cleared his throat, glanced at Indy as if hoping he would pick up the conversation, then looked back at the woman. "It's nice to meet you. Walter didn't, ah . . ."

She smiled and turned. "I thought as much. I guess Walter likes to surprise people. This way, gentlemen."

They entered the vast Piazza San Marco, and she directed the conversation immediately to the matter at hand. "The last time I saw your father we were in the Marciana Library. That's where I'm taking you now. He was very close to tracking down the knight's tomb. I've never seen him so excited. He was as giddy as a schoolboy. He was certain the tomb would contain the map leading to the Grail."

Dr. Henry Jones—Attila the professor—giddy as a schoolboy? That was a side of him he'd never seen, Indy thought. "He was never giddy, even when he *was* a schoolboy."

Maybe working with Elsa Schneider had deranged the old man, Indy thought. Indy couldn't take his eyes off her, and he had to admit he felt a bit giddy himself. As they strolled along, he noticed a vendor selling flowers from a cart. He reached back and pulled out a red carnation from a corner bouquet. The vendor was busy with a customer and missed his quick fingers.

He held out the flower to Elsa and smiled. "Fraulein, will you permit me?"

She eyed the flower, then glanced up at Indy. "Well, I usually don't."

"I usually don't, either."

She regarded him a moment longer. "In that case, I permit you."

"It would make me happy."

She took the carnation from Indy. "I'm already sad. By tomorrow it will have faded."

"Then tomorrow I'll steal you another. That's all that I can promise."

She laughed again, that beautiful laugh, that laugh Indy suddenly craved. He started to say something else, but Brody spoke up. "Look here, I hate to interrupt, but the reason we are here . . ."

"Yes, of course," Elsa said in a serious voice, and reached into her purse. "I have something to show both of you. As I was saying, I left Dr. Jones working in the library. He sent me to the map section to fetch an ancient plan of the city. When I got back to his table, he was gone, and so were all of his papers. Except for one thing."

She held up a scrap of paper and looked from Brody to Indy. "I found this near his chair."

Indy took the paper from her and unfolded it. The only thing that was written on it were the Roman numerals III, VII, and X.

Indy contemplated that bit of information.

Elsa pointed her gloved hand to her right. "Here's the library."

They climbed the front steps, and Elsa led the way inside. Their shoes clicked against the polished marble floor. It was the sort of place, Indy thought, that encouraged you to speak in hushed, almost reverent tones. "I've been trying to figure out those numbers all week," Elsa whispered. "Three, seven, and ten. They don't appear to be a Biblical reference. I've checked every combination of chapter and verse in the gospels."

Indy glanced up at the ceiling fifty feet overhead and at the stone walls interspersed with towering stained glass windows. The library was immense and shadowy, huge enough to get lost in.

Maybe his father was still here, he mused, absorbed in some ancient manuscript. He wouldn't even know he was missing.

"Now I'm looking into the Medieval *Chronicles* of Jean Froissart," Elsa continued. "This library has copies of the original text. Perhaps three, seven, and ten represent volume numbers."

Indy nodded. He was impressed with the library, but he also felt uneasy here, knowing this was where his father vanished.

It was ironic in a way. He recalled Professor Henry Jones lecturing him about libraries. Storehouses of knowledge, junior. Spend more time in libraries, and you'll be the wiser for it. His father thrived in libraries, immersed himself in books, but he didn't lose himself. Indy was sure of that. He had disappeared under duress, not voluntarily. He wasn't the type who ran from trouble. He was too stubborn for that.

They walked between two massive granite pillars and entered a room with tall rows of bookshelves. Elsa led them to the corner of the room and stopped by a table, where she ran her hand lovingly over a couple of precious leather-bound books.

"Your eyes are shining," Indy commented.

"A great library almost makes me cry. Even a single book. It's almost sacred, like a brick in the temple of all our history."

"Yeah. I like a good book," Indy quipped.

"Like being in a church, I'd say," Brody chimed sympathetically.

"In this case it's almost the literal truth. We're on holy ground. This used to be the chapel of a Franciscan monastery." Elsa pointed toward several marble pillars. "Those columns were brought back as spoils of war after the sacking of Byzantium during the Crusades."

Indy noted the columns, but at the moment he was more interested in the window above the table. It was stained glass and depicted a knight of the Crusades. He walked around the table to take a closer look at it, then turned to Elsa. "Is this the table where you last saw my father?"

She nodded, moved her fingertips over the edge of it. "He was working right here. That reminds me. I have to check with the reference counter. I left a picture of Henry. They said they'd be watching in case he showed up again."

The moment Elsa was out of sight, Indy grabbed Brody by the arm and pointed at the stained glass window. "Marcus, I've seen this window before."

Brody frowned. "Where?"

Indy took out the Grail diary and opened it to the sketch he had noticed during the plane flight. He tapped the diary. "Right here."

Brody studied the sketch, looked up at the window, down at the sketch again, and nodded slowly. "Good God, Indy. It's the same."

"Do you see it?"

"Yes, the Roman numerals are part of the window's design."

"Dad was onto something here."

Brody handed the diary back to Indy. "Yes, but what? We know where the numbers came from, but we still don't know what they mean."

Indy saw Elsa approaching and quickly tucked the diary back into his pocket. "Dad sent me this diary for a reason. So until we find out why, I think we should keep it to ourselves."

"Agreed," Brody said.

Elsa shook her head. "No sign of him." She frowned slightly, looking from Indy to Brody and back again. "You two look like you've found something. What is it?"

"Is it that obvious?" Indy asked.

He was scanning the walls and the ceiling. Somewhere around here there had to be a clue; he was sure of it. He had never been as sure of anything in his life.

Brody pointed to the window. "Three, seven, and ten. There it is, the source of the Roman numerals."

"My God, you're right."

"Dad wasn't looking for a *book*, but the knight's tomb. He was looking for the tomb itself."

Elsa's expression was utterly blank. She finally shook her head. "What do you mean?"

"Don't you get it, Elsa? The tomb is somewhere in the library. You said yourself that this place used to be a church."

Indy's eyes rested on one of the marble columns. "There." He jabbed his finger at it and strode across the room as Elsa and Brody hurried after him.

"Three." Indy pointed at the Roman numerals embedded in the column and smiled triumphantly. "I bet they're all numbered. Spread out. Let's find the others—seven and ten."

They headed off in separate directions, each one making a beeline toward a column. A moment later, Brody motioned to Indy. He found VII.

They kept looking, but none of them could find the last one—X.

They regrouped in the center of the room, about halfway between the III and VII columns. "Damn, it has to be here," Indy muttered. "It's got to be. I'm sure of it."

He walked over to a ladder leading to a loft, climbed up it, and looked down, hoping that his new perspective would offer a clue. It took only a moment to see it, it was that obvious. The floor where Brody and Elsa stood was an elaborate tile design that contained a huge X that was visible only if you were above it.

"X marks the spot," he said aloud, and grinned. He rushed down the ladder and found the center tile where the X intersected. He bent down on one knee and started prying the tile with his knife.

"What're you doing?" Elsa whispered, and looked about anxiously to see who might be watching the crazy foreigner who was ripping up the floor.

"I'm going to find the knight's tomb." The words hissed through his gritted teeth as he struggled with the tile. "What do you think?"

After several moments the tile popped free, revealing a two-foot square hole and proving him right. Cold air and a wet, rancid smell escaped from the dark cavity.

Indy looked up at Elsa and Brody and smiled broadly. "Bingo."

CHAPTER NINE

◄◄ ►►

THE CRUSADER'S TOMB

"You don't disappoint, Dr. Jones," Elsa said, brushing a strand of blond hair back in place. "You're a great deal like your father."

"Except he's lost, and I'm not."

Indy peered down into the blackness of the hole, then took a coin from his pocket and dropped it. He heard a soft plop a second later. The bottom was about six feet down. "Be back soon."

He was about to climb into the hole when Elsa touched him on the shoulder. "Ladies first, Indiana Jones. Please lower me down."

Indy tipped his fedora, impressed by the woman's spirit. She sat down, swung her legs over the lip of the hole, then dropped her head back and looked up at him. "Ready?" she asked.

"Ready," he said.

She lifted her arms above her head. He gripped her hands, and she pushed away from the edge. For a second or two she hung in the center of the blackness; then Indy slowly lowered her until she told him to let go. He did and heard her drop to the floor an instant later.

Indy glanced over his shoulder at Brody. "Keep an eye on things, Marcus."

Brody nodded. "I'll put the tile back in place so we don't attract any attention."

"Good idea." He reached in his pocket for the Grail diary and removed the folded piece of paper. He stuffed it in his shirt, then passed the diary to Brody. "Take care of this for me."

"Will do."

Indy glanced down the hole, then back to Brody. "Be back soon. I hope."

He dropped down into the hole, and the tile slid back in place. Instantly the darkness collapsed around him. Overhead, he heard a clatter of footsteps. What the hell was Brody doing, taking dance lessons?

"Elsa?" he whispered.

Her cigarette lighter flicked on; the tiny yellow flame looked like some sort of weird, glowing insect. He blinked and saw her peering at him.

"Did you hear that?" he asked.

"What?"

He glanced up, torn between going back and moving on. Maybe a librarian or the police had found Brody messing around with the tile. If they went back up now, they might never get another chance to look for the knight and the second marker. "Nothing, I guess."

He took the lighter from Elsa. "Come on. Let's get this over with."

It was cool and still, and the air smelled like wet socks. They moved along a stone-walled corridor as Indy sheltered the lighter's flame with his palm. It didn't offer much light, and every now and then he had to look slightly to the right or the left of the flame to see what lay ahead of them.

He stopped and gazed a moment toward a niche carved in the wall. He took a couple steps closer, at first not believing what he saw in the flickering light. He held the lighter slightly to one side and peered ahead, directly at a leering skull attached to blackened skeletal remains that were covered in rotting strips of linen.

"I think we've found a catacombs," Elsa said from behind him. "There's another one of these guys on the other wall."

Indy looked over his shoulder. "Nice. Let's keep going. I don't think either of these fine fellows is our fabled knight."

They moved on, passing several similar burial sites before Elsa pointed to symbols carved on the wall near one of the skeletons.

"Look at this," she said. "Pagan symbols. Fourth or fifth century."

Indy held the lighter up and stepped closer to examine the markings. "Right. About six hundred years before the Crusades."

"The Christians would have dug their own passages and burial chambers centuries later," Elsa added.

He knew she was right and told her so. "If a knight from the First Crusade is entombed down here, that's where we'll find him."

They moved on down the tunnel. "We're on a crusade, too, aren't we?" Elsa's voice was hushed and sincere.

Funny, he thought. She took this Grail stuff as seriously as his father did. "I guess we are. You could say that." He paused. "Hold my hand."

"Why?"

She didn't sound very enthusiastic, he thought, but what the hell. "I don't want to fall."

She laughed, and her fingers brushed his, and Indy clasped her hand.

The passageway wound to their left for another hundred yards or so, then opened into a section of the catacombs that was wider and wetter. They were soon slogging through ankle-deep water that was dark and slimy.

Indy noticed the water percolating in spots. He dipped his fingers into it and rubbed them together. "Petroleum. I could sink a well down here and retire."

"Indy, look." Elsa pointed to another marking on the wall. "A menorah. During the tenth century a large Jewish ghetto formed in Venice."

"I guess that means we're headed in the right direction."

Elsa stopped in front of another carved symbol. "I don't recognize this one."

Indy perused the wall and knew instantly what the etching depicted. He had not only seen it before but had pursued what it represented halfway around the globe, barely escaping death a handful of times.

"That's the Ark of the Covenant."

"Are you sure?"

He glanced over at her, a slight smile forming on his lips. "Pretty sure."

They continued deeper into the catacombs. The passageway narrowed. The water rose to their knees. Indy stopped. He heard a thrashing in the water and a squealing sound. He held up the lighter.

"Rats."

Two, three, four of them. No big deal. As soon as he had discounted them, he saw a couple more, then others. There were dozens of them diving from ledges into the water. He cautiously stepped ahead and saw the water churning with rats. He recalculated. There were hundreds, maybe thousands, of them pouring into the passageway.

He was getting worried.

He looked over at Elsa. Shadows and light danced across her face; her expression was one of disgust, not squeamishness, for which he was grateful. The last thing he needed was a woman who would faint at the sight of a rat. He suggested they climb up onto the ledge, and she readily agreed.

The outcropping of rock was just wide enough for them to gain footing. It was wet and slippery, and they inched forward holding hands, their backs flat against the wall. Below them the river of squealing rats rushed by, and occasionally Indy booted a few from the ledge. At least it wasn't snakes. Ever since he had fallen into a vat of snakes as a kid, he had had an aversion to them. A couple of years ago, during his search for the Ark of the Covenant, he had been trapped in a den of snakes and still had nightmares about that experience.

Adrenaline surged through him as he sidled along the ledge. Danger was a two-sided experience: apprehension on one side, thrills on the other. He squeezed Elsa's hand and smiled to himself. If he had to be prowling through slimy, rat-infested catacombs, he couldn't think of a better choice of companion than Elsa Schneider. She was bright, lovely, and didn't seem to be any more disturbed about their tenuous circumstances than he was. He liked that. Besides, he knew the shared experience was bonding them together, and he thoroughly enjoyed the thought of what might develop—provided they survived the excursion.

Encounters with beautiful women in exotic, dangerous circumstances were hardly everyday experiences in his profession. They never rated mention in his university lectures. But maybe someday he'd write a book and turn his more interesting encounters in the field into an eye-opening adventure tale.

The passageway turned and opened into an expansive chamber that was flooded with black, briny water but appeared devoid of rats. Their eyes had adjusted to the darkness, and Indy no longer needed the lighter. They paused a moment, gazing in silence toward the center of the cavern. Jutting up above the water on a stone platform were several ancient caskets. An "island altar," Indy thought.

They waded toward the coffins, the putrid water deepening with every step. It was up to their knees, and they were still fifty feet away.

"Be careful," Indy said. "Stay behind me. The bottom's slippery."

As soon as he said it, he lost his footing and fell to his knees. "See what I mean?" He stood up, smiled sheepishly, then took another step forward, and instantly the water rose to his chest.

"It's only water. C'mon."

They carefully moved ahead, the water remaining at Indy's chest and Elsa's shoulders. "If this gets any deeper," Elsa warned him, "I'm climbing on your back."

"Yeah. Fine. But whose back am I going to climb on?"

When they reached the center of the chamber, they crawled onto the elevated platform and immediately forgot about the water and the rats. The two scholars began examining the ancient, ornately carved caskets, which were made of oak and held together by straps of etched brass.

"It must be one of these," Indy said.

"This one," Elsa said.

Indy nodded. He wasn't sure she was right, but she seemed confident about her choice.

"Do you doubt me? Look at the artistry of the carvings and the scrollwork. This is the work of men who believed that devotion to God and to beauty were one and the same," she said, placing her hands gently on the coffin.

Indy leaned over and strained to open the lid. Elsa joined him. The top groaned as it slowly rose. Then suddenly it slid away from the coffin and banged against the stone platform.

He peered down and saw a rusted suit of armor and an intricately carved shield. The hood of the helmet was turned up, and inside it, the hollow eyes of a skull stared up at him.

"This is the knight," Elsa proclaimed. "Look at the engraving on the shield. It's the same as Donovan's Grail tablet."

Indy was elated. He clasped her arm, and the words spilled out of him. "The shield is the second marker. We found it."

"I just wish he was here now to see this."

"Who, Donovan?"

"No, of course not. Your father. He would be so thrilled."

He glanced around the chamber and tried to imagine his father here. He couldn't. Libraries were his idea of an excursion.

"Yeah, thrilled to death."

He leaned over the coffin and brushed away the dust and corrosion from the knight's shield. Despite Indy's enthusiasm, the past and his difficult relationship with his father were never far from his mind.

"He never would have made it by those rats. He hates rats. He's scared to death of 'em." He recalled an incident from his childhood. "Believe me, I know. We had one in the basement once, and guess who had to go down there and kill it? Yours truly, and I was only six."

Indy reached into his shirt and took out the paper impression of the Grail tablet. He unfolded it and laid it over the shield. The portion missing from the tablet was there on the shield. "A perfect match. We've got it."

"Where did that come from?"

"Trade secret."

"Oh, I thought we were partners."

She sounded miffed, and Indy, who had started making a rubbing of the missing portion of the Grail tablet, paused long enough to glance up and smile.

"No offense, Elsa. But we just met." He went back to work on the rubbing.

"This is no time for professional rivalry, Dr. Jones. Your father is missing. Quite possibly in serious danger, and here . . ."

Indy's head snapped up. "Hold it." It wasn't what she said that had made him shout at her.

He looked around, tilted his head, listening. Something was wrong. He heard a distant squealing. It was getting louder, closer. Rats again.

Then he saw the glow of firelight dancing across the walls of the catacombs. A moment later he saw the rats. Thousands of them squirmed through the narrow passage, stampeded into the chamber, and headed toward the stone platform.

Within seconds the rats washed over the platform and caskets, a squirming, squealing tidal wave. Then Indy saw what they were scurrying to escape. An enormous fireball roared around the corner—it was feeding on the oil slick and depleting the oxygen, an elemental monster devouring everything in its path. It was spreading across the chamber and heading toward them.

Elsa screamed.

Indy stuffed the rubbing from the shield inside his shirt, then braced his back against the altar and toppled the coffin with his feet. It crashed against the stone platform and splashed into the water. It sank, then bobbed to the surface.

"Jump," Indy shouted.

For a second Elsa didn't move. Indy grabbed her hand and yanked her along after him. They struck the water, inches from the bobbing, overturned coffin. Fingers of flame licked across the surface, sizzling masses of shrieking rats.

Indy grabbed on to the coffin. "Get under it. Quick. Air pockets."

When Elsa hesitated, Indy fit his palm over her head, dunked her, and dragged her under the coffin. She surfaced in the air pocket, sputtering and coughing, clawing her hair from her eyes so she could see. She gasped as she found herself face-to-face with the ghastly, decomposed skull of the Grail knight, whose armor had remained attached to the coffin.

Indy popped up next to her, grimaced at the skull, then struggled to detach the corpse. He jerked it from the coffin, pushed it down. However, there were air pockets in the armor, and the grisly skull popped to the surface and stared blindly at them.

"Get lost." Indy struck the top of the head with his fist, like a hammer, and pounded it back down. This time it slowly sank beneath them. He kicked the armor and it drifted away.

The heat rose. Hundreds of rats scrambled across the top of the coffin. The scratching of their claws and their relentless squealing created a deafening din. The coffin rocked back and forth and started to sink beneath the weight of the rats. Some of them surfaced inside the coffin, still chattering, squealing.

"Indy. My God."

Elsa swatted at a rat that was swimming toward her, then swatted another that had scrambled onto her shoulder from behind. The rats seemed to be everywhere, and there was no end to them. They were panicked and biting at anything near them.

Indy punched one rat after another on the snout as they neared him. Above them, sawdust rained as the rats above desperately tried to burrow through the top of the coffin. One rat dropped through a hole. Several more followed, plopping down on them.

Some of the rats were on fire and hissed as they struck the water. The stench of burned hair and flesh filled the coffin. The heat of the fire pressed down on them, sucking greedily at the air, gobbling it up. Indy coughed and knuckled an eye.

Elsa screamed as she was bitten.

It can't last much longer. It can't, Indy was trying to convince himself.

"The coffin's on fire," Elsa yelled above the shriek of rats.

"There go the rats," Indy said as nonchalantly as possible. But he knew their situation was desperate. "Can you swim?"

"Austrian swim team. 1932 Summer Olympics. Silver medal in the fifty-meter freestyle."

"A simple yes or no would've sufficed. Take a deep breath. We'll have to swim under the fire."

They filled their lungs and dove under. As he swam, Indy wondered why the fire had started. Maybe a spark from the lighter had ignited it. But they would have noticed it much sooner.

Thirty seconds. What if someone had followed them? If so, then what happened to Brody?

Forty-five seconds. Indy felt the side of the chamber. He saw a faint light to his left and headed toward it.

One minute. The light was filtering through a storm drain that opened into the wall.

Indy paused and looked back to Elsa. The source of light must lead outside. But would they fit through the opening? He swam into the drain and had gone less than fifty feet when he reached a hole in the top of it. A spindle of light pierced down through it, and the opening was just large enough for his shoulders.

He took one more look back for Elsa, pointed at the hole, and urged her to go up. She shook her head, and motioned him to go first.

Indy wasn't about to argue. He had been underwater at least a minute and a half, maybe longer, and his lungs were ready to burst. He kicked hard, shot up, and his head broke the surface. He gulped at the air. Nothing had ever tasted so sweet.

A moment later, Elsa surfaced next to him. To his surprise, she didn't even seem out of breath.

He looked up. A shaft rose twenty feet up to daylight. Indy pressed his back against one side of it, his feet against the other and worked his way up.

Elsa mimicked his style. "Don't fall on me, Indy," she yelled.

"Wouldn't think of it."

He glanced down only once. Elsa looked like a crab of some kind, working her way up the shaft beneath him, her blond hair wet and tangled. She sensed his eyes and tipped her head back. She grinned, and Indy chuckled and kept on climbing.

When he reached the top, he pushed up on one side of the grating. It lifted a couple of inches, then fell back. He tried again with no better success. He could see feet walking by, and yelled. Someone looked down, and he called for the man to pull off the grating.

The stranger complied and gave him a hand.

As soon as he was out, he swiveled around and reached down inside the sewer, shouting for Elsa to grab his hand. She did, and he hoisted her up onto the sidewalk.

The man looked at them and asked in Italian if they were all right.

Elsa answered in a reassuring voice, telling him everything was fine.

Indy glanced around. They were in the corner of Piazza San Marco a few feet from a sidewalk café, where the people were gawking and talking excitedly among themselves.

Indy smiled broadly as he gazed at the postcard-perfect scene. "Ah, Venice."

His good humor, however, was short-lived.

CHAPTER TEN

◄◄ ►►

LETHAL AGENTS

Indy turned from the gawking patrons of the café to the man who had helped him from the sewer. He was about to thank him when he realized something was wrong. Unlike everyone else nearby, the man's attention was turned away from them. He was staring across the plaza toward the library. Indy followed his gaze and saw four men running in their direction. He noticed the one in front wore a fez. Then he saw something else. One of them was sporting a machine gun.

"Oh, oh."

Suddenly several things clicked together: the clatter he had heard after Brody had lowered the tile; his question about the source of the fire; and the direction from which the men were running. Indy had the distinct impression that they were being hunted. He grabbed Elsa by the hand and ran in the opposite direction toward the Grand Canal.

Elsa lagged behind him, confused by Indy's abrupt sprint toward the water. "What are we doing now? Are you crazy?"

He tugged on her hand. "We've got some company on our trail."

She glanced back, then suddenly surged ahead of him. "You're right."

Indy leaped into a motorboat. He fired the engine. It sputtered and died.

"Hurry, Indy. They're almost . . ."

He pulled again and the engine fired. He shoved it into gear, and at that moment the boat rocked violently and Elsa shouted.

Indy pulled down on the throttle and glanced back just in time to block a punch. One of the men had boarded just as he pulled away. The boat veered wildly as the two men exchanged punches. Elsa crawled past them, grabbed the wheel, and turned sharply, barely missing several gondolas. Gondoliers stopped singing and shook their fists as they careened along the canal. One of the gondolas flipped over in the sudden backwash of the speedboat.

"Sorry," Elsa called out.

Indy, meanwhile, battled as best he could on the bouncing speedboat. He took a savage punch to his stomach and doubled over, holding a rib. The attacker rose up, pulled his arm back for the finishing blow, but Indy struck first. He caught him squarely in the jaw, hurtling him over the side.

He brushed his hands off, wiping them clean of the ordeal. He wished the man had stayed around so he could question him, but then again he hadn't seemed very cooperative.

"I guess that takes care of that," he yelled forward to Elsa.

"Think again."

Behind them a pair of speedboats was giving chase and gaining rapidly on them. He crawled toward the wheel. "Let me handle this."

"Wait until I . . ."

He looked up, and his jaw dropped. They were moving toward an enormous steamship straight ahead. The hull of the ship was drifting toward the dock, and the gap ahead of them was narrowing.

"Are you crazy?" he shouted. "Don't go between them. We'll never . . ."

But Elsa only caught snatches of what he'd said. "Go between them? Are you nuts?"

Indy shook his head, confused. He took another step toward the wheel, but Elsa had already committed the speedboat to the perilous course between the steamship and the dock. He frantically waved his hands. "No. Elsa, I said go *around* them!"

"You said go *between* them."

"I did not."

At this point it no longer mattered. The hull of the ship and the side of the dock loomed on either side of them like cavern walls. Indy crouched down, grabbed the side of the boat, and squeezed his eyes closed, waiting for the impact.

He heard a piercing screech of metal. But they were still in one piece. He opened his eyes and looked back. Just behind them one of the other boats had smashed into the hull.

Indy breathed a sigh of relief. But a moment later he saw the other boat emerge from the far side of the steamboat. "Let me handle this," he said, taking over the steering. "You scare me."

That said, he jammed the wheel to the right in a diversionary move. The boat swerved sharply, but the one pursuing them smoothly matched the turn. It was still gaining on them, moving up on their left side.

"All right, guys," Indy said through gritted teeth. "Let's see what you're made of."

He jerked the wheel to his left, hoping to drive the other boat into the side of the canal. Suddenly a machine gun chattered, and splinters flew away from the side of the boat.

"Okay. I get your point."

He quickly changed his course, zigzagging ahead of his pursuers. But the machine-gun blasts battered the engine. It coughed, sputtered, and then it died.

Indy grabbed his pistol and fired at the other boat until he was out of bullets.

"Indy, look!"

"What?"

Elsa was pointing to the side of the boat. They were drifting and heading right toward the rotating blades of an enormous propeller on the stern of another steamship.

The other boat drew close to them. One of the men held a machine gun on them. The other, who was behind the wheel, stood up and smiled at Indy. He was swarthy, in his late thirties, with a mustache and black, wavy hair protruding from beneath his fez. His dark, compelling eyes seemed to bore right through Indy. The boat bumped against them, pushing them closer to the churning propeller.

Indy was almost too exhausted to think. He had unraveled the ancient code, battled rats in slimy water, found the Grail knight, and narrowly escaped a fire. Then the flight and battle on the water had followed in rapid succession. Now, as he stared eye to eye at the man, he just wanted to know what the hell was going on.

Then he remembered Brody. "What did you do to my friend back in the library?"

The man laughed; his eyes were now dark pools that revealed nothing. "Your friend will be okay. You better worry about yourself."

Indy glanced over his shoulder and saw they had drifted closer to the propellers. "Who are you, and what do you want anyhow?"

"My name is Kazim, and I'm after the same thing you are, my friend."

"Your kind of friends I don't need. I don't know what you're talking about."

"Oh, I think you do, Dr. Jones."

The boat rocked in the turbulent waters near the propeller. Indy turned to Elsa and signaled her with his eyes that it was time to act.

"Enough talk," Kazim yelled over the noise of the propeller as it slapped against the water. "Better luck in the next world." He motioned for the man with the machine gun to shoot them.

Elsa jumped to the other boat, momentarily distracting the man with the gun. Indy leaped the gap, and his forearm came up under the machine gun, which fired harmlessly into the air. As they battled for control of the gun, the engine started.

The boat sped forward, and Indy lost his balance. He fell over the side, pulling the man with the machine gun with him. He let go of the man and swam as fast as he could away from the pull of the propeller. The gunman, desperate and panicking, yelled for help.

Behind him Indy heard a loud crunch as the other boat was dragged underwater. With a deafening crash the propeller blades of the steamship violently tore it apart like a piece of balsa wood, scattering shredded bits of the boat across the surface of the water.

Kazim swung the boat about and edged as close as he could to the steamship. Indy swam for it as Elsa leaned over the side, stretching her hand until he grasped it.

The gunman wasn't so lucky. He was already floundering

in the bubbling maelstrom a few feet from the slicing blades. He screamed again to Kazim, but it was too late. Indy looked back just as the man was sucked into the blades.

The water abruptly foamed red.

Kazim shoved the motor into gear, and the boat tore away from the pull of the steamship. He zigzagged, trying to shake Indy from the side. But Elsa clutched his arm, dragging him until he grabbed the side of the boat. Then, with a final burst of energy, he pulled himself out of the water and flopped onto the floor of the boat gasping for breath.

He looked up and saw Kazim trying to load his gun and steer the boat at the same time. He crawled forward and shoved him against the wheel, causing the boat to spin a hundred and eighty degrees back to the direction of the steamboat.

"Indy, we're going back toward . . ."

Before Elsa could finish, he switched off the ignition, and pulled out the key. He pressed his thumb against the man's throat.

"Okay, Kazim, you and I are going to have a little chat."

Kazim stammered as Indy let up on his throat. "You foolish man." He tried to sound calm and dignified. "What are you doing, Dr. Jones? Are you crazy?"

"Where's my father?"

"Let go of me, please."

"Where . . . is . . . my . . . father?"

"If you don't let go, Dr. Jones, we'll both die. We're drifting back toward the steamship."

Indy heard the chop of the blades cutting through the water. He didn't even bother to look back. His eyes were wide and his voice sounded hysterical. "Good. Then we'll die."

"My soul is prepared, Dr. Jones." Kazim's voice was even, smooth as cream. "How about yours? Is *your* soul ready, Doctor?"

Indy grabbed the front of Kazim's shirt. "This is your last chance, damn it." Kazim's shirt ripped open, revealing a tattoo on his chest in the shape of a Christian cross that tapered down like the blades of a broadsword.

He stared placidly back at Indy, undisturbed.

"What's that supposed to be?" Indy asked.

Kazim raised his head high. "It's an ancient family symbol. My forebears were princes of an empire that stretched from Morocco to the Caspian Sea."

"Allah be praised," Indy said quietly.

"Thank you, and God save *you* too. But I was referring to the Christian empire of Byzantium."

Indy smiled gamely. "Of course. And why were you trying to kill me?"

Elsa tapped him on the shoulder. "Indy, you're going to kill all of us if we don't get out of here."

"Hold on." Indy sounded irritated. "Keep talking, Kazim. It's just getting interesting."

"The secret of the Grail has been safe for a thousand years. And for all that time the Brotherhood of the Cruciform Sword has been prepared to do anything to keep it safe."

"The Brotherhood of the Cruciform Sword?" Elsa seemed to have forgotten about their precarious situation, her curiosity whetted.

Indy's eyes narrowed as he looked again at the tattoo on Kazim's chest. Then he met the man's gaze, held it for a long moment. The roar of the blades was as loud now as it had been when he was treading water. The boat rocked violently beneath them.

"Ask yourself why you seek the cup of Christ, for his glory or yours," Kazim said.

"I didn't come for the cup of Christ. I came to find my father."

Kazim nodded, glanced over Indy's shoulder toward the steamship. "In that case, God be with you in your quest. Your father is being held in the Brunwald Castle on the Austrian-German border."

Indy suddenly pushed Kazim aside, jammed the key into the ignition. He felt the spray from the steamship's giant propeller on his back as he turned the key. The engine sputtered and died.

"C'mon. Start."

He tried again. This time the engine revved to life, and they pulled away just seconds before the blades would have chewed into the hull.

"You're dangerous!" Elsa shouted at him, her pretty face

flushed red, as though she were sunburned. "You could've gotten us killed."

He smiled. "I know. But I got what I wanted. Ask Kazim where we can drop him off."

Indy's thoughts were already miles ahead of him.

CHAPTER ELEVEN

◄◄ ►►

DONOVAN'S PLACE

After a hot shower, food, and nine hours of sleep, Indy was ready to explore the apartment Donovan had allowed them to use during their stay in Venice. "Apartment," however, was something of a misnomer: the place was a virtual palace.

The ceilings were vaulted, and the floors were made of thick slabs of marble. The antique furnishings were worth a fortune. There was a courtyard and balconies and at least a dozen rooms altogether. Covering the walls were some of the finest paintings of sixteenth-century Venetian artists: Veroneses, Tintorettos, and Titians as well as a variety of works that were mostly of historical importance.

It was obvious to Indy that most of the paintings were designed to bolster the egos of the sixteenth-century aristocracy, who spent most of their time showing off the riches of their independent state for visiting dignitaries. He smiled, thinking that Donovan was cut from the same mold, a twentieth-century patrician.

Indy was impressed by it all, but at the same time found it too pretentious for a private home. Some of the works should have been in museums, where they could be appreciated by more people. In some ways it was even a little obscene that so much beauty should be enjoyed only by the people who came into these rooms.

He wandered into the library. Shelves climbed from the floor to the ceiling on each of the four walls. Impressive, he thought. His father would've loved it. He perused the books and picked up a volume called *The Common-wealth of*

89

Oceana, by James Harrington. It was an original edition and had been published in 1656. He flipped it open to a marked page and read a sentence describing Venice. "There never happened unto any other Common-wealth, so undisturbed and constant a tranquility and peace in her self, as is that of Venice."

"Right." Indy chuckled. Tranquillity, peace: things had changed a bit in three centuries. An image of the brutal Fascists he had seen flashed into his head. He rubbed absently one of his bruised ribs and tried not to think too much about his own less than tranquil experiences in the city.

Maybe the city was still undisturbed for some people, but he wasn't one of them.

It was his second day in Venice, and he, Elsa, and Brody were all still recovering from the incidents of yesterday. An egg-size lump had risen on the back of Brody's head where he had been struck. Indy was recovering from an odd combination of combat and travel fatigue. His jaw was tender, and two of his ribs were sore from a couple of punches that had connected. Elsa, meanwhile, was suffering from minor rat bites and a slight burn on one arm from the fire in the catacombs.

Indy had been impressed that she hadn't even mentioned the burns or bites until after they had found Brody wandering about the library in a daze and had made their way to the apartment. She was pensive today and kept looking at him as if she wanted to say something. But every time he tried to start a conversation, she abruptly found an excuse to do something else.

"Indy!"

Brody stood in the doorway of the library. He held an ice pack to his head with one hand and had a sheet of rumpled paper in the other.

"How's the head, Marcus?"

"Better, now that I've seen this. It finally dried. You've got to take a look."

In spite of the ice pack, Brody sounded as excited as Indy had ever seen him. He hurried into the library and dropped the piece of paper on the massive mahogany table that dominated the room. The paper was what remained of the rubbing from the knight's shield. It was smeared and faded from the soaking in the tunnel, but was still in one piece. Now that it was dry, Indy could see that it was fairly legible.

"We know that what was missing from Donovan's Grail tablet was the name of the city, right?"

Indy nodded.

Brody pointed at the ancient lettering, and Indy leaned close. But Brody couldn't contain himself. "You see, it's Alexandretta."

"You sure?"

"Positive."

Indy walked to a shelf and searched until he found an atlas.

"What are you doing?" Brody asked.

"Looking for a map of Hatay."

Indy knew that the knights of the First Crusade had laid siege to Alexandretta for more than a year, and the entire city had been destroyed. Today, the city of Iskenderun on Hatay's Mediterranean coast was built on its ruins.

He found the page he wanted and stabbed at it. "Here. Look, Marcus, this is the desert, and this is the mountain range. Just the way the Grail tablet described it. Somewhere in these mountains must be the Canyon of the Crescent Moon." He paused, studying it. "But where? *Where* in these mountains?"

"Your father would know," Brody said quietly.

"He would?"

"Let me take a look at the diary."

Indy passed it to him.

"Your father *did* know. He knew everything except the city from which to start. He drew a map with no names. Here it is."

He set the diary on the table and opened it to a pencil-drawn map that covered two pages. Indy had looked at it briefly on the airplane, but since there were no names, it hadn't meant anything to him.

Brody's fingers moved across it. "Henry probably pieced this together from a hundred different sources over the last forty years."

"What is it?" Indy asked, even though he had a fairly good idea.

"It describes a course due east, away from the city, across

the desert, to an oasis. Then turning south to a river which leads to a mountain range, here, and into a canyon. But because he had no names, he didn't know *what* city. Or *which* desert. Or *which* river."

And now they knew, for all the good it would do his father.

"I'm sure there're enough details here to find it. Indy, I'm going after it." Brody looked up at him, his spirits soaring after his discovery. "I hope you'll come with me."

Indy shook his head and closed the Grail diary. "I'm going after Dad. I'm leaving first thing in the morning for Austria."

Brody nodded, understanding. "Of course. What was I thinking. I'd better..."

"No. You go ahead, Marcus. I'll... We'll catch up to you."

"Are you sure?"

"Yes."

Brody was quiet a moment, as if he was wondering if he had made the right choice. Then he brightened. "Well, we've got a few more hours in Venice. Let's make the most of it. I'd love to visit the Galleria dell'Accademia. It has the best collection of Venetian paintings in existence. Let's go, okay?"

"You sure you feel up to it?"

Brody took the ice pack from his head. "I'm feeling fine. Do you know that collection has Giorgione's *Tempest*, Carpaccio's *Saint Ursula Legend*, and Titian's *Presentation of the Virgin*? Everything is there," Brody gushed, "from the first masters of the fourteenth century to the great pieces of the mid-eighteenth century."

Indy shrugged. "Let's go. I'll ask Elsa if she wants to join us."

Elsa couldn't seem to make up her mind about joining them. It was as if she were suffering from delayed shock or something, the aftereffects of their tumultuous experiences. Or maybe it was depression, as if their survival were a letdown somehow.

"I think I'll skip the galleries," she finally said. "I'm going out to buy a few groceries for dinner. I hope that's okay."

"You want company?" He wouldn't mind one bit spending the rest of the afternoon alone with her while Brody toured the museum. Hell, he'd even help make dinner.

She shook her head. "You and Marcus go on. I'll meet you back at the apartment."

So much for a romantic dinner, he thought, and went off to get dressed.

After a five-minute walk from the apartment, Indy and Brody reached the Ponte dell'Accademia, a wooden bridge crossing the Grand Canal. There were four hundred bridges in Venice, but only three crossed the Grand Canal. The bridge had been built five years earlier, during the Depression, and supposedly was a temporary structure.

They stopped at the summit to take in the view. On their left, they could see as far as Basilica di San Marco—a Byzantine monument from the eleventh century. The exterior of the church dated back to the thirteenth century and the sacking of Byzantium during the Fourth Crusade. On the right was the Palazzo Balbi, a palace with obelisks on its roof.

"I've been thinking, Marcus. I don't like the idea of you going off on your own."

"Indy, I'm sure your father would approve. If we wait any longer, those violent people from that strange brotherhood might find it, and who knows what would happen to the Grail Cup."

"I won't stop you. But before you leave, contact Sallah. Have him meet you in Iskenderun."

Brody nodded in agreement. Sallah was an old friend of both men. When Indy had pursued the Ark of the Covenant in Egypt, Sallah had saved his life more than once. He would feel a lot better about Brody chasing after the Grail Cup if he knew that Sallah was with him.

The two men spent the next hour wandering about the rooms of the Accademia. Brody was an enthusiastic and knowledgeable tour guide, pointing out the significance of one painting after another. He noted that the Renaissance for Venetians was something of a paradox. Unlike the rest of Italy, they had no Roman heritage. Founded on the cusp between East and West, antiquity and the Middle Ages, the city had preserved its traditions from the early Christian era. As a result, the Renaissance was more an adaptation of style and intention than a rebirth. Yet, Venice produced some of the best works of the Italian Renaissance.

Indy found them interesting but was less enthralled than Brody. He always told his students that there was an overlap between art and archaeology, but with the latter the remains of preserved feces could be as interesting and notable as painted ceramics or finely crafted gold.

Near the end of the hour Indy could tell that Brody was tiring and reminded him that his head injury was still fresh and he had better take it easy.

"I'm all right, Indy. Just a minor concussion and a bit of a headache. I'll be fit in the morning."

But he agreed that it was time to leave.

As they neared the apartment, Indy felt increasingly anxious. It was as if dozens of tiny needles were poking the back of his neck. Over the years he had learned to pay attention to that sensation. It was a sort of inbred warning signal, one that had given him a helpful edge more than once.

As soon as they reached the apartment, he knew the intuitive sensation had proved itself again. The door was slightly ajar. He peered inside, then cautiously entered the apartment and looked around.

"Elsa?" he called out tentatively.

The silence threw his own voice back to him, an empty echo.

"Elsa?" He raised his voice this time. Again there was no answer.

Just like Dad. A chill sped down his spine.

"I'll check the kitchen," Brody said.

Indy rushed over to his bedroom and swung open the door. The room had been ransacked. The mattress was on the floor, and the drawers had been dumped.

Oh, God. What happened to her?

He hurried down the hall to Elsa's room. He paused, took a breath, and slowly turned the doorknob. Someone had rifled through her room as well. The intruder had tossed things from her drawers, jerked clothes from the hangers, torn the sheets away from the mattress.

But where the hell was she?

He backed out of the room and heard a distant, muffled

voice. He crept down the hallway. The voice grew louder, more distinct. It was a woman's voice, singing, and coming from the bathroom.

He opened the door a crack. "Elsa?"

"Hello, Indy."

She was in a bathtub full of bubbles, smiling brightly at him. Bubbles encircled her throat like a necklace of translucent pearls. A smooth white shoulder lifted from the foam.

"Listen, kid. People are trying to sleep." He backed out, relieved she was okay. He'd let her enjoy her bath.

"I'll be right out," she called after him.

He returned to his room and looked over the mess. Whoever had rummaged through the place must have been hiding when Elsa returned from her shopping trip. The intruder probably fled when she went into the bathroom.

He waited as he heard Elsa singing in the hallway en route to her room. He looked at his watch, estimating how long it would take her to change her tune.

She shrieked, and he smiled. He waited for her to run to his room. He heard footsteps. She swung open his door. She was dressed in a bathrobe; her hair was still wet.

Her jaw looked as though it had come unhinged. "Indy, my room . . ."

"Yeah, mine, too."

She shook her head. "What were they looking for, anyway?"

"This."

He took the Grail diary out of his pocket and tossed it onto the table.

"Your father's Grail diary. You had it."

"Uh-huh."

"You didn't tell me." She shook her head. "You don't trust me."

Over Elsa's shoulder Indy saw Brody peeking into the room and signaled that everything was okay. Brody, sensing that matters were turning personal, quickly backed away, slipping out of sight.

"I didn't know you." He looked into her soft blue eyes; his thumb ached to trace the pout on her mouth. Christ, but she was hard to resist. "Or maybe I wanted to know you better."

"It was the same for me." Her voice was breathy now. "From the moment I saw you."

"Does this sort of thing happen to you all the time?"

"No. Never. It's a nice feeling."

He moved closer to her, touched her face. "Don't trust it, Elsa."

"What do you mean?"

"Shared danger. Coming out of it alive. That's what did it."

"Yeah?" She smiled coyly, and Indy moved toward her, touched her chin, lifting it, and kissed her gently. Her mouth tasted faintly of toothpaste. He loved the scent of soap on her skin. She moved up against him, and suddenly he was kissing her harder, and she responded passionately, letting herself go.

"Look after me, Indy," she whispered, her breath warm against her ear.

His hands worked at the belt of her robe. "You looked after yourself pretty well yesterday. For an art historian."

"You don't know anything about art historians, Dr. Jones? Do you?"

"I know what I like."

"I'm glad you do, Indiana Jones."

She grabbed the hair on the back of his head and pulled his face toward hers. She kissed him long and deep, holding him close to her. Her kiss was so hard that Indy cut his lip on his own tooth.

He rubbed away a drop of blood with the back of his hand. "You're dangerous."

"Maybe I am. Just like you."

Her eyes flashed. She was breathing hard, waiting for him to move. A smile changed the shape of her mouth. Her hair lifted gently in the evening breeze that blew through the open window. Outside, a gondolier was singing.

"Ah, Venice," Indy said half-aloud and closed the bedroom door.

AUSTRIA/
GERMANY

CHAPTER TWELVE

◄◄ ►►

THE BRUNWALD CASTLE

The Mercedes-Benz Indy had rented glided smoothly around the sharp mountain curves of the Austrian Alps. When they started out, the sky had been crisp, clear, a smooth, even blue. But by late afternoon, as he and Elsa neared the German border and the grounds of the Brunwald Castle, storm clouds climbed the horizon, and thunder rumbled in the distance.

A perfect day for a friendly visit, Indy thought, casting an eye toward Elsa.

She was staring straight ahead along the curving road. Her blond hair was tied back, and the waning light struck the sharp promontories of her face—high cheekbones, that pouty mouth, a straight nose, which was, at the moment, pink at the tip from the cold. He thought back to their passionate love-making in Venice and reached out, touching the back of her neck. The skin was cool and dry, and she turned her head, smiling absently, as if she had a lot on her mind.

When this was over, he thought, he and Elsa would . . . well, he didn't know. He would think of something. She had asked him about the university, its archaeology and art history programs, and hinted that she might like to visit him—who knew what might happen.

He pulled into the courtyard. The place loomed in the windshield, menacing and impregnable. The dark windows on the upper levels revealed nothing; the castle was as impregnable as a block of stone. He wondered which one was his father's room. Did he even have a room? Maybe he was in chains in a dungeon. Maybe he wasn't even alive.

No. Bad thought.

This wasn't the time for bad thoughts. He had no idea how he was going to find out where his father was being held, much less how he was going to rescue him. Maybe he wasn't even here. Maybe it had simply been a ploy by Kazim to turn him away from the trail of the Grail Cup.

"Here we are," he said quietly. He felt an all too familiar tingling on the back of his neck, alerting him to danger. Yes, his father was here. He was sure of it.

"Imposing, isn't it?" she said.

"You know anything about the place?"

"It's been in the Brunwald family for generations. They're very powerful in this region, but not particularly well liked."

He noticed a pond next to the castle; gliding across its surface was a solitary swan. Its long neck was gracefully arched, and its snowflake-white feathers seemed luminous against the pond's dark waters. He was reminded of the swan in his father's Grail diary. It represented one of the levels of awareness in the search for the Grail and meant something about overcoming weaknesses of the mind and heart.

Elsa was his weakness. He had quenched his desires like a man who had found an oasis after days in the desert without water. He had taken her greedily, and she had fulfilled his every wish. Why would he, or anyone, want to overcome such pleasures?

"What are you thinking?" she asked.

"Oh, nothing."

"Yeah, I bet," she said softly.

He frowned, hating the idea that his feelings were so obvious.

Elsa brought her hand up under her hair and flicked it off her collar. Indy sensed it was a dismissal of some sort or maybe a signal to just get on with things. He reached into the backseat for his bullwhip, focusing his thoughts on the matter at hand. He attached it to his belt as he got out of the car.

"What're you going to do?" she asked as they headed toward the castle.

"I don't know. I'll think of something."

Indy knocked on the door and waited. Fingers of lightning blazed and sutured the sky. Thunder grumbled almost instantly, and it started to rain. The drops beaded on Elsa's long, well-tailored coat and glistened.

"Let me borrow your coat, okay?"

"You're cold?" she drolled.

"Got an idea."

She shrugged off the coat, and he quickly draped it over his shoulders, covering his leather jacket and bullwhip, just as the heavy wooden door swung open.

A uniformed butler said, "Yes?" in a voice that would have chilled Jell-O.

Indy adopted the haughty manner of an upper-class English barrister and regarded the butler with a properly arrogant expression. "And not before time. Did you intend to leave us standing on the doorstep all day? We're absolutely drenched."

As Indy spoke, he pushed his way past the startled butler, pulling Elsa with him. He sneezed. "Now look. I've caught a sniffle."

He dabbed at his nose with a handkerchief as Elsa looked on in amazement.

"Are you expected?" The butler's voice remained frosty and terse.

"Don't take that tone with *me*, my good man, just buttle off and tell Baron Brunwald that Lord Clarence Chumley and his assistant are here to view the tapestries."

"Tapestries?"

Indy looked over at Elsa. "Dear me, the man is dense. Do you think he heard me?"

He looked back at the butler and continued. "This is a castle, isn't it? You have tapestries?"

"This is a castle, yes. We have tapestries, and if you're an English lord, I'm Jesse Owens."

"How dare you!" Indy responded in a stilted, English falsetto, and knocked the man cold with one powerful punch to the jaw.

The butler crumpled to the stone floor like a windup toy that had suddenly run down. Indy brushed his hands together. "The nerve of it!" He was still chattering in his stilted English voice. "Did you hear him speaking to me like that, impugning my breeding, my honor, my gift for impression?"

Elsa laughed and shook her head as she helped him drag

the butler to a corner closet. "Unbelievable. Very convincing, my lord."

Indy dropped his pose, grabbed Elsa's hand, and tugged her along toward a wide, vaulted hallway. "Okay, let's get down to business." He slipped off her coat as they hurried across the foyer. She pulled it on and started to whisper something, but he touched a finger to his mouth.

Voices.

They stopped. He glanced around quickly, and they ducked into an alcove behind a large piece of statuary. They watched as a pair of uniformed Nazi soldiers walked by. One of them laughed loudly at something the other said, and his voice echoed down the hallway.

"S.S., I should have known," Indy whispered to Elsa as the men disappeared.

They slipped out of their hiding place and continued down the hallway. "Now, where do you suppose they're holding Dad?"

"The dungeon?"

"Very funny." Just a little too close to what he'd been thinking.

A servant appeared in the corridor, wheeling a large trolley that contained the remains of a feast. Indy and Elsa ducked behind a staircase and watched. They hadn't eaten in a few hours, and their eyes widened at the extent of the leftovers. Indy placed a hand over his stomach to keep it from growling. He wondered if it had been his father's dinner. He hoped so; at least he wouldn't be starving in his captivity.

They hid for a long time under the stairs. Indy wanted to get a feel for the place. He needed to have some idea of how many people were on the staff, what the routines were, or if there *were* any routines, and if so, how he might use them to his advantage.

He heard thunder rumbling, and rain thrashed against a window above their heads.

Elsa's stomach growled with hunger.

His own responded.

They looked at each other and laughed silently.

Footsteps on the stairs above them caught Indy's attention. A servant, escorted by an armed German soldier, descended with a cheap tray. On it was a tin bowl with a metal spoon chained to the bowl. *Dad's lunch just sailed past.*

"Now *that* looked more like a prisoner's meal," he whispered as soon as the two were out of sight.

"Yeah, I'm afraid so."

It was time to act. They stepped out from their hiding place and began to ascend the stairs. But just as they reached the first landing, more Nazis approached. This time they concealed themselves behind a massive pillar and waited until the sharp click of the soldiers' boots faded away.

They hurried along and, when they reached the next floor, paused and looked both ways. A door stood ajar nearby; Indy heard voices from inside the room. He peeked through the crack; Nazis were busy examining works of art. Looted booty, he thought.

Hitler was interested in amassing as many of Europe's works of art and primitive artifacts as he could, but not solely for the value of the ancient treasures. Indy was well aware that Hitler had a special interest in obtaining ancient mystical objects that he believed would enhance his power and thus expand his empire.

It was Nazis who had opposed Indy in his pursuit of the Ark of the Covenant. In fact, he had found the Ark only to discover the Führer's goons waiting to take it away from him. He never understood Hitler's motives until he experienced the power of the Ark, something he still couldn't explain. Although he had finally succeeded in getting the Ark to the States, bureaucrats had confiscated the priceless and mysterious artifact. By now he figured it was stored away in a dusty warehouse somewhere, waiting.

He had also heard that Hitler was after the ancient spear that had pierced the side of Jesus Christ. And, no doubt, the leader of the Third Reich would also like to get his hands on the Grail Cup that had held the blood of Jesus. And that, he knew, was why his father was being held captive here.

He backed away from the crack, and he and Elsa moved silently down the corridor. At the end of it were three doors. Indy looked from one to the next, then jabbed his forefinger at the door on the left.

"This one."

"How do you know?" Elsa whispered.

He pointed to an electrical wire. "Because this one's wired. I'll have to find another way in." He stepped back, studied the situation a moment, then decided to try the adjoining door.

He turned the knob; the door was locked. He reached into the pouch on his belt and took out his lock-picking tool. It seemed a lifetime had passed since he had used it on the captain's door to get to the safe with the Cross of Coronado. Yet, it had been less than two weeks ago. He slipped the long, slender tool into the lock, fiddled with it a moment, then turned the knob. The door creaked open.

The room was dimly lit and empty except for a bed and dresser. He closed the door again as soon as Elsa was inside.

"What was that?" she asked as he slipped his burglar's tool back into his pouch.

"A trade secret."

"Oh, you mean you don't tell your students about it?" she asked in mock surprise.

"Only the advanced ones," he said, and walked over to the window.

The rain pounded furiously against the pane. He raised the shade, then the window, and stuck his head out. It was almost dark. The rain splattered against his face, soaking his head. He blinked, clearing his vision. Beneath the window of the next room was a narrow ledge. It ended abruptly several feet away.

Indy pulled his head back into the room and loosened his bullwhip.

"What are you going to do?" Elsa asked.

"Take a shower."

Elsa looked out the window a moment. "You can't mean you're going to..." She saw Indy uncoiling the bullwhip from his belt. "I don't believe it."

"Watch me. It's a snap."

He leaned out the window and flicked the bullwhip at the gargoyle that protruded from the castle wall above the adjoining window. It was a perfect shot; the whip wrapped around the gargoyle's thick neck. He tugged hard, making sure it would hold his weight.

He swung his leg over the window frame and looked back

through the window at Elsa. "Stay there. I won't be long."

"Indy, this is crazy. You can't . . ."

He held up a hand. "Don't worry. This is kid's stuff. Be right back."

Indy swung out from the window, his legs dangling in midair. He was right. It was an easy swing for him, but he hadn't taken one thing into account. The rain had soaked the ledge, and his feet skidded on the slick surface as he landed. One slipped over the ledge, his knee bent, and he wobbled precariously for an instant. Then he pulled on the whip, and recovered his footing.

Next, he had to figure out a way to open the shutters, which were closed over the window. He jerked on them, but they held tight. He was about to try again when he heard a noise. He looked down and saw two Nazi guards prowling with their dogs and flashlights.

They found the butler.

One of the beams bounced along the castle wall, heading in his direction. He pressed himself into the recess of the window and stood perfectly still. *The bullwhip*. He should have loosened it, but it was too late now. The beam skipped over him. He waited, holding his breath. Then he heard the Nazis moving on. They had missed him and the whip.

He turned his attention back to the shutters. He slid his fingers into the opening between them and tugged as hard as he could. They still wouldn't budge. He tried to use his shoulder, but he couldn't get the proper leverage.

Okay, he thought. More drastic measures were in order. But his timing had to be perfect. He watched for a bolt of lightning and noted that the rain was not quite so hard. When he saw the flash, he counted the seconds until he heard the clap of thunder.

He waited until the next bolt lit the sky. He grasped the bullwhip with both hands, counted to himself, then pushed off from the castle wall. He added an extra number in his calculation, figuring the storm was starting to recede. He curled in his legs as he swung back, and crashed through the shutters with both feet. The impact was timed precisely with the thunder.

He tumbled into the room, falling on his hands and knees.

Rain and cold air whipped into the room through the broken shutters. He rose to his feet, looked around to get his bearings. Just as he realized his father was nowhere in sight, something heavy crashed down on the back of his head and shattered.

Indy stumbled, sank to one knee. Stunned, his vision blurred, he looked up helplessly as someone stepped out from the shadows.

"Junior!"

"Yes, sir," he said, responding with a reflex reaction left over from his childhood. He rubbed his head, focusing on his father.

"It's you! Junior!"

Indy's head cleared. Now he was annoyed. "Stop calling me that."

"What the devil are you doing here?"

He wondered if the Nazis had done something to his father's mind. "What do you think? I've come to get you out of here."

Henry looked down at his hand, suddenly distracted and alarmed by what he saw. "Wait a minute."

Indy sucked in his breath, tensed, glanced around. "What's wrong?"

"Late fourteenth century, Ming dynasty," he muttered to himself.

Indy frowned as he realized the fuss was about the broken vase his father was holding.

"It breaks the heart," Henry exclaimed.

"Also the head," Indy interrupted. "You hit me with it, Dad."

Still looking at the vase, Henry continued. "I'll never forgive myself."

Indy misunderstood his father, who was still talking about the vase. "Forget it. I'm fine."

"Thank God."

Henry looked relieved as he examined the broken end of the vase. "It's fake. You see, take a look, you can tell by the . . ."

". . . cross sections," Indy and Henry said simultaneously.

They looked at each other, and both of them grinned. "Sorry about your head," Henry said, frowning a little, as if noticing his son for the first time. "I thought you were one of them."

"*They* come in through the door," Indy said. "They don't need to use the window."

"Good point, but better safe than sorry. This time I was wrong. But by God I was right when I mailed you the diary. I felt something was going to happen. Did you get it?"

Indy nodded. "I got it, and I used it. I found the entrance to the catacombs."

Henry was suddenly excited. "Through the library. You found it?"

"That's right." Indy smiled, pleased to see his father impressed with something he had done.

"I knew it." He stabbed at the air with his fist. "I just knew it! And the tomb of Sir Richard?"

"Found it."

Henry was breathless. "He was actually there. You saw him?"

"What was left of him."

Henry's voice fell to an excited whisper and trembled with expectation. "And the shield . . . the inscription on Sir Richard's shield?"

Indy nodded again, paused a beat, then answered in one word. "Alexandretta."

Henry's mouth came unhinged. He stepped back, rubbing a hand over his beard, considering everything he'd just been told. Lost in thought, he mumbled to himself. "Alexandretta, of course. It was on the pilgrim trail from the Eastern Empire." He turned back to Indy, a jubilant expression on his face. "Junior . . ."

Indy winced. He would have chided his father for calling him by his childhood name again, but he knew this wasn't the moment.

Henry continued: ". . . You did it."

"No, you did, Dad. Forty years of scholarship and research."

Henry's eyes glazed; he stared at a spot just over Indy's

shoulder. "If I only could have been there." His eyes flicked back to his son. "What was it like?"

"There were rats."

"Rats?" He suddenly didn't look so interested in hearing details of the adventure.

"Yeah. Big ones."

"I see."

"Speaking of rats . . . how have the Nazis treated you here?"

"Okay, so far. They've given me one more day to talk, then they get tough. But I wasn't going to say a word, Junior. I figured if I died, you would take over the search. I knew I could count on you keeping that book as far away from the Nazis as possible."

Indy's hand twitched toward his pocket. His fingers traced the outline of the diary. *Guess what, Dad. It's not too far away.*

"Yeah, I suppose." He suddenly felt uneasy. "We'd better get out. . . ."

A resounding thud silenced him. His head snapped toward the door just as it burst open, and three Nazis marched into the room. Two of them held machine guns aimed at them. The third was an S.S. officer.

"Dr. Jones!" the officer shouted.

"Yes." Indy and Henry answered at the same time.

"I'll take that book now."

"What book?" they both said simultaneously.

The officer turned to Indy and sneered. "You have the diary in your pocket."

Henry's laugh was straight from the belly, and Indy thought, *Aw, God, I'm going to be sick.*

"You dolt! Do you really think that my son would be stupid enough to bring the diary all the way back to the very place from where . . ."

Henry stopped and slowly turned to Indy. "You didn't, did you, Junior?"

Indy smiled uneasily. "Uh . . . well."

"Did you?" Henry thundered.

"The thing is . . ."

"You did! My God."

"Can we discuss this later, Dad? I don't think that right now is . . ."

"I should have mailed it to the Marx Brothers," he fumed.

Indy held up a hand, patted the air. "Dad, please, take it easy."

"Why do you think I sent it home in the first place?" He pointed toward the Nazis. "To keep it out of *their* hands!"

"I came here to save you," Indy said lamely, then glanced at the machine guns.

"And who is coming to save you, Junior!" Henry roared, his face turning red.

What happened next took place so fast that when it was over, Indy hardly believed what he'd done. His eyes blazed; his nostrils flared with anger. He looked as if he was about to punch his father and was so convincing, Henry drew back, anticipating the blow. But instead, Indy's arm shot out and ripped one of the machine guns from a startled guard. With a quick kick, he knocked the barrel of the second machine gun in the air. Bullets sprayed the ceiling.

An instant later Indy's finger squeezed the trigger of the machine gun. "I told you before," he yelled as the three Nazis stumbled back under the impact and crumpled to the floor, "don't call me Junior."

Henry stared in disbelief as the three Nazis bled and died. He was shocked and horrified. "Look what you did! You killed them!"

Indy grabbed him by the arm and pulled him out of the room. He placed his hand on the knob of the adjoining room, where Elsa was waiting, and turned it.

"I can't believe what you did," Henry whispered hoarsely, his eyes wide with astonishment. "You killed those men!"

Indy paused in the doorway. "What the hell do you think *they* were going to do to *us*?"

His father frowned, as if he was trying to justify his son's violence in his mind.

Indy swung the door open and raised his hand to signal Elsa that it was time to flee. His hand froze. He was staring into the face of a Nazi. One of the man's muscular arms was coiled around Elsa's waist like a thick snake. His other hand held a Luger, its muzzle pressed behind her ear.

"That's far enough, Dr. Jones."

A big man. A colonel. Lantern jaw, small, dark eyes, an insect's eyes. He redefined the word *brute*, no doubt about it.

"Put down the gun. Right now," the colonel ordered, his accent thick, but not awkward. "Unless you want to see your lady friend die."

"Don't listen to him," Henry said.

"Drop it now," the colonel demanded.

"No," Henry shouted. "She's with them."

"Indy, please," Elsa pleaded, her eyes wide with fear.

"She's a Nazi!" Henry countered.

"What?" Indy shook his head, confused. He didn't know what to do. He looked at Elsa, then back to his father. Everyone was yelling at once.

"Trust me," Henry shouted.

"Indy, no," Elsa begged.

"I'll kill the Fraulein," the colonel spat through clenched teeth.

"Go ahead," Henry told him.

"Don't shoot her," Indy yelled.

"He won't," Henry answered.

"Indy, please!" Elsa implored. "Please do what he says."

"For God's sake, do not listen to her!" Henry roared at his son.

"Enough. She dies." The colonel jammed the barrel of his Luger into Elsa's neck.

She screamed in pain.

"Wait." Indy dropped the machine gun to the floor and kicked it away.

Henry groaned.

The colonel released his grip on Elsa and shoved her toward Indy. He caught her in his arms, and he held her tightly as she buried her face in his chest.

"I'm sorry, Indy."

He comforted her. "It's okay."

"I'm so sorry."

Her hand slipped into his coat pocket and removed the Grail diary.

She smiled sadly at him. "But you should have listened to your father."

"He never did," Henry uttered in an exasperated tone. "He never did."

CHAPTER THIRTEEN

◀◀ ▶▶

BETRAYED

Elsa moved away from him and over to the Nazi colonel. Indy just stood there, stunned, speechless, hating the smirk on the Nazi's face and the sweet innocence in Elsa's eyes. He wanted to grab her by the shoulders and shake her until she explained everything to him. He had to know why.

But the colonel raised his Luger threateningly, and Indy stayed where he was and simply stared. How could you do this to me? he thought at her.

She smiled a little, almost as if she had heard the thought. Indy finally averted his eyes and glanced at his father.

He wished he hadn't.

The expression on Henry's face could have turned stone to dust. No wonder he still calls me Junior. Indy was as astonished by the shift of events as his father had been a few minutes earlier when Indy decimated the opposition in the adjoining room.

"You two better come along with Colonel Vogel and me. Now."

Elsa's voice was hard and cold, the voice of a woman he didn't know. Even her face looked different now, not as he remembered it. Her jaw seemed more square, more stubborn, her skin whiter, bloodless, like china, and her eyes were cubes of ice that would never melt.

The colonel stabbed at the air with his weapon, and Indy said, "Yeah, I guess we better."

"Like we have a choice," muttered his father, his voice laced with blame.

As they were marched through the castle at gunpoint, Indy could feel his father's disgust. It radiated from him like heat or an odor, strong enough to track. It didn't diminish until they entered a large baronial room at the other end of the same floor.

Here the walls were decorated with ancient tapestries and suits of armor. A fire crackled and hissed in an enormous fireplace, casting shadows that eddied across the walls and ceiling. He caught a whiff of Elsa's skin as she fluttered past, making way for the two Nazi guards who joined them.

The guards tied their hands behind their backs. They definitely meant business, Indy thought, wincing as the ropes cut painfully into his wrists. While the guards worked on the ropes and Elsa conferred quietly with Vogel, Indy looked around furtively. There were several windows, but they were on the third floor. Besides, as long as their hands were bound and the goons were guarding them, their chances of escaping were minimal. Still, he thought, it never hurt to exercise the imagination.

When he ran out of ideas, he thought about Elsa and what he'd like to do to her if he got free. He watched her as she crossed the room toward a high-backed chair that faced the fireplace. She stopped next to the chair and held out the Grail diary. As a hand reached for it, Indy realized the chair was occupied. His eyes slid over to Henry, and he edged closer to him.

"How did you know she was a Nazi?" he asked in a whisper.

"She talks in her sleep."

"What?" His head snapped toward his father. "You mean you—you and that, that woman—were . . ."

"Silence!" Vogel bellowed.

Elsa and my old man . . .

The pieces fell into place. Elsa had ransacked his room in Venice, looking for the diary, then had torn through her own room, making it look as though someone had broken into the apartment.

And I fell for it.

"I didn't trust her. Why did you?" Henry muttered, tilting his head toward Indy.

The man in the chair rose to his feet and answered Henry's question. "Because he didn't take my advice. That's why."

Indy gaped as Walter Donovan strolled over to them, his bearing as regal and aristocratic as the room. Jesus. He couldn't believe it.

"Didn't I tell you not to trust anyone, Dr. Jones?" Donovan smiled benignly as he flipped casually through the Grail diary.

Indy had no snappy response; he didn't say anything at all. This was the man who had told him his father was missing, the man who had told him to meet Dr. Schneider in Venice, the bastard behind the whole scheme. What could he possibly say that would make any difference?

Everything was moving too fast. In the past few minutes, he had been betrayed by Elsa and by Donovan. To top it off, he had found out Elsa had gone to bed with his father, who had inadvertently clobbered him over the head with a vase.

Henry gave an indignant snort, but when he spoke, his voice was old and tired. "I misjudged you, Walter. I knew you'd sell your mother for an Etruscan vase; I didn't know you'd sell your country and your soul to this bunch of madmen."

Donovan ignored Henry. The crease in his forehead deepened as he paged through the diary faster and faster. Something was obviously wrong.

"Dr. Schneider!" he stammered.

Elsa rushed over to him. "What is it?"

Donovan held up the Grail diary and shook it in her face. "This book contained a map—a map with no names—but with precise directions from the unknown city to the secret canyon of the Holy Grail."

"Yes," she said. "It's known as the Canyon of the Crescent Moon."

"Where *is* the map?"

Elsa shrugged and looked a little uneasy. She said she didn't know, she thought it was in the diary. Donovan, his face pink with anger, looked from Elsa to Indy. "Well, where are the missing pages? We must have them."

Henry glanced at Indy, looking surprised and quite pleased. Indy smirked.

"You're wasting your breath asking him," Elsa said. "He won't tell us. And he doesn't have to. It's perfectly obvious where the pages are."

She flashed a triumphant smile at Indy and turned to Donovan. "He gave them to Marcus Brody."

Henry squeezed his eyes closed as if to shut out what he had just heard. When he opened them again, he turned them on Indy. "Marcus? You dragged poor Marcus along? My God, Junior, he's not up to the challenge."

"We'll find him," Donovan said, and turned away, dismissing them.

"Don't be so sure," Indy called after him. "He's got a two-day start on you, which is more than he needs."

Donovan paused, considering what he had just heard. Indy rushed on. "Brody has friends in every town and village between here and the Sudan. He knows a dozen languages and every local custom. He'll be protected. He'll disappear. You'll never see him again. With a little luck on his side, he's probably found the Grail Cup already."

Henry grinned. "That's very impressive," he muttered. "I hope you're right."

Donovan walked up to Indy and studied the man as if he were looking for flaws in a work of art. "Dr. Jones, it's too bad you won't live to find out what happens. Neither of you will."

The way he looked at him made Indy feel as if Donovan knew more about him than he was letting on. Maybe he did. He suddenly wondered if Donovan had anything to do with the Cross of Coronado. He recalled that the man in the Panama hat had said the buyer wanted him dead. Maybe the reason had not only been to stop him from looking for the cross but to keep him from looking for his father. Then, when things had gone wrong—when the diary had disappeared, when Indy survived—everything had changed.

But that was just speculation. He was certain, if he asked, Donovan would deny knowing what he was talking about. The man was too arrogant ever to admit that anyone could outwit him.

"Something on your mind, Dr. Jones?"

Indy stared back and remained silent.

Donovan turned to the guards. "Take them away."

Indy and Henry were tied back-to-back in a pair of chairs and watched over by two hulking Nazi guards. They had been moved to another room in the castle, one in which heavy, floor-length drapes hung from all the windows blocking out the wet night. As in the room in which Donovan had condemned them, an immense fireplace dominated one wall. But here there was no cheery fire; the room was dark and cold.

They had been bound for several hours when Elsa and Donovan entered the room. Donovan addressed the guards in German and asked if the captives had behaved themselves.

"Must we be tied up like this?" Henry complained after one of the guards told Donovan that the prisoners weren't going anywhere. "We're gentlemen, not common criminals."

Donovan laughed. "I've seen your son's handiwork upstairs, and so have these guards. I wouldn't call that the behavior of gentlemen. Would you, Henry?"

"You're hardly one to comment, Walter, considering your associates."

Donovan crossed his arms. "It won't be long now, and neither of you will be tied any longer. Everything will be all over."

Indy didn't like the sound of that. Nor did he like Donovan's gleeful chuckle, a kind of rolling, mad sound that made him realize Donovan, in his own way, fit in well with the Nazis. It wasn't hard for him to imagine the man chatting with Hitler as they talked about relics and antiquities, their values and uses.

Indy turned his attention to Elsa. She stood in the shadows, off to one side. There was just enough light for him to see her eyes, which were fixed on him. He thought she seemed sad, withdrawn, introspective, but maybe that was just wishful thinking. Besides, why should *he* care what she felt? She had tricked him. Used him. Betrayed him. And slept with his father.

So maybe she doesn't like herself for it.

A door swung open, and Indy heard the voice of Colonel

Vogel. "Dr. Schneider, a message from Berlin. You are to return immediately—a rally tomorrow at the Institute of Aryan Culture."

"So?"

"Your presence on the platform has been requested." He cleared his throat. "At the highest level."

"Thank you, Herr Colonel."

Her eyes slid toward Indy, then away from him as she addressed Donovan. "I'll meet you at Iskenderun as soon as I can get away."

Donovan handed her the Grail diary. "Take this with you. It's no use to us without the map, but it will show them we're making progress. Take it to the Reich Museum. It'll be a nice souvenir."

Vogel stepped between Donovan and the captives. "Allow me to kill them. Then we'll have no more accidents like upstairs."

"No," Elsa said. "If we fail to recover the pages from Brody, we will need them alive."

Donovan hesitated, uncertain. He regarded Indy and his father as though they were interesting and possibly valuable artifacts. To Vogel, he said: "Always do what the doctor orders. We'll wait. Then they are yours."

The colonel frowned, stared coldly at Indy, then nodded to Donovan without comment. It was obvious to Indy that he thought they should be executed immediately. He was probably more concerned about punishing the ones who were responsible for the deaths of his men than with finding the Grail Cup.

"Come along," Donovan said, and walked over to the fireplace. He stepped into it and opened a hidden door. Vogel and the guards followed him. Donovan allowed them to go on through and glanced back at Elsa.

"You coming?"

"I have a couple of things to take care of before I leave. I'll be ready in a few minutes."

Donovan nodded, and smiled at Indy and his father as if they were simply friends or business partners. He's a madman, Indy thought, as Donovan disappeared through the fireplace.

Elsa watched the fireplace until she was sure they were gone. Then she turned to Indy, her expression a perfect duplicate of their most intimate moments together in Venice. *What the hell was she up to now?*

He looked away.

"Indy, that wasn't my real reason for keeping the colonel from killing you."

He raised his eyes and grinned. "Yeah? You must be the good Nazi I keep hearing about."

"Don't look at me like that. We both wanted the Grail Cup. I would have done anything, and you would have done the same."

"Too bad you think that way, Doctor." His voice was as flat as stale soda water.

She ran a hand down the side of his face, but Indy jerked his head away. Elsa bent closer to him and spoke quietly, her breath warm against his ear, and the side of his face. Her skin smelled faintly of soap and perfume and stirred memories he preferred not to think about.

"I know you're angry, and I'm sorry. But I want to tell you, I'll never forget how wonderful it was."

Henry, who could see none of Elsa's actions, but could hear the voice, responded as if she were talking to him. "Yes, it was wonderful. Thank you."

Elsa ignored him. "Indy, you've got to understand my situation."

Indy wanted to spit in her face, but instead, he nodded, playing along with her in the hope that she would loosen the knots and give them a chance to get away.

She leaned forward and kissed him passionately, stroking his head with her hand.

"Dr. Schneider!"

Elsa abruptly stood up, and turned toward the fireplace. Vogel had returned through the hidden entrance.

"Yes, Herr Colonel?" She turned her head but kept her back to the Nazi.

"Your car is waiting."

"Thank you."

She smiled at Indy and brushed strands of her hair from her cheek. "That's the way Austrians say good-bye."

Elsa walked over to Vogel. "I'm ready now." She slipped through the door behind the fireplace.

This time the colonel stayed behind. He marched over to Indy, a good soldier, his rhythm perfect. His mouth slid into a sneer. "And this is how we say good-bye in Germany, Dr. Jones."

He jerked his arm back and punched Indy in the jaw. Hard. His head snapped back, blood trickled from the corner of his mouth, from his nose. Vogel turned and vanished through the fireplace.

Indy blinked his eyes, clearing his head. "I like the Austrian way better," he muttered to himself.

"Stop chattering!" Henry admonished. "I need time to think."

"Oh, that's great. And while you're thinking, let's try to loosen these knots again. We've got to get to Marcus before the Nazis do."

"I thought you said Marcus had a two-day start, and that he would blend in—disappear."

"Are you kidding? I made that up. You know Marcus. He got lost once in his own museum."

Henry swore under his breath. "That's just great. Bad enough that monster Vogel is itching to kill us, but now we're going to get Marcus killed and lose the Grail Cup to the Nazis."

"Something to think about, isn't it?" Indy said as he struggled with the ropes.

Now his father started pulling from his side. But the harder they pulled, the tighter the knots got, and the deeper the rope sliced into their wrists.

Finally, they let their arms relax. That was better. Less pain. But just sitting there like a couple of mummies wasn't going to get them out.

Blood oozed over Indy's upper lip from his nose and over his chin from his mouth. One side of his jaw was numb. His nose itched, and his wrists throbbed. His head felt as if it were tied in knots.

Think. Think.

There were probably Nazi guards posted outside the door and others beyond the fireplace. But right now that didn't matter. He knew there had to be a way to get free of the ropes. So why couldn't he think of it?

The silence in the room seemed to stretch toward tomorrow. He wondered if his father had fallen asleep. Then Henry shifted on his chair and tilted his head back until it hit Indy's.

"Junior, what ever happened to that cross you were chasing after?" Henry asked.

The Cross of Coronado had been a sore point between father and son since Indy was a kid. Henry had refused to believe Indy's story that he had recovered the fabled cross from thieves and had actually brought it home, then lost it again. Indy had vowed to his father that he would recover the cross if it took a lifetime. Over the years, his father had treated the subject like a joke. If he wanted to annoy Indy, he'd ask him where the cross was.

Usually Indy just simmered and said it wasn't any more humorous than his father's search for the Grail Cup. This time he had an answer. "I gave it to Marcus for the museum before we left New York. I finally got it back," he said evenly. "Just like I said I would."

Henry was silent a moment. When he spoke, he sounded conciliatory. "Marcus was very interested in your search for that cross. I can imagine how excited he must have been. But now . . . now if Donovan catches him, he'll never even have a chance to see it on display."

"That's the least of his worries."

And the least of my worries. He thought about telling his father his theory about Donovan and the cross. But that could wait. Right now, he needed to find a way out of their predicament.

Donovan and Colonel Vogel stood near a causeway in an underground storage depot in the bowels of the mountain beneath the castle. They watched as Elsa was driven away in a Nazi staff car. A second staff car pulled up, and Donovan was about to climb into the backseat when he paused momentarily to exchange a final word with Vogel.

"We'll find Brody. No problem. Go ahead and kill them now."

CHAPTER FOURTEEN

◀◀ ▶▶

BURNING DESIRES

Indy's head jerked up. He suddenly knew how to get the ropes undone.

Damn. And all along, it was right there and I just didn't realize it.

How could he have been so thick-skulled? If his hands hadn't been tied, he would have pounded his fists against his head.

"Dad, can you reach into my coat pocket?"

Henry came alert. "What for?"

"Just do it."

"All right, all right."

Indy squirmed against his restraints to shift his right hip as close to his father's hand as he could. It took a couple of minutes before Henry could touch the top of the pocket. Finally, after more shifting around, his fingers slipped inside it.

"What am I looking for?"

"My good luck charm."

"Feels like a cigarette lighter to me."

Indy didn't answer, waiting for his father to figure out his plan.

"That's it. Junior, you're a pip!"

Indy's impatience burned through him. "Dad, just try to burn through the ropes, will you?"

Henry fumbled to open the lighter, cursed as the top remained closed, and tried again.

Exasperated, Indy said, "Just don't drop it, Dad. Please."

"Confidence, Junior. Where did you get a lighter? You don't smoke."

"It's Elsa's. I forgot to give it back to her after we were in the catacombs."

On the next try, the lighter's top sprang open. Henry's thumb flicked at the wheel. Indy felt sparks, but the lighter didn't ignite. "Damn thing," Henry grumbled. "I think it needs fluid."

Wonderful.

"C'mon, *work*." Henry shook the lighter, tried again. "There we go. I got it."

Instantly, Indy felt the flame on his fingers. "Dad, burn the rope, not my hand."

For the next few minutes, Henry held the lighter against the rope. Once, the flame went out, and he fumbled again until he reignited it.

Indy's back ached from holding the awkward position. He gritted his teeth and tried to hold his hands steady. The stink of the burning rope saturated the air and made his nose itch again.

As the rope finally began to smolder and burn, Indy heard Henry curse.

"What happened?" Indy asked.

"I dropped it."

Indy craned his neck, but couldn't see where the lighter had fallen. He knew the only way to retrieve it was for them to tip the chairs over. Then they'd have to work on their sides. He said as much. "You ready to try it?"

Henry didn't answer him.

"Dad?"

"Junior, there's something you ought to know."

Indy misinterpreted his father's apologetic tone. "Don't get sentimental now, Dad. Save it until we're out of here. Okay?"

Indy smelled something. "Hey, what the hell's burning?"

"That's what I was going to say. The, uh, floor is on fire."

"What?" Indy cranked his head as far as he could and saw the tongues of fire. "All right, let's move. Rock your chair. Do what I do."

They inched their way slowly across the room and away

from the burning carpet. The chairs scraped against the floor and nearly toppled.

"Head for the fireplace."

They rocked and hopped in their chairs, moving toward the only safe place in the room. Behind them the fire seemed to feed itself, spreading fast, racing across the rug.

Indy rubbed his hands up and down, trying to get them free of the rope. As they wobbled into the fireplace, nearly toppling their chairs, Indy's foot kicked out and accidently hit the lever that opened the hidden door. The fireplace floor rotated like a lazy Susan, and they found themselves in a communications room. Four Nazi radiomen wearing headphones sat behind an elaborate panel of dials, switches, and meters. Their backs were turned to them, and for a moment they didn't see Indy or Henry.

"Our situation has not improved." Henry whispered his sentiments, but his voice was still too loud.

One of the radiomen glanced over his shoulder and was startled to see the two men tied back-to-back in their respective chairs.

Henry groaned. "Now what, Junior? Got any more good ideas?"

Indy looked around frantically for the lever that would turn them back. The radioman was already rising from his chair and alerting his partners. Indy spotted the lever directly in front of them and kicked out a leg. It was too high to reach with his foot. There was only one other way that he could think of to activate it.

"Push off with your feet," he yelled. He rocked forward as hard and fast as he could. His head struck the lever, and the floor rotated again just as the radioman pulled out a revolver and fired several shots.

The bullets pinged against the closing door.

Indy and Henry were out of the proverbial frying pan and into the fire. The carpet, drapes, and furniture were all ablaze. Greasy plumes of smoke burned their eyes; fire leapt for the ceiling. Indy coughed; he could hardly breathe.

"We were better off back there," Henry shouted above the roar of the blaze.

Indy didn't waste his breath answering him. He had been

working at the burned rope around his wrists, and suddenly his bonds broke. He slid off the chair and quickly unraveled the ropes around his father's wrists.

He hurriedly looked around. He spotted a grating inside the chimney, and tested it with his hand. The fireplace started to rotate again. "Quick, up here." He stood on one of the chairs, and grabbed the grating and pulled himself up through the opening in the center. He wedged himself between the walls, reached down and grasped his father by the arm. He pulled him up through the grating just as the four radiomen revolved into the burning room.

Their pistols were drawn. They looked at the empty chairs, conferred a moment; then two of the men returned to the communications room. The other pair shielded their eyes and moved cautiously toward the flames.

Indy knew they weren't going to be able to remain much longer in the chimney. Besides the fact that their positions were awkward, the heat of the fire was funneling up the chimney. A minute passed, and the radiomen returned from the communications room. As soon as they ventured away from the fireplace, Indy, then Henry, dropped from the chimney.

Indy immediately pulled the lever to rotate the fireplace. As they started to revolve, he saw the door across the room open and momentarily glimpsed the startled face of Colonel Vogel. Flames swept toward the Nazi as air from the corridor was drawn into the room. The colonel leapt back, barely escaping the rush of fire and smoke.

"Halt!" one of the radiomen yelled as he spotted Indy and Henry disappearing behind the fireplace.

"They're going to be coming back again," Henry warned as soon as they were inside the communications room.

"I know. I know."

Indy smashed a wooden stool against the floor, breaking off a leg. The wall started opening just as he reached over his head and jammed it into the gears controlling the movement of the wall. The door stopped after only opening a few inches. The radiomen were sealed inside the burning room.

Henry stared at the door, listening to the men's screams. Indy knew his father was horrified at what he had just done. It was that or die. That was the reality. Kill or be killed.

He turned away and searched for a way out. There had to be another exit, another secret door, a window, something. He ran his hands over the walls, knocked his knuckles against them, listening for a hollowness.

"You won't find the way out *that* way," Henry told him. "Let's sit down and work this out."

"Sit *down*?" Indy's eyes widened. "Are you crazy?"

"Stop panicking. I often find if I sit down calmly, the solution soon presents itself."

Henry slumped down into an overstuffed sofa. As he did, it budged slightly, and started to tilt forward as a section of the floor opened.

Indy leaped onto the sofa, realizing that his father had found the exit. "I see what you mean," he yelled as they slid down a ramp for several hundred feet until they were deposited on a dock. They were inside an enormous cavern that covered an underground causeway. The cavern obviously had been transformed into a Nazi storage depot.

They hurried over to a stack of large shipping crates. "We must be inside the mountain, below the castle," Henry whispered.

Indy perused the array of gunboats, speedboats, and supply vessels. "Great. More boats."

They waited until a Nazi patrol had passed, then darted across the dock to one of the boats. Indy revved up the engine just as Vogel appeared on the dock.

The colonel stopped and glanced over the boats as the engine roared to life. He ran with several Nazis to the nearest speedboat and climbed aboard. A moment later Vogel's boat sped away from the dock in search of the two Dr. Joneses.

Indy and Henry had already abandoned the boat and appropriated a motorcycle and sidecar. Indy was at the bike's wheel, and his father squashed into the little connecting car.

"Would you say this has been just another typical day for you?" Henry shouted as they roared along the dock.

"Better than most," Indy yelled back, accelerating toward a circle of light he hoped was the way out of the mountain. If it wasn't an exit, he wasn't sure what the next move would be.

Maybe there wouldn't be any next move.

The road and waterway suddenly came together at the

mouth of the cove. The rattle of machine-gun fire exploded from a boat. "Get down!" he shouted to his father, who complied without argument.

Indy ducked low on the motorcycle, and a moment later they burst into the bright morning sunlight. The road veered sharply away from the canal and away from the immediate threat.

Indy glanced down at Henry, who was peeking up over the side of the car now, checking to make sure the coast was clear. "And we're just starting a new day."

As the motorcycle raced toward a crossroad, the sign indicated Budapest to the right and Berlin to the left. Indy slowed at the intersection and turned right.

"Hold it!" Henry yelled. "Stop!"

"What's wrong?" Indy braked the motorcycle and glanced over at his father.

Henry just kept motioning him to stop so Indy pulled off the road and into the bushes, out of sight from any curious eyes.

He dismounted from the motorcycle and stretched as Henry climbed out of the sidecar. "So what are you waving your hands about?"

"Turn around. We've got to go to Berlin."

Indy pointed in the other direction. "But Brody is *that* way, Dad."

"My diary is *this* way," Henry answered, jerking his thumb in the other direction.

"We don't need your diary."

"Oh, yes we do. You didn't tear out enough pages, Junior." He glared defiantly at Indy.

"All right, tell me. What is it?"

"He who finds the Grail Cup must face the final challenge —devices of a lethal cunning."

"You mean it's booby-trapped?"

"Eight years ago I found the clues that would take us safely through the traps. They were in the *Chronicles of St. Anselm*."

"Well, can't you remember what they are?"

"I wrote it down in the diary so I wouldn't have to re-member."

Indy heard a roar and glanced out to the road just in time to see two Nazi motorcycles racing by, headed in the direction of Budapest.

"The Gestapo and half of Hitler's Wehrmacht is after us now, and you want to turn around and head right into the lion's den."

"Yes. The only thing that matters to me is the Holy Grail."

"What about Marcus?"

"Marcus would agree with me. I'm sure of it."

Indy rolled his eyes. He'd heard *this* litany so many times, he could have recited it in his sleep. "You scholars. Pride and plunder. Jesus Christ."

Henry's hand stung Indy's cheek. The blow wasn't hard, but it surprised him. He had been joking, but his father had obviously taken offense. He touched his cheek and frowned at him.

"That's for your blasphemy," Henry snapped. "Don't you remember anything from reading *Parzival*? Didn't you learn anything from Richard Wagner or Wolfram von Eschenbach? In the hands of the knight, Sir Parzival, the Grail is a scared talisman of healing. But under the control of the malefic Klingsor it is a tool for black magic."

He shook his head scornfully at Indy. "The quest for the cup is not archaeology. It's a race against evil. If the Grail is made captive to the cult of the Nazis, the armies of the dark-ness will march over the face of the earth." Henry glared at him. "Do you understand me?"

Myth and reality were intertwined in his father's world. They were virtually inseparable. He was living the myth. "I've never understood this obsession of yours, and Mother didn't, either."

He glared back at his father. The mention of his mother was a challenge. For the first time in more than thirty years, he heard his father talk about her.

"She did. Too well. Because of it, because she didn't want me worrying about her, she kept her illness from me until all I could do was mourn her."

Their eyes locked, and for those few moments Indy knew they were equals. At last his father had spoken to him of his mother's death and told him his feelings, even admitted fault. The very mention of her resolved an old wound between them.

He clasped a hand on his father's shoulder. "C'mon. Let's get on our way to Berlin, Pop."

CHAPTER FIFTEEN

◄◄ ►►

BERLIN FIREWORKS

Flags, banners, and standards displaying the swastika were waved frantically back and forth, over and over again, in a rhythmic motion that reflected the mounting frenzy of the massive crowd. At the center of the rally was a bonfire fueled by a ten-foot-high mound of books. At the periphery of the fire college students and Nazi Brownshirts fed the flames with more and more books. Many of them were classics that had been deemed blasphemous or unpatriotic by the Nazis and their sympathizers.

Indy walked toward the square, buttoning the tunic of a Nazi uniform that was several sizes too large for him. When they had arrived in Berlin, they had driven around on the motorcycle until they found a uniformed Nazi who was separated from his unit. Henry had acted as if he were ill and collapsed on the sidewalk a few feet away from the soldier. When the man had stopped to see what was wrong, Indy had rushed up and asked him to help carry his father to someplace quiet. When they reached the alcove of a building, Indy had knocked the Nazi cold and stripped off his uniform.

Henry, still dressed in street clothes, hurried along beside Indy, gawking at the chaos around them. "My boy, we are pilgrims in an unholy land."

"Yeah, too bad it's real life, not just the movies," Indy said, nodding toward a motion picture cameraman who was filming the scene.

Indy suddenly stopped dead and stared ahead at the platform.

"What is it?" Henry asked.

Indy nodded toward the raised dais. It was occupied by high-ranking officials of the Third Reich, who gazed out over the rally like royalty overseeing their subjects. Among them were two familiar faces: Adolf Hitler and Dr. Elsa Schneider.

"Oh, my God," Henry moaned, and shook his head. "On the right hand of the fiend himself. Do you believe she's a Nazi now?"

Indy said nothing. He threaded his way through the crowd, Henry right behind him like a shadow, and moved as close to the platform as he dared.

A woman stood next to a cameraman who was trying to get a shot of Hitler, Elsa, and others in the High Command. Indy pegged her as the director, because she kept shouting and waving her hands to attract the attention of those on the dais. There was so much noise and confusion, she was having a hard time of it.

"One step forward, please, Mein Führer," she called out in German.

Hitler took a step back.

"All right. That's fine. That's fine. Everybody else, one step back now."

Instead, everyone took a step forward, and Hitler was barely visible.

The director threw up her hands and shook her head. "Please, please. You are blocking the Führer."

Indy laughed to himself. "Looks like I understand German better than the High Command," he remarked to his father, who had forced him to learn several foreign languages before he was eighteen, something he resented at the time but appreciated now. "Thanks to you," he added, elbowing his father gently in the side.

Henry snorted. "*Now* he thanks me. *Now* he listens to me."

Indy laughed.

The rally was breaking up, and Indy pressed his way past a throng of torch-bearing Nazis. The zealots repelled him, but outwardly he maintained a placid look of indifference. He skirted the platform and snaked through Nazi officers and their staff cars. He perused the dispersing crowd and spotted Elsa walking alone, her hair thick and gold in the sunlight.

Henry trailed behind, keeping a discreet distance. He had agreed that Indy should be the one to approach Elsa, and they decided to meet in half an hour near one end of the platform.

Indy hurried after Elsa, approaching her from behind. He slowed as he neared her, waiting until she was well away from anyone who could overhear them.

"Fraulein Doctor."

"Indy," she gasped.

His voice was quiet and tough, his eyes hard and unforgiving. "Where is it?"

"You followed me."

She said it in a way that made him wonder if she was still attracted to him. It was as if her emotions pulled her one way, while her logic and her orders directed her on another course —a deadly one for Indy and his father.

Her hand touched his face, her mouth opened slightly, and her eyes shone with longing. "I missed you really bad, Indy."

He brushed her hand aside and slipped his hands over her body, searching her pockets for the Grail diary. "I want it. Where is it?"

His voice and the roughness of his search snapped her back to the reality of the situation. For a moment he thought she was going to beg him to forgive her. Her mouth quivered, her face seemed to come undone at the seams. But then something changed; he could see it happening, a pulling together somewhere deep inside her. Her reply was cool and crisp.

"Everything is right where it was the last time you looked."

Indy continued with his search, ignoring her. He slid his hand along her legs and stopped as he felt something. He glanced around, then quickly reached up her dress and pulled out the Grail diary, which she had strapped to her leg.

"Sorry about the inconvenience."

Elsa shook her head, confused by Indy's urgent search. "I don't understand, Indy. You came back for the book? Why?"

"My father doesn't want it incinerated in one of your parties here."

She glared back at him. "Is that how you think of me, like I'm one of these Brownshirts?"

"I don't know why I would think any other way," he answered coldly.

"I believe in the Grail, not the swastika."

"Yeah." He jerked his thumb over his shoulder toward the platform. "And you stood up to be counted with the enemy of everything the Grail stands for. Who cares what *you* believe?"

"You do," she snapped.

Indy's hand shot out and clutched her throat. "I only have to squeeze."

"I only have to scream."

It was a standoff, and he knew it. Love and hatred, back and forth, a tug-of-war. He wouldn't follow through on his threat, and she knew it, just as he knew she wouldn't scream. In spite of everything, the allure and fascination of her presence was as strong as ever.

Indy released her and backed away. They shared a look that said everything, that told of lovers whose lives met and diverged through matters that appeared beyond their control. But at the same time some part of him knew it was their own choices that had brought them together and would separate them.

"Indy," she called out.

He took another step backward, then spun around and left. He found his father waiting near the platform. "Come on. Let's get out of here."

"Well, did you get it?" Henry asked as they walked away.

"Yeah. I got it."

"Wonderful. How did you get it away from that Nazi whore?"

The comment angered him. For some reason he felt compelled to defend her. He was about to lash out at his father for the crack when he realized that the crowd they were walking through consisted of Hitler and his entourage. About fifty kids surrounded the Führer, pushing autograph books at him for his signature.

Hitler paused to sign them, then looked at Indy, who towered well above the heads of the youngsters. Their eyes locked. The contact lasted only a moment, but Indy felt the pull of Hitler's charisma. For the first time, he understood the attraction and allegiance the man drew from his followers. But he also knew the horror of Hitler's regime, the devastation and suffering, and the horrible potential for worldwide chaos. And that made his appeal all the more frightening.

Hitler broke the spell when he took the Grail diary from Indy's hand to autograph it. He opened it before Indy could react, but his father's groan was clearly audible behind him. Then Hitler signed the diary and handed it back to him.

Indy quickly recovered his sense of place. He clicked his heels and delivered a straight arm salute. At the same time, he secretly countered his show of fealty. He held his other hand behind his back, and crossed his fingers.

A moment after Indy withdrew his salute and stepped back, Hitler was whisked away into the backseat of a waiting limousine and the crowd of students dispersed. But his direct encounter with Hitler had created enmity from other Nazis who witnessed the incident. One of them, an S.S. officer whose obesity was wrapped in a long overcoat, lingered behind to castigate the low-ranking Nazi.

"What are you doing here?" the officer demanded in crisp German. "This is a restricted area. Get back to your post at once."

Indy stood bolt upright, raised his hand in another "Heil Hitler" salute. Realizing there was no one else around, he jerked back his arm, balled his fingers into a fist, and smashed the officer in the face.

Henry groaned again.

"Now we're going to do things my way," Indy announced to his father.

"Meaning what?"

"We're getting out of Germany."

Indy pulled up to the main terminal of the Berlin airport and parked the motorcycle. As he hopped off, he adjusted the overcoat he had taken from the overweight S.S. officer.

"If you're going to keep taking other people's clothes," Henry said, as they entered the terminal, "why don't you pick on somebody your own size?"

"I'll remember that next time."

They got in line at one of the boarding gates and waited to buy their tickets. "Any luck, we'll be out of this country in an hour, and we'll find Marcus tomorrow," Indy said confidently.

"Oh, oh." Henry nodded toward an area to the side of the ticket counter. Each passenger buying a ticket was being questioned by Gestapo agents.

"Yeah." Indy took Henry by the arm and turned away from the line. They had taken a half dozen steps when he spotted more trouble. Colonel Vogel was striding across the terminal. "Look who's here."

Both men quickly turned up their coat collars and lowered their hat brims, then briskly veered away from Vogel. Indy glanced back once and saw Vogel showing a couple of Gestapo agents a photograph.

"It's probably not a family portrait," he muttered to himself, and they left the terminal. The adjoining building was another terminal, but it was smaller, newer, and decorated in a florid art deco style.

They headed for the counter and stood in line behind several well-dressed men and women. Must be first class, Indy thought.

"Why this line?" Henry asked.

"Because, nobody's checking it."

The line inched forward. Minutes ticked by. Indy kept glancing around, anxiety churning across the floor of his gut. He hated this. He hated waiting around for something to happen. He would rather be confronting it—and getting it over with.

He started feeling conspicuous and forced himself to stare down at his shoes for a while. Then he raised his eyes and looked around again, but slowly, like a bored traveler who was wondering where he was going to sit once he was checked in for his flight. To keep from turning around, he read a plaque that was on a nearby pillar. It commemorated the zeppelin *Hindenburg*, which had flown from Lakehurst, New Jersey, to Friedrichshafen, Germany in forty-two hours and fifty-three minutes, August 9–11, 1936—a world record.

He looked back down at his shoes, tapping his foot impatiently. Then he couldn't stand it anymore, and his eyes roamed through the terminal again, hungry, curious. A burly woman, who was next in line, glared at him. He looked back at the plaque and read the last line: Certified by Federation Aeronautique Internationale.

"What are you doing?" Henry barked.

Indy jerked his head around and saw that the line had moved ahead, and his father was waiting at the window. They purchased their tickets, asking for the next flight. As they walked toward the door of the terminal, Indy asked his father if he knew where the flight was headed.

Henry rolled his eyes as if it was a foolish question, but to Indy's surprise said, "As a matter of fact, no. Do you?"

It didn't really matter where they were going at this point, as long as it was *out* of Germany. But he consulted his ticket. "Athens. Not exactly within walking distance of Iskenderun, but at least it's in the right direction."

"Athens, of course." Henry repeated, nodding his approval of their destination. "Things are starting to look up."

Indy stopped as he noticed the drawing on his ticket and realized they weren't taking an airplane to Athens. "Hey, Dad."

Henry kept walking and didn't hear him. Indy hurried after him. They stepped out onto the tarmac and saw their ride to Athens parked in front of them.

"Well, well," Henry said.

A zeppelin that was more than ten stories high and two football fields in length was moored on the tarmac. They not only hadn't bothered to find out where they were headed, but neither of them had realized they were taking a zeppelin. As they approached the boarding stairs, Indy and Henry exchanged glances. Both were excited and surprised by the turn of events.

"Hey, look at that," Indy said, pointing to a pair of biplanes suspended on large hooks below the zeppelin. "How'd you like to ride down there?"

Henry's answer was succinct. "No, thanks."

They found an empty compartment and made themselves comfortable as the zeppelin prepared to take off. Indy sank down in his seat, folded his arms across his chest, and exhaled.

"We made it, Dad."

Henry took out a handkerchief and wiped it across his forehead. "When we're airborne and Germany's behind us, I'll join you in that sentiment."

Indy gazed out the window. "Relax. In a few hours we'll be in Athens and on our way to Iskenderun, and Marcus. Sit back and enjoy the scenery."

Just as he finished speaking, he saw a now too familiar figure rushing across the tarmac. It was Vogel, followed by one of the Gestapo agents Indy had seen in the airport. His body suddenly felt leaden as he watched the pair board the zeppelin.

He sensed it was going to be a rough flight.

CHAPTER SIXTEEN

◄◄ ►►

AEROBATICS

"Stay here," Indy said to his father.

He flew out of the compartment before Henry could say anything, his mind racing, seeking a plan. His only advantage was that he knew Vogel was on board. He didn't know how he could use it for leverage but felt sure he'd come up with something before it was too late. He always had before, so why not now?

He felt like a cat with nine lives. Nine lives. Do I have any left?

He was barely out of the compartment when he spotted Vogel headed down the passageway in his direction. He ducked through a door marked Crew Only. As the Nazi colonel walked past the door, Indy heard a steward tell him that the zeppelin was about to take off and that he must find a seat. He opened the door a crack and saw Vogel following two other late-arriving passengers into a compartment, the same one he had just vacated.

"Oh, God," he whispered, wondering how his father would deal with Vogel.

Before he could do anything, the steward slid open the door and nearly ran into Indy. "What are you doing here?" the man asked loudly in German. "This is the crew room, can't you see? We're about to take off. Please . . ."

Indy pointed toward the ceiling, and the man glanced up. As he did, Indy connected with a short punch under the jaw. He disliked assaulting innocent bystanders, but with Vogel seated only a few feet away, he knew he had to deal quickly with the man.

Unlike the butler, the steward only stumbled back a step. In his concern about not hurting the man, he hadn't hit him hard enough. The steward gave Indy a startled look, then threw his own punch. Indy blocked it, and this time connected with a powerful blow to the man's cheek. He slumped to the floor, unconscious.

When the zeppelin rose from the tarmac a few minutes later, Indy returned to the compartment where his father was. But now he wore the hat and jacket of the steward. For a change, the borrowed apparel fit perfectly.

"Tickets please. May I have your tickets?" he said in German.

Henry peeked over the top of a magazine, and his eyes widened as he saw who was collecting tickets. Indy nodded as his father passed him his ticket.

"Your ticket, sir," he said to Vogel and held out his hand.

The colonel glanced up, recognized Indy, and reached for the gun inside his coat. But Indy grabbed his arm, collaring him, and jerked him out of his seat. He removed his Luger and, with a boost from his father, shoved Vogel out the window and onto the tarmac.

The other passengers in the compartment drew back, startled and frightened by the aggressive behavior of the steward with the foreign accent.

Indy smiled and shrugged. "No ticket."

Everyone in the compartment immediately produced his ticket and held it up in Indy's face.

As he collected them, Indy glanced out the window to see Vogel on his hands and knees, peering up as the zeppelin lifted off. "Next time, you get a ticket first," Indy yelled at him.

He moved out of the compartment and ducked back into the crew quarters. He wondered what he'd do next. Vogel hadn't been alone.

A few minutes later the Gestapo agent hurried down the passageway. He stopped a few steps past the crew quarters. He looked worried and disgruntled, and it didn't take a genius to figure out why. After all, the poor sucker hadn't been able to find him or his father, and now he couldn't even find Vogel.

Indy stepped out of the crew quarters and tapped him on the shoulder. He was about to club him with the butt of the Luger when one of the passengers who had seen him toss Vogel out the window emerged from the nearby compartment. Indy asked the Gestapo agent for his ticket.

"I don't need one," the man snapped.

The passenger walked by, heading for the bathroom. "You'll be sorry," he mumbled to the agent.

"He's right," Indy said, and cracked him behind the ear with the Luger. The agent crumpled. Indy dragged him into the crew quarters, took his gun, and opened the storage closet. Inside, the steward was bound and gagged.

"Company." He lowered the agent into the corner.

The steward was wide awake and yelling into his gag. Indy brandished the gun over his head, and he immediately calmed down.

He noticed a cluster of wires running into a box marked Radio Transmitter and yanked them out. Then he saw a leather jacket hanging from a hook. It looked a lot like his own. He couldn't resist trying it on.

Another perfect fit.

At the bar in the zeppelin's lounge, Indy eavesdropped as a World War I German flying ace relived his daring exploits, using a pair of model airplanes as props. Several enthralled onlookers bought him one drink after another, and the stories grew more and more fantastic.

The steward arrived with drinks for Indy and his father, who were seated several tables away from the now drunken flying ace. Both men had settled for non-alcoholic beverages. Neither was now certain their ordeal with the Nazis was finally over. If it was, fine. But if more trouble was ahead, they wanted to remain as alert as possible.

Henry was so absorbed in the Grail diary, he didn't even know his drink had arrived. He was studying the pages that described the lethal devices defending the Grail. Now and then, he would mutter to himself, and all of it brought back old childhood memories for Indy, of his father in his study, lost in the ancient past. Some things, he thought, would never change.

Indy stared out the window, watching bright wisps of clouds sail past the zeppelin. He wondered what Elsa was doing and if she was thinking of him. Despite the fact that she had been standing up there with Hitler, he believed her primary interest was in the Grail, an obsession he could understand, since it was something she shared with his father. But he couldn't condone her association with the man who was quite possibly the most heinous human being to walk the face of the earth since Genghis Khan.

He turned away, shutting off his secret longings. He looked down at the Grail diary and focused on his father's tiny handwriting, which was inscribed in medieval Latin. There were three complex diagrams that made no sense to him. The only thing he understood was their labels. The first was called The Pendulum, the second, The Cobbles, and the third, The Invisible Bridge.

He was about to ask his father to explain the devices, when Henry looked up at him. "Sharing your adventures is an interesting experience."

"That's not all we shared," Indy said, thinking of Elsa again. "By the way, what *did* she say in her sleep?"

"Mein Führer."

"I guess that's pretty conclusive." He thought back to his last moments with Elsa in Berlin. He was sure that she had been sincere and yet . . .

"Disillusioned, are you? She was a beautiful woman, and I'm as human as the next man."

"Yeah. I was the next man."

Henry smiled as if he was thinking about his own experience with her. "Ships that pass in the night. Can we drink to that?"

He raised his glass, and Indy did the same. They clinked glasses. "Ships that pass in the night," Indy repeated. He thought a moment. "Also the afternoon."

Henry cleared his throat and straightened his shoulders. "Well, back to work."

He leaned over the diary and began reading. "'The challenges will number three. First, the Breath of God; only the penitent man will pass. Second, the Word of God; only in the footsteps of God will he proceed. Third, the Path of God; only in the leap from the lion's head will he prove his worth.'"

"Meaning what?"

Henry tapped the page. "I think we'll find that out when we get there."

Sunlight broke through the clouds, casting a beam through their window and dividing the table into equal parts of light and shadow. As Indy reached for his drink, he noticed that the ray was moving across the table like the hand of a clock. He stared at it, puzzled by the phenomenon. Then suddenly he understood what it meant.

"Dad."

"What is it?"

"We're turning around. They're taking us back to Germany."

They quickly rose from the table and made their way to the crew quarters. The storage closet door was smashed open, and the Gestapo agent and steward were gone. Indy looked around and saw that the radio wires had been repaired with tape.

"Shit."

"Ah, Junior. I think we've got a problem here."

"I know. I know. You don't have to tell me," he said, as he tried to figure out what they should do.

"No, you don't understand. I forgot the diary in the lounge."

"You *what*?"

Henry smiled weakly at him and stammered: "Yeah, I'm afraid so."

Good going, Dad. "Okay, stay right here. I'll be right back." Indy hustled down the passageway, back toward the lounge. He started to push open the door but heard voices and stopped. He peeked inside and saw the agent and several crewmen standing in the center of the lounge near the table Indy and Henry had just abandoned. The diary was on it, but no one had noticed it.

The agent called for everyone's attention. "There are spies aboard the airship! Everyone loyal to the Führer, the Reich, and Deutschland come immediately with me."

Blasé passengers looked up, then returned to their conversations and cocktails, ignoring the agent's command. The only one who responded was the World War I ace, who struggled to his feet from his bar stool and wobbled forward.

Indy knew he had to act fast. He turned the collar up on the leather jacket and took out a handkerchief. He sneezed into it as he walked into the lounge, keeping his head down. He heard the agent giving orders.

"You," he pointed at Indy. "You come with us. We're looking for American spies."

Indy kept the handkerchief to his nose. "I've got a cold," he said in German. Sorry." He reached around behind him and slipped the diary into his back pocket. He recognized the steward he had knocked out standing near the agent. He was wearing an undershirt, and his face was a question mark as he looked over Indy.

"I'll guard my compartment," Indy said, and hustled toward the door.

"That's him," the steward yelled. "Stop him." But Indy was already out the door and racing down the passageway.

He ducked back into the crew quarters and looked around for Henry. "Dad, where are you?"

Henry poked his head out of the storage closet. "Did you get it?"

"Yeah, but I think I got a lot more, too." Indy hurriedly prowled around the quarters, looking for a hiding place. He glanced up at the ceiling.

"Trouble, you mean?"

"No more than usual."

Quickly he pulled a chair across the floor, stepped on top of it, and hoisted himself up through a hatchway. He reached down to help his father.

"Not another chimney," Henry complained.

Indy lifted him through the opening, then climbed to the top of the hatchway. They crawled out the top of it and found themselves in the belly of the zeppelin. Its skin was attached to an elaborate metal framework, and narrow catwalks connected the huge helium gasbags that gave the airship its lift.

Henry paused in wonderment and awe. Indy glanced down the hatchway and saw the agent and steward peering up. He grabbed his father by the arm, and they rushed along one of the narrow catwalks.

But they weren't fast enough.

The agent pulled a small gun from an ankle holster and aimed it at Indy. He was about to fire when the steward knocked his arm aside.

"Nein! Nein!"

Indy looked over his shoulder and saw the steward point to the gasbag, then gesture with his arms. "Kaboom!"

The catwalk ended at a pair of doors framed on the outer skin of the zeppelin. Behind them Indy heard the pounding of feet along the catwalk. He opened one of the doors, and gripped the frame as the wind pounded him. He was staring into the blue sky and white clouds.

Several feet below, he saw the biplanes suspended on hooks that were attached to a steel framework. Indy pointed to the nearest one, which had an emblem on the fuselage of a pelican with its wings spread wide. "Climb down, Dad. We're going for a ride."

Henry looked terrified as he peered out the doorway. "I didn't know you could fly a plane."

Fly, yes. Land, no. "Let's go."

Henry ventured out of the zeppelin, climbing down a metal ladder to the biplane. Indy watched anxiously, then looked away. If his father fell now, he couldn't help and didn't want to see it.

He glanced back to Henry and saw he had made it safely to the biplane. He started to follow, when the Gestapo agent grabbed him by the arm and attempted to pull him back. He twisted free and pushed the man away. He was about to resume his descent when the steward scampered down the ladder and dropped on top of Indy, wrapping his arm around his neck.

Indy clung to the ladder and, to his surprise, saw his father climbing up toward him. Henry grabbed the man by the back of the collar and jerked him away. At the same moment Indy bucked as hard as he could.

The steward lost his grip and tumbled into space, arms pinwheeling, grappling for anything to break his fall. He caught hold of one of the struts just above the hook that attached to the plane. His legs pumped in midair.

Indy stared at his father in amazement. "Look what you did!" he shouted.

Henry climbed down into the rear cockpit, and Indy leaped the last few feet, landing in the front one. He found the starter and switched it on. The propeller sputtered, coughed, then roared to life.

As Indy searched for the lever to release the hook, Henry shouted something. Indy's head snapped up, and he saw the agent standing in the doorway above him, aiming the gun at him, trying to hold it steady in the wind. He fired, but missed. Indy found the lever and pulled back on it, releasing the biplane.

Suddenly they soared away from the zeppelin, leaving the agent and dangling crewman behind.

Indy circled about and saw the World War I ace walk out onto a catwalk outside the zeppelin and climb down into the second plane. He signaled the Gestapo agent to join him.

The agent, mimicking Indy, walked out on the catwalk, and jumped into the rear cockpit. He struck hard, and his feet burst through the bottom of the fuselage, and the lower half of his body was suspended in midair below the plane.

The World War I ace didn't realize what had happened, and released the plane from its hooks. He was so drunk that he had forgotten to start the engine first. Instantly it spun straight for the ground. Indy knew there was no way the ace pilot, even with all of his experience, could start the engine and recover from the spin.

Less than a minute later the plane crashed into the side of a mountain, spewing flames and debris.

Indy's plan was to fly as far away from Germany as the biplane would take them, and as near as they could get to Iskenderun. He wasn't looking forward to landing. He decided he would take it down in a field rather than an airport, and that way they would avoid any questions. The last thing they wanted to do was attract attention and get the Nazis on their trail again.

He heard his father yell something to him. He turned back to him and saw Henry jerking his thumb up and down. Indy smiled and flashed the thumbs-up sign back to him, and beamed with confidence. But Henry shook his head.

Indy finally understood. His father was pointing up and yelling something he couldn't hear. What he did hear, though, was a sound that was both a roar and a wail. He couldn't see anything above them, but the sound was growing louder, eerier. He tilted his head back again.

Two Messerschmidt fighter bombers streaked out of the clouds and raced across the sky. Indy and Henry sank down in their seats as the fighters screamed toward them.

"Fire the machine gun," Indy yelled.

Henry puzzled over the gun, trying to figure out how it worked.

Indy turned in his seat and pointed at the gun. "Pull back on that lever, then jerk the trigger."

The plane's slow speed and small size worked to their advantage. The speeding Messerschmidts overshot them and whizzed by in a blur. Indy knew it would take the fighters miles to turn around. But he also knew the pilots would find them again.

On the second sweep Henry framed one of the fighters in his sight. He pulled back on the trigger and fired at the first one. The gun exploded with such force that he was nearly shaken out of his seat. The Messerschmidt banked to the left, and Henry swung the gun around. He kept firing, missed the fighter, and inadvertently cut his own rear stabilizer.

"Oops."

"Are we hit?" Indy bellowed.

"More or less," Henry yelled back.

Indy looked over his shoulder at the missing tail section, then at his father, and his heart plunged to his toes, then zipped up again. *Bad news, Pop. Real bad.*

"Son, I'm sorry. They got us."

Indy struggled to control the plane as it rapidly descended.

"Hold on. We're going in."

At five hundred feet Indy saw a paved road. It was their only hope, their only choice at all, in fact, because that was where the plane was headed. He did his best to stabilize the craft, and they belly-flopped onto the road. The plane skidded out of control and crashed into the parking lot of a roadside tavern.

Indy was shaken by the impact, but still managed to crawl out of the plane. He helped Henry out. "You all right, Dad?"

"I'm in one piece, I think," he said as they stumbled away from the plane.

Indy knew they had to get away as fast as possible. He spotted a customer who was about to drive off, and signaled him. As the man stepped out of his car, Indy leapt behind the wheel. He circled around the parking lot, picked up Henry, and shoved down hard on the gas pedal.

The man chased after them, shaking his fist and shouting. A moment later, the Messerschmidts screamed low, guns blazing. Through the rearview mirror, Indy saw the car owner dive headfirst off the road and roll down a ditch as the fighters strafed the parking lot, ripping holes through the parked cars.

Indy shoved the throttle down and gripped the steering wheel tightly with both hands. He concentrated on the road as Henry twitched and turned and fretted.

"Are we out of the woods yet?"

"Hope so."

Indy heard the peculiar roar of a Messerschmidt again and glanced into the side mirror. One of the fighters was swooping toward them.

"Oh, shit."

"What is it?"

Gunfire ripped through the car, miraculously missing Indy and his father. As the Messerschmidt screeched away, beams of sunlight streamed into the car through the bullet-riddled roof.

"Good Lord," Henry moaned. "Take me back to Princeton. This is no way to live."

The whine of the second Messerschmidt raised the hair on the back of Indy's neck. "Here comes the other one."

Then he saw a tunnel cutting through the mountainside. He slammed his foot against the gas pedal and raced for it. But the fighter bore down on them, its machine guns chattering.

They sped into the tunnel, out of the range of the guns. "Let's stay in here," Henry said.

But even the tunnel wasn't safe. An instant later, they

heard a resounding crash. The Messerschmidt couldn't pull up in time. It slammed into the mouth of the tunnel, the mountain shearing off its wings. The fuselage rocketed like a bullet down the muzzle of a gun. Sparks flew as it scraped the pavement and sides of the tunnel. Then the fuselage burst into flames.

A fireball grew in the rearview mirror, gaining on them. The accelerator was flat against the floor; the car was going as fast as it could. Indy leaned forward, as if the thrust of his body could somehow speed up the car. He gripped the steering wheel so tightly, his knuckles turned white.

Just as the fireball was about to slam into them, the car flew out of the tunnel. Indy swerved sharply to the shoulder of the road and struggled to maintain control of the car. The flaming fuselage shot past them, struck a tree, and exploded.

Indy swung back onto the road and raced into a wall of flames and greasy smoke. He shot out the other side, eyes wide, heart slamming against his chest.

Henry looked as if he was on the verge of a stroke. "They don't come any closer than that."

"Don't count on it," Indy said as he saw the other Messerschmidt screaming out of the sky toward them.

The fighter dropped a bomb; it exploded in the road directly ahead of the car, missing it by several feet. Indy turned the wheel hard to the right. The car smashed through a guardrail and bounced down an embankment. For several seconds they were airborne. It was all over, he thought, and squeezed his eyes shut.

As quickly as the car had pitched off the road, it landed with a thud, sinking into the soft sand of a deserted Mediterranean beach. The two men staggered out of the car. Indy held his head where he had cracked it against the steering wheel. There wasn't another person in sight for miles. The beach was populated by sea gulls, which had turned the sand into a virtual snowfield of white, feathered bodies.

Indy heard the deadly sound again and looked back, to see the Messerschmidt coming in for yet another pass. Father and son exchanged a wordless glance. They didn't even think about running. There was no place to hide.

Indy checked his gun. It was empty.

The fighter was coming in low, less than a hundred feet over the surf.

Suddenly Henry ran toward the sea gulls, waving his hands. He was a madman, screaming, shouting.

The gulls took to the air en masse, thousands of them rising in fright, wings beating the air just as the Messerschmidt howled overhead, its machine guns spitting, tearing into the beach, kicking up sand.

Then the fighter and the sea gulls met. It was a massacre. Hundreds of gulls were shredded apart by the whirling propeller blades. A feathery, white-and-red puree smeared the windshield and clogged the engine.

The Messerschmidt stopped firing just short of Indy and Henry. Its engines sputtered. The plane stalled and disappeared beyond an embankment.

A brief moment later an explosion shattered the silence. Smoke and flames rose in the distance.

Indy sank into the sand, completely drained.

Henry walked back to him and sat down next to him. "I remembered Charlemagne. 'Let my armies be the rocks and the trees and the birds in the sky.'"

Indy gazed off into the distance toward the burning fighter. "Good advice then; good advice now."

HATAY

CHAPTER SEVENTEEN

◄◄ ►►

CONVERGING FORCES

The same day Indy and Henry were fleeing Germany, Marcus Brody arrived by train at Iskenderun. He was utterly exhausted and wished he was back home in New York in the safety of his museum. The problems he faced in his everyday life seemed minor to the frustrations he had already experienced on this trip. And who knew what was ahead for him and Sallah.

That is, if he even found Sallah.

He should have arrived at least a day earlier, but he had taken the wrong train out of Venice and found himself in Belgrade before he realized it. There, he wasted another day in confusion before finally boarding the right train. He had traveled nonstop through the day, the night, and half the following day. He was finally here, and as he disembarked from the train, he sensed that his bold proclamation that he would find the Grail Cup was brash and unrealistic.

His eyes burned as he moved along the railway station platform, through a crowd of Hatayans and Arabs. Bodies in flowing robes blurred into a collective mass. They seemed part of some mysterious coordinated activity, and only he, Marcus Brody, stood apart, confused and out of place. He rubbed his throbbing eyes. What he wanted most of all was a hot shower, a good meal, and about twenty hours of sleep.

He felt anxious and depressed because he had failed Indy and Henry. He should have found the Grail by now, or at least been close to it. Instead, he couldn't even find Sallah. But he was a scholar and a museum director, not a geographer . . . not an explorer. And certainly not an adventurer.

He needed a guide.

"Mr. Brody! Marcus Brody!"

He looked up, amazed to see Sallah making his way through the crowd toward him. He was so relieved by the familiar face, he almost threw his arms around Sallah. That was something he would never even consider doing in New York or in his native London.

"Old fellow, it's good to see you!" You have no idea how good, Sallah.

They shook hands; then Sallah embraced him. Brody patted his back, although his arms barely reached halfway around him. He blushed and grinned sheepishly, embarrassed by the public show of affection.

"Marcus, where have you been?" Sallah held Brody at arm's length and looked him over. "I've been waiting for you here. I've been worried."

Sallah was a bear of a man with black hair and eyes and distinctive Mediterranean features. His rich baritone voice and hearty laugh went a long way toward making Brody feel better, as did his reputation for loyalty. He was known for his fierce dedication to his friends and as a formidable enemy to anyone who opposed them.

"I was turned around for a while. Is Indy here?"

Sallah shook his head. "No, I thought he would be with you."

Now Brody didn't feel so bad. He had still managed to beat Indy here. "He's been delayed."

"Ah, yes. Delayed." Sallah laughed. He picked up Brody's luggage with such ease, the bags could have been empty. "Perfect British understatement, that," he added with a grin.

They left the station and emerged in an open-air market. Vendors' carts were everywhere, and people were shouting and waving their wares. The smell of ripe fruit and vegetables baking in the warm sun swirled around Brody, making him nauseous and dizzy. He felt as though he'd stepped off onto another planet and longed for the quiet solitude of the museum, for the cool silence of the artifacts that were entrusted to him. This, he thought, was not his world, not his way of life.

Sallah said everything they had discussed when Brody had called him in Cairo was ready, and he was anxious for the journey to begin. "As soon as we—" He stopped in midsentence. Two thugs in trench coats were blocking their path.

"Papers, please," one of them said in a foreboding tone, and held out his hand.

"Papers?" Sallah nodded. "Of course. Have one right here. Just finished reading it myself."

Sallah took out a newspaper from under his arm and shoved it in front of the agents' faces. *"Run!"* he hissed at Brody.

Turning to the men, he grinned and waved the newspaper. "The *Egyptian Mail*. Morning edition. Lots of good, timely news."

Brody frowned at Sallah. "Say again?"

"Run!" This time he yelled it.

Brody spun but didn't even move a step before one of the men grabbed him by the collar and pulled him back. Sallah bulldozed into both thugs with a flurry of punches. Bystanders scattered, and vendors' stands were overturned as the fight spilled into the open-air market. Fruits and vegetables fell to the ground and rolled away. Spools of costly silk and colorful cotton tumbled into the mud.

Brody pushed his way through the excited, chattering crowd. He tried to come up with a plan to help Sallah, but nothing came to mind. He didn't have the strength to overpower either man, and besides, Sallah *had* told him to run. He threaded his way through stalls, past vendors, and finally took refuge in a doorway.

He could still see the fighting and spotted Sallah just as he bumped into a camel. The impact stunned him long enough for the thugs to lunge at him. But Sallah quickly recovered and slapped the camel on the nose. The ornery beast jerked its head back and unleashed a huge gob of spit that splattered in one of the thug's faces. Sallah raced away, and Brody waved his arms, hoping to catch his eye.

Sallah raised a hand in recognition and cut toward him,

jabbing a finger at a darkened doorway at the top of a ramp. A curtain hung over it. "Get away, fast! Go!"

Brody didn't feel particularly disposed toward hiding there, but Sallah kept shouting. So Brody stepped out of the doorway and ran up the ramp. He slipped behind the curtain and peeked out. In the moment Sallah had turned his attention from the thugs, they had caught up with him. They pounced on him like animals, pounding him with their fists and short, heavy clubs. But Sallah wasn't fighting back. He was still waving frantically at Brody and yelling something he couldn't understand.

Nearby, a couple of Nazi soldiers moved in to back up the thugs. Brody knew Sallah didn't have a chance. He hesitated, wishing he could do something for his friend, but knew it was useless. He didn't want to look any longer. He ducked behind the curtain and turned around. Before he realized where he was, he heard metal doors slamming shut behind him. He was inside a truck, and on the wall was a red-and-black Nazi banner.

Sallah lifted his head. He hurt all over, he was bleeding, dust filled his nostrils. The thugs were gone, but they had captured their target after all. Brody had misunderstood him and run right into the Nazis' grasp instead of away from it. Now the truck had disappeared—with Brody in it.

One day later, in a center of a courtyard in Iskenderun, the sultan of the region was seated on his royal chair. It was purple and high-backed and made the sultan appear larger than life. He was an aloof-looking man with eyes that somehow defined his royal bearing. His full beard was silky white and fell to his chest. He wore a deep-red coat embroidered with golden braids on the front and sleeves, and ornate epaulets on the shoulders. His midsection was wrapped in a wide, gold-and-red sash, and his hat was flat-topped and cylindrical and matched his coat.

He was surrounded by his minions, and standing before him was an American he had met more than once in his travels. "What can I do for you, Mr. Donovan? As I told you the last time we talked, I am not interested in selling any works of art."

Donovan nodded. "I understand that. Your Highness, I have something I'd like to show you."

He handed the sultan the missing pages of the Grail diary. "These pages are taken from the diary of Professor Henry Jones. They include a map that pinpoints the exact location of the Grail Cup."

The Sultan studied the map with superficial interest. The fact that the cup was in his territory didn't surprise him. Nothing really did, not since he had realized as a child that he had been born into a wealthy, powerful family in a land where most people were born into families with little or nothing. He was privileged. He accepted that as fact.

He folded the map and casually handed it back. "And where did you obtain this map?"

Donovan turned and nodded toward the group standing near the entrance of the courtyard. Among them were Elsa Schneider, several Nazi guards, and Marcus Brody. It was obvious that Brody was being guarded.

"The man in the center is an emissary to Dr. Jones. He was given the pages by Dr. Jones's son, Indiana Jones."

"And what was he doing with them?"

"We captured him in Iskenderun. He was on his way to steal the Grail Cup from your territory."

"I see."

The cup didn't mean much to him. He had heard of it, of course, and was aware there was an old story that it was supposed to possess great power. But he didn't believe in superstitions—as far as he was concerned, it was just another gold cup destined for a museum or a private collection. He was a modern man and much more interested in newer, up-to-date things, objects with real, believable power.

But he was also well aware of the law of supply and demand. It was obvious that Donovan was interested in the Grail Cup himself. With more than one party pursuing it, the cup's value was greater than if only one party was after it. He knew exactly where he stood in the matter—right in the middle— and if Walter Donovan wanted to go into the desert and find the old cup, it was going to cost him dearly. The sultan had no doubt about that.

"And what do you want to do?" he asked, as if he didn't already know.

Donovan cleared his throat. "As you can see, the Grail is all but in our hands. However, Your Highness, we would not think of crossing your soil without your permission, nor would we remove the Grail Cup from your borders without suitable compensation."

The sultan looked past Donovan. "What have you brought me?"

Donovan turned and signaled the Nazi soldiers. "The trunk, please."

Two of them lugged a huge steamer trunk to the feet of the sultan.

Donovan motioned them to open the lid.

They unlocked the trunk and lifted the top. When the sultan made no move to inspect its contents, Donovan told the soldiers to empty it. For the next several minutes, they removed a wide-ranging assortment of gold and silver objects. There were goblets and candle holders, bowls, plates, and cups, precious boxes of varying sizes, and swords and knives.

"These valuables, Your Highness, have been donated by some of the finest families in all of Germany."

The sultan rose from his chair and walked right past the trunk and the "donations." He headed directly to the Nazi staff car parked in the corner of the courtyard and began to inspect it.

"Daimler-Benz 320L." He lifted the hood and studied the engine. "Ah, 3.4 liter, 120 horsepower, six cylinders, single solex updraft carburetor. Zero to one hundred kilometers in fifteen seconds."

He turned to Donovan, who had trailed after him, and smiled. "I even like the color."

Donovan quickly sized up the situation. It was obvious the sultan wasn't going to settle for the gold and silver, and since they needed his help, there was really only one choice. However, he could still bargain. "The keys, Your Highness, are in the ignition and at your disposal. It is yours, along with the other treasures. I would only ask that you loan us some of your men and equipment."

The sultan smiled appreciatively. "You shall have camels, horses, an armed escort, provisions, desert vehicles. And a tank."

Donovan nodded, pleased with the agreement.

Elsa hurried across the courtyard toward Donovan. "We've got no time to lose. I'm sure Indiana Jones and his father are on their way."

The proceedings at the sultan's court had not been overlooked by another party interested in the Grail Cup. Standing off to one side under an arch was the man who nearly killed Elsa and Indy in Venice, the same man who told Indy where his father was being hidden.

Kazim slipped a hand inside his tunic and ran a finger over the outline of the cruciform sword tattooed on his chest. No one was going to take the Grail Cup from its hiding place as long as he was alive.

The train arrived in Iskenderun at dawn. Despite the early hour, the platform was crowded with arriving and departing passengers. Indy glanced around. He hoped to see Marcus waiting for them but knew that was unlikely. Even if he was in Iskenderun, he would have no idea they were arriving at this hour.

Henry apparently was thinking along the same lines. "I wonder where we'll find Marcus."

"No sign of—Look!"

Indy pointed at the heavyset bearded figure bounding through the crowd toward them.

"Indy," Sallah bellowed. "How I have missed you." He embraced him, lifting him off the ground.

He put Indy back on the ground and turned to Henry. "Father of Indy?"

"Why . . . er . . . yes."

"Well done, sir! Your boy has blessed my life. He is a wonderful man." He threw his arms around Henry, who looked as if he didn't quite know what to make of Sallah, or any of the rest of it. "I'm so glad I have met you."

Indy noticed the bruises and lumps on Sallah's face. "What the hell happened? It looks like a camel kicked your face."

"Something like that. I'll tell you all about it very soon."

Indy frowned, almost not wanting to ask. "Sallah, where is Marcus?"

"We can't talk here, Indy," he whispered, leaning closer. "Hurry. Into the car." Sallah pointed at a battered, dusty coupe parked at the edge of the market.

After they had all climbed into the car, Sallah gunned the engine, and the coupe shot forward. A moment later they were racing through the crowded, narrow streets, threading through animals and cars, bicycles and wagons, and throngs of pedestrians. He honked, accelerated, downshifted, and swerved.

Henry was speechless with terror; he gripped an armrest in the backseat, certain that at any second Sallah was going to smash into a cart or plow through a crowd, killing everyone.

He finally found his voice and sat forward. "Please," he gasped. "Please, slow down. I've had enough crazy driving for a lifetime on my way here."

"Sorry, father of Indy."

He motioned frantically with his hand and stuck his head out the window. "Move that goat!" he shouted at someone in the street.

The goat moved, they sped forward, and Sallah looked over at Indy. "About Marcus. There were too many for me to handle."

"Watch out!" Henry bellowed from the backseat.

Sallah slammed on the brakes and cursed as a man with a cart pulled into their path. "Get a camel!" he yelled, poking his head out the window.

The man ignored him, and Sallah veered around the cart and sped on again. He returned to the matter of Marcus. "My face will tell you I did what I could with what I had." He raised a bruised fist. "I am not the only one who is feeling sore."

"What about Brody?"

"They set out across the desert this afternoon after getting supplies and soldiers from a sultan. I fear they took Mr. Brody with them."

Henry jerked forward, leaning over the front seat. "That

means they have the map and are on their way. They'll reach the Grail Cup before us."

"Calm down, Dad. We'll find them," Indy reassured him. At the same time he worried they were too late, for Marcus, and for the Grail.

"There's no silver medal for second place in this race, my boy." Henry had suddenly changed his mind about Sallah's driving and patted him on the shoulder. "Faster. Go faster, please."

Sallah grinned, pounded the horn, and stuck his head out of the window. "You blind Ottoman rug merchant. Out of my way."

Henry rolled down his window and joined in the haranguing. "Road hog! Move along now."

Indy was pensive. He knew that once Donovan and his gang of Nazis were certain they were on the right trail to the Grail Cup, Marcus's life would be worthless. "Can we catch them?"

Sallah gave Indy a knowing smile. "There are always shortcuts."

He leaned on the horn, shaking his head and cursing in three languages. He turned to Indy. "You'll see."

CHAPTER EIGHTEEN

◄◄ ►►

CONFRONTATIONS

Marcus Brody pushed his head up through the hatch of the World War I tank and peered into the blazing sun. He wiped his forehead with his handkerchief and muttered, "Nazi mad dogs."

They were moving through a desert canyon that looked just like the last one. To Brody, who thrived in urban environs, it was the end of the world—barren, harsh, ugly, and relentlessly hot. The irony didn't escape him: there was a good chance that this ghastly, forsaken land would be the end of *his* world.

"Care to wet your whistle, Marcus?"

Brody turned at the sound of Donovan's voice. An open-topped car trailed the tank. Seated with Donovan was Elsa Schneider, the betrayer, and a Nazi whom Elsa had called Colonel Vogel. Behind the car was the remainder of the caravan—camels bearing soldiers from the sultan's private army, each of whom was armed with a saber and carbine and garbed in billowy desert dress; spare horses; a supply truck, a German sedan, a jeep; and a couple of troop carrier trucks packed with Nazi soldiers.

Donovan thrust the canteen at him and grinned. Brody felt like spitting in his face rather than accepting his offer. But since he didn't have any spit, he caught the canteen when Donovan tossed it up to him, and took a swallow. They had stopped briefly at an oasis a couple of hours ago, but he was already parched. The sun had turned the inside of the tank into an oven, and up on top it was like a broiler.

The water ran down his throat, and he couldn't remember anything having tasted this good in a long time. He took a breath, turned the canteen to his lips again, and drank deeply.

Donovan held out his hand for the canteen, evidently worried that Brody was going to deplete it. "According to your map, Marcus, we are only three or four miles from the discovery of the greatest artifact in human history."

Brody wiped the back of his hand across his mouth and considered hurling the canteen into the bastard's face. But he knew that would only reduce his chances of surviving even further. Instead, he simply lobbed the canteen to him.

"You're meddling with powers you cannot possibly contemplate, Walter."

Donovan started to say something about power but stopped.

Brody followed his gaze. In the distance, somewhere in the hills, he glimpsed a reflection. He had a good idea what it was, and figured that Donovan did, too.

The sun glinted off the binoculars as Indy spied on the caravan moving across the canyon basin. Sallah and Henry were on either side of him, and the car containing their supplies was parked beside a rock outcropping thirty yards behind them.

"They've got a tank . . . six-pound gun. I see Brody. He looks okay."

Henry shaded his eyes and squinted. "Be careful they don't see you."

"We're well out of range."

At that moment they saw a flash as the tank fired a shell in their direction. Indy dove to the ground and covered his head. The others did the same. The shell whistled past and exploded less than a hundred feet away. Pieces of Sallah's car, destroyed by the direct hit, rained down on them.

Sallah groaned. "That car belonged to my brother-in-law."

"Bull's-eye," Colonel Vogel shouted. "Let's go claim the bodies."

Elsa took the binoculars and looked for herself. Part of her felt like weeping at the possibility that Indy might be dead.

But another part felt immensely relieved: if he was dead, her own internal conflict would be over. She could get on with finding the Grail and wouldn't constantly be battling with herself. Ever since she met Indy, she had been on an emotional roller coaster. One moment she hated him, the next moment she didn't want to live without him. If he was dead, so be it.

The Grail, she reminded herself, was her true passion. Men and politics were simply means to another end. She would go along with Donovan, but only to a point. She needed Donovan to get her to the Grail, but somehow she had to get the cup away from him. The promises the cup held were too wondrous to pass up. It would be hers, or she would die trying to get it.

When they arrived at the spot where the car blew up, Elsa saw that there were no bodies. Oddly, she felt better. Indy was alive.

As Vogel hurriedly organized the soldiers to begin a search, Donovan walked over to her. "Well, maybe it wasn't even Jones."

"No. It's him, all right. He's here." She looked around, feeling that they were being watched. "Somewhere. I'm sure of it."

Donovan must have felt it, too. He looked around anxiously, then told one of the soldiers to put Brody in the tank. He turned back to Elsa. "In this heat, without transportation, they're as good as dead."

Suddenly, a bullet ricocheted off a nearby rock, and the crack of gunfire filled the air. Donovan ran for cover, forgetting about Elsa. She scrambled after him, angered more by the possibility that Indy might be firing at her than by the fact that Donovan had only been concerned about saving his own neck.

"It's Jones," Donovan yelled. "He's got guns."

Indy was hiding behind a massive rock when the gunfire began. He saw Elsa and Donovan rush to cover and the soldiers return the fire.

He exchanged puzzled looks with his father and Sallah. Who could be firing on them?

"C'mon. Let's take a look," Indy said.

They climbed down from their hiding place and, after a couple of minutes, reached a rock overlooking a chaotic scene, as Nazis and the sultan's soldiers exchanged gunfire with an unseen enemy positioned in caves on the canyon wall. Sallah gazed through a pair of binoculars, then passed them to Indy.

One of the figures emerged from the shadowy mouth of a cave, and Indy saw the man had a symbol on his shirt, a cross that tapered down like the blades of a broadsword. The man stepped boldly into the open, defying death. Indy focused on his face and recognized him. It was Kazim.

So the brotherhood of the Cruciform Sword was more than just one man's fanatic enterprise.

Indy handed the binoculars back to Sallah, then conferred with Henry. The three men agreed on a plan, and Henry moved off toward the tank where Brody was being held. Indy and Sallah, meanwhile, crawled down to the outskirts of Donovan's hastily made encampment.

From their position they could see the horses, and Indy picked out the one he wanted. They waited for the right moment to race across the open span.

"Look," Sallah said, pointing toward the canyon wall.

Kazim was climbing down the rocky face and firing as he ran from boulder to boulder.

"Now," Indy said, and signaled Sallah.

They were halfway between the rocks and the horses when one of the Nazi soldiers who had been firing at the caves turned away to reload his weapon. He spotted them and was about to alert the others when Kazim rushed forward and fired, killing the soldier. Kazim spun wildly around, firing like a madman until he was cut down at close range by a hail of bullets.

Indy and Sallah ducked down among the horses as Donovan rushed over to Kazim. He was standing just a dozen feet away from them.

"Who are you?" he demanded as Kazim lay bleeding.

"A messenger from God. For the unrighteous, the Cup of Life holds everlasting damnation."

Those were Kazim's last words.

Abruptly more shots rang out from the caves, and Donovan darted for cover as bullets kicked up dust within feet of him.

Indy and Sallah slipped onto the backs of two of the horses and rode off undetected amid the gunfire.

Brody was sweltering in the tank. He had been left alone and was searching for a spare key. He wasn't sure he would be able to figure out how to operate the tank, but he knew he needed the key before he was going to get anywhere. He heard the hatch open and quickly moved away from the front of the tank.

"Marcus."

The voice was familiar. He looked up at the hatch in surprise, and before he could respond, Henry dropped down feet-first next to him.

He grinned at Brody and recited an old University Club toast: "Genius of the Restoration . . ."

". . . aid our own resuscitation!" Brody finished.

They threw their arms around each other. "Hope you don't mind my dropping in this way, unexpected and all," Henry said, and laughed.

"Not at all. Glad to see you alive, old boy. What are you doing here?"

"It's a rescue mission, my good man. You thought I was coming for tea, or what?"

"You're a little late for that."

Suddenly a Nazi dropped through the hatch and aimed his Luger at the two men. Two more Nazis joined him, followed by Vogel.

"Search him," the colonel ordered.

One of the Nazis frisked Henry, but found neither weapons nor the Grail diary. Vogel was infuriated. He slapped Henry across the face.

"What is in the book? That miserable little book of yours."

When Henry didn't reply, Vogel's hand slammed across his face again. "We have the map. Your book is useless. And yet you went all the way back to Berlin to get it. Tell me why, Dr. Jones."

Henry remained mum, and Vogel smacked him across the face a third time. "What are you hiding? What does the diary tell *you* that it doesn't tell us?"

Henry's look burned with loathing. "It tells me that goose-stepping morons like yourself should try reading books instead of burning them."

Vogel slapped him again, much harder this time, and Henry staggered back under the impact.

"They've got your father in the tank," Sallah said, passing Indy the binoculars. "I saw the soldier go after him."

Indy cursed himself. He shouldn't have listened to his father. He should have gone after Brody himself and worried about the horses later. He gazed toward the tank, then turned in the direction of Donovan and the other soldiers. He saw they were still busy fighting the remaining members of Kazim's band.

"Let's get them before it's too late."

"Herr Colonel!"

One of the soldiers, who had moved to the driver's seat of the tank, motioned for Vogel to come to the viewing port.

Vogel looked out and saw Indy and Sallah charging toward the tank on horseback, through a cloud of dust. He turned back to the Nazi who guarded Henry and Brody. "If they move, shoot them both."

He took command of the tank's gun.

"Watch out, Indy. The guns!" Sallah bellowed.

Indy saw the six-pound cannon on the tank revolving and pointing in their direction. He suddenly realized that attacking the tank wasn't such a good idea. He pulled back hard on the reins and headed in a different direction—away from the tank.

Sallah was right behind him, yelling at the top of his lungs. "Smart move, Indy. Horses against a tank are no good. I totally agree."

They zigzagged across the desert as the tank gave chase, firing several rounds at them. Each time, Indy and Sallah emerged from a plume of dust as the rounds missed them.

Indy's head snapped around. The tank was gaining on them. Then he noticed they had company. A small German sedan with two soldiers was heading their way. It was going to take more than two of those guys to stop him. He knew that for a fact.

Just then another shell was fired, barely missing Indy this time. "Damn."

"That was close, Indy," Sallah yelled. "Ride for your life."

Sallah charged ahead, but Indy was starting to get angry. He scowled, glancing back, and this time realized that the gun that was firing on them could only pivot so far. It gave him an idea.

He jerked back on the reins and turned the horse. The tank turned and followed him, but now it was heading on a collision course with the small sedan carrying the two Nazi soldiers. The driver of the sedan tried to avoid the tank, but Vogel didn't see him; he was only concerned with keeping Indy in the sights of his gun.

With an earsplitting screech of metal, the sedan was struck from the side and lodged between the front treads of the tank. Not only was the tank stopped by the collision, but the sedan had blocked the front port and jammed the turret on the six-pound cannon.

Indy, meanwhile, reined in his horse. He leaned down and scooped up an armful of rocks from a wall along a culvert, then urged the horse on. He galloped up to the starboard cannon and jammed several of the rocks down the barrel. Then he steered the horse so that he was directly in front of the gun, close enough to be an easy target.

"I see him." Henry jerked his head up as he heard the side gunner's excited yell.

He knew the Nazi was talking about his son.

"Well, shoot him," Vogel ordered.

"No," Henry yelled, and lunged toward the gunner. But the guard blocked his way and shoved him against the bulkhead. He pointed his Luger between Henry's eyes just as the side gunner aimed the cannon at Indy and fired.

The gun backfired, blowing the breech into the face of the gunner. He stumbled backward, his face ripped apart by the blast. He was dead before he hit the floor.

Smoke poured into the tank. Henry and the others choked and gasped for air. Vogel stepped over the dead gunner, reached up, and threw open the hatch to let out the smoke.

"Fire the turret gun," he yelled at the driver, taking no chance himself.

Henry grabbed Brody by the arm, and together they crawled on hands and knees until they were underneath the hatch. Henry was about to stand up and climb out when he bumped into the guard, who was also on the floor of the tank. The guard raised his Luger and pressed it against Henry's forehead.

The driver of the sedan was dead upon impact with the tank, but the passenger survived the crash and was attempting to cut his way out through the cloth top. He managed to cut away a flap, and pulled it down. He stuck his head through the hole and stared directly into the barrel of the six-pound cannon.

At that moment the cannon fired, emulsifying everything in its path and blowing bits of the sedan seventy-five yards through the air.

Indy was behind the tank. He had just spotted Sallah galloping toward him when the cannon blasted the sedan. Chunks of the car landed all around Sallah. His horse reared up, and Sallah tumbled off.

He quickly remounted, glanced once toward the tank, and charged off in the opposite direction.

Indy had the feeling he wasn't going to get much more help from Sallah.

Free of the car, the tank trundled ahead.

Vogel took over the turret gun and swiveled it around, looking for Indy. But now the turret would only move in a ninety-degree arc. He was sure Indy was behind the tank, and if the other horseman joined him, they might try boarding.

If they did, he would shoot Jones's father, right in front of him.

But he needed reinforcements. He grabbed the microphone on the radio and called Donovan. "Forget about those crazies in the hills," he said tersely. "Bring the troops now."

There was a moment of silence, then Donovan barked,

"Are you telling me you haven't taken care of Jones, even with that tank?"

Vogel fumed, and spoke between gritted teeth. "Not yet."

He stared out above the turret gun, looking again for Indy. He saw a narrow canyon opening on the port side, and an idea struck him. He smiled to himself and ordered the driver to turn into the canyon.

He clicked on the radio again. "By the time you get here, Jones will be taken care of, as you say."

He turned the turret gun as far as he could, as they entered the canyon. He aimed it at the canyon wall and waited for the right moment. He spotted a rock overhanging the wall and adjusted his aim. He fired a volley directly at it, and suddenly tons of rock tumbled down.

Vogel grinned. That should take care of Jones.

CHAPTER NINETEEN

◄◄ ►►

ONE AGAINST MANY

Moments before the landslide Indy lagged behind the tank, looking for loose rocks again. His plan was to jam the tank's port gun in the hope that it would backfire as the other had done. This time, when the hatch opened to clear away the smoke, he would overpower Vogel and commandeer the tank. A simple plan, if Vogel fell for it.

But the tank had maneuvered into a narrow canyon, and he couldn't find any sizeable rocks. There were pebbles and there were boulders, most of them half the size of the tank or larger. And that wasn't the only problem. The canyon had also cut him off from Sallah, who had galloped well out of the range of the tank's big gun. Now Sallah probably wouldn't know what had happened to him or the tank.

He concentrated on the ground. Rocks. I need rocks.

Just then, the cannon fired into the cliff, and suddenly more rocks than he cared to think about were careening toward him. He reined the horse sharply, turning, and galloped away from the landslide. Rocks bounded by on either side of him, barely missing him. But he escaped unharmed.

If he had been keeping pace with the tank, he wouldn't have been so lucky—he would be dead. No doubt about that.

But now he had another problem. The route through the narrow canyon was cut off. He would have to backtrack and go around the canyon to find the tank, and that would take precious time, maybe hours.

He didn't have hours.

Then he saw an alternative route. The landslide had

worked to his advantage, creating a rugged trail along the side of the cliff. Time to take the high road.

He followed it as quickly as he could, maneuvering the horse around the rubble. He found that it not only allowed him to cross the canyon but it was also a shortcut. Before long he was nearing the tank, approaching it from above. He passed it and was wondering how he could work his way down to the canyon base when, unexpectedly, his luck ran out. The trail abruptly ended in a rock wall.

He glanced down as the tank motored along below him. He would have to turn around, or . . . He dropped from his saddle and, before he had time to change his mind, ran to the cliff's edge and leapt. He landed on his feet on top of the tank, and dropped to his hands and knees. He made it—but now what?

The tank cleared the canyon, and the desert opened again to the right. Indy glanced back and saw a cloud of dust on the desert floor. He squinted against the bright light. A jeep was rapidly approaching. Behind it, in the distance, were two carrier trucks filled with Nazi troops.

Company was arriving.

"Welcome aboard, Jones."

He turned and saw Vogel's face peering through the hatchway. His beady eyes speared Indy like darts. He stared back at him and held his gaze. He felt waves of hate from the man but refused to look away, to let him win the contest of wills.

Suddenly he felt a familiar prickling sensation on the back of his neck—a warning. He spun around and saw a soldier crawling behind him. He realized Vogel had been trying to distract him while the soldier boarded from the jeep. The man leapt like a spider and overpowered him, pinning him to the top of the tank.

He struggled to free himself, but his cheek was pressed against the hot metal. The position gave him a chance to see one of the troop carriers moving alongside the tank. A handful of soldiers vaulted aboard like pirates stealing their way onto a galleon. The odds were not looking good.

Indy shoved the soldier and grappled with him for his Luger. They rolled over, and Indy pinned him to the tank with the Luger wedged between them. He twisted the soldier's hand, trying to loosen his grip on the gun. They rolled over again, and the barrel of the gun neared Indy's head. He used the leverage of the tank and forced the gun away until it was turned toward the soldier.

He squeezed with all his strength, forcing the soldier to fire a round into himself. The bullet passed through the man's neck and continued through the stomach of another soldier and the groin of a third. The three bodies fell away, tumbling over the side of the crowded tank.

Three down, plenty more to go. He saw that Vogel had emerged from the hatch to join the huddle of Nazis surrounding him.

"That's my boy. Go get 'em, son."

Indy heard his father's voice, then spotted him looking up through the open hatch. He reached for the bullwhip on his hip, but realized it was too crowded to use it. The lack of space, however, was his one advantage. The soldiers came at him from all sides, wielding knives and guns, but he was an elusive target. He dodged the blade of a knife, which missed his side and slammed into the thigh of another Nazi. A blow struck him in the jaw, and he spun around and kicked a gun out of the hand of a second Nazi, who fell off the tank. A third soldier fired at him, missed, and hit one of his own men. A few more down.

"Go get 'em, Junior," Henry yelled.

Suddenly, Indy literally saw red. He seethed, his anger spurted through him like a shot of adrenaline, and he slammed his fist into the jaw of the nearest soldier. The man fell back into another soldier, and they both tumbled off the tank. Indy kicked at the next one, who fell onto the tank's tread and took one more with him. The two rolled forward, hit the ground, and were instantly crushed by the tread.

Indy, still infuriated, looked at the hatch. "Don't ever call me Junior again!"

No sooner had he spoken the words than Vogel swung a length of chain and snapped it twice around Indy's shoulders. A white hot pain burned through him; he crumpled to his knees, grimacing in agony. Still, he managed to keep his wits about him. He saw the Luger the first soldier left behind and kicked it toward the hatch. It was a shot that would have pleased a soccer champion. The gun skittered across the tank and fell right into Henry's lap.

Indy rose to his feet and faced Vogel and the one remaining soldier. The chain was still wrapped around his shoulders but he could move his arms, and neither of his opponents was armed. He smiled gamely at Vogel. After overcoming all the others, he was confident he could handle these two.

But Vogel smiled back, and then Indy saw the reason for his cockiness. A second troop carrier was about to pull alongside the tank with a host of reinforcements. More men than he could handle. Hell, more men than a half dozen of him could fight.

When the gun fell into his lap, Henry grabbed it by the barrel, just in time. Brody yelled for him to watch out. He heard a thud as his friend was knocked to the floor. The guard wrapped his arms around Henry's waist and pulled him down from the hatch.

"Let go of me," he yelled.

When he didn't, Henry acted decisively. "Fair warning, fellow."

He clubbed him over the head with the butt of the gun, and the guard dropped to the floor next to Brody. Henry climbed to the top of the hatch, and was about to join Indy when he saw the troop carrier. There was no way they could overcome that horde of Nazis. They needed help, and lots of it.

He ducked back inside and ran over to the port turret just as the guard stumbled to his feet. Henry aimed the cannon at the troop-laden truck and fumbled for the trigger. Just as he found it, the guard jerked his arm away and dragged him away from the turret.

Brody crawled over on his hands and knees, and the guard tripped over him. Henry slipped out of his grasp and lunged toward the turret. He quickly aimed at the troop carrier, and squeezed off a round.

Beginner's luck was with him: he scored a direct hit on the gas tank, and the carrier exploded, spewing soldiers and debris through the scorched air.

*   *   *

The blast blew Indy, Vogel, and the last soldier off the top of the tank. The soldier fell to the ground, but Indy and Vogel landed on the moving tread. Both were shuttled quickly forward and were inches from being crushed under the tank when they rolled onto the cannon mounting.

Vogel's feet slammed into Indy, forcing him off the narrow ledge of metal and back onto the tread. Indy latched a hand onto the cannon, then wrapped his other arm around it. His feet dangled over the edge of the tread as he fought to keep from falling.

Vogel, meanwhile, crawled forward, and kicked at Indy's hands.

Inside the tank the guard picked Brody up and hurled him viciously against the bulkhead, smashing his head into it. He slumped to the floor, lingering on the edge of consciousness, fighting the blackness that crept up on him like a nightmare. Vaguely he was aware that the guard was aiming his Luger at him. He closed his eyes, not wanting to see any more. He waited for the explosion, and death.

Henry jumped the guard, knocking his arm aside. The weapon fired, and the bullet ricocheted several times. Suddenly the tank veered out of control as the driver pitched forward into the gears, struck dead by the bullet.

Henry fought. He gasped for breath. The guard's powerful arm was wrapped around his neck, and he was squeezing. Both of Henry's hands gripped the guard's other arm, keeping the gun from turning toward him. Desperately he tried to stay conscious. If he passed out, he was dead.

Brody was jarred awake as the tank bounced over a large rock. He felt as if he had been raised from the dead. His body ached fiercely in a dozen places, and his head throbbed as though a spear were piercing it. But he pushed himself to his feet despite the pain and saw Henry struggling with the guard. Brody kicked the guard's hand, and the gun skidded across the floor.

The tank bounded over another rock, and Brody fell to the floor. "Who's driving this thing, anyhow?" he muttered.

* * *

Henry reached into his pocket the moment Brody kicked the gun away. His fingers were inside the pocket, moving, searching, groping for a fountain pen. His other arm clung to the guard, who was now trying to get away and retrieve the Luger. He pulled out the fountain pen and stabbed the guard again and again, but the man didn't seem to feel it. He finally managed to get the top off, raised his arm, and squeezed. A burst of ink shot into the guard's eyes.

The man bellowed, staggered back, clawing at his eyes. Henry gulped for air, filling his lungs, then smashed his fist into the stunned guard's face. The man's head jerked back and cracked against the bulkhead. He pitched forward and was out cold.

"The pen *is* mightier than the sword," Henry crowed, and helped Brody to his feet. This nonsense was a damn long way from the study of ancient languages and antiquities. But now the adrenaline was pumping through him.

They climbed through the hatch and onto the top of the tank. Neither Indy nor the soldiers were in sight. Then Henry peered over the side of the tank. Vogel and his son were locked in a deadly embrace on the cannon mount, and both were now fettered by Vogel's chain.

And Indy's head was only inches above the tread.

Henry carefully lowered himself over the side of the tank, determined to help his son in a way he had never dreamed possible. He would make up for his shortcomings as a father, all right. And when this was over, he would stand in front of Indy and spell out those shortcomings, just as he should have done years ago.

I'm a stiff ole coot whose stubborn ways never did him any good. That's what he'd tell him, he thought. It was time at long last to admit to it.

Sallah had galloped away from the tank after he had nearly been killed by the parts of the demolished car. A horse was no challenge to a tank, he had told himself over and over. But where was Indy? The tank and Indy had disappeared. Sallah backtracked and found the narrow canyon but was baffled when he came to the landslide. Fearing that Indy had been trapped in the rubble, he searched the rocks.

Finally, certain that Indy wasn't in the rubble, he had backtracked again and spotted the tank in the distance. As he neared it, he knew something was wrong. The tank was speeding directly for a gorge less than two hundred yards away, and he didn't see Indy. He spurred his horse and tore toward the tank. As he galloped alongside it, he spotted Brody clinging to the top. *"Jump!"* he shouted. *"Jump, man!"*

Brody heard Sallah yelling. He snapped his head around and saw the gorge for the first time. He slid down to the cannon mounting on the side where Sallah was galloping.

"Jump, I said!" Sallah roared.

He figured he was going to die, but leapt anyhow. He grabbed Sallah's neck as he landed half-on the horse, half-off. Sallah reached back, pulled his ankle over the horse.

"Hang on, Marcus."

"The other side," Brody yelled. "They're on the other side."

Indy and Vogel were still tangled in the chain, at an impasse. If one threw the other from the tank, they would both go over the side.

Then Indy saw the gorge barely a hundred yards away. *Who the hell is driving the tank?*

He fought to rip the chain from around his chest just as Vogel, who had also seen the cliff, tried to jump. But to Indy's surprise, his father appeared from nowhere and grabbed Vogel by the leg.

Vogel spun and jerked his leg away, then kicked Henry in the face, knocking him onto the tank's tread. Indy saw his father rolling toward the front of the tank and reacted instantly. He unhitched his whip and snapped it toward his father. The whip coiled neatly around Henry's ankle just as he was about to roll over the front of the tank.

Indy reeled in the whip with every bit of strength he had left, and Henry bounced back along the tread, a huge fish hooked on the end of a line.

Sallah drew his horse up next to the tread. "Indy, hurry. Get off the tank."

Indy glanced over at him. "Here. Give me a hand." He passed him the whip.

Sallah snatched it, reined back on the horse, leaned away from the tank.

Henry tumbled off the tread and rolled in the dirt. Sallah was about to dismount to help him, when he looked up to see Indy and Vogel racing to the rear of the tank. They were tangled in a chain, and both leapt at the same time. They would have made it, too. But one end of the chain hooked on the superstructure of the tank and both men were dragged toward the cliff.

"Oh, no. Indy," Sallah shouted.

In a final act of desperation, Indy struggled to slip out of the chain as he was dragged across the ground. But now the chain was caught on his leg. He ripped open his pants, and pushed them down over his hips and then his knees. He was like a stage magician performing a sensational death-defying escape trick. But it wasn't a trick, at least not one *he* had ever performed.

Next to him Vogel screamed in despair as he fought the chain.

Indy's pants were almost off when the tank hit the edge of the cliff and plummeted over the side, plunging toward the deep gorge.

In the distance Elsa saw a plume of black smoke rising from the gorge. She lowered the binoculars and ordered the driver to start the engine of her sedan.

"The tank is finished," she said to Donovan. "All of them are finished."

"What about Vogel?"

"What about him, Herr Donovan?" Her voice was terse and utterly cold. She had shed her emotional concerns, stripped herself of them. The point was the Grail. She couldn't expect Indy to be alive, and what if he was? What would it change?

Nothing.

Donovan nodded and joined Elsa in the car. "I guess it's destined that you and I would find the Grail Cup together."

Elsa remained silent, staring ahead, watching the heat ripple across the desert floor. *Dead. Indy's dead. Nothing matters but the Grail.*

"Make sure the supply truck and the others are ready," she said at last. "We've got work to do."

Henry stared down at the flaming wreckage of the tank, fighting a wave of emotion that threatened to drown him. He was cut, bruised, battered. But that didn't matter. He had lost his only son, lost him before he had ever had a chance to put things right, to make up for the years of misunderstandings.

"I have to go after him," Sallah said. "He's my friend." He started to charge toward the cliff, but Brody grabbed his arm, restraining him.

"It's no use, Sallah."

The big man pulled himself away from Brody, then sank to his knees and buried his face in his hands. Henry looked from Sallah to Brody, not knowing what to say, barely able to place his own grief in any sort of perspective, much less anyone else's.

Brody tried to comfort him. He slipped an arm around Henry's shoulder, offering his condolences. Henry's eyes burned with tears. Dust swelled around them. The hot sun beat down.

I never even hugged him, Henry thought miserably. *I never told him I loved him.*

Dazed and bewildered, Indy staggered from behind a cluster of rocks. He was carrying his pants, which had been slit from the waist to the ankles. Remnants of the pants were gathered around his boots.

He joined the others and gazed over the cliff at the wreckage. One by one they became aware of his presence. First Brody, then Sallah, then Henry.

Indy shook his head and whistled softly. "Now *that* was close."

"Junior!" Henry shouted, and threw his arms around Indy, hugging him hard. "I thought I'd lost you," he said over and over again and babbled on about love.

It took a moment for Indy's head to clear enough for him to realize his father was embracing him, telling him he loved him. It was something he hadn't heard in a long time. In fact, he couldn't recall ever hearing it, or his father ever embracing him.

He hugged him back, hugged fiercely, a young boy swept up in a blind love for his father. "I thought I'd lost you, too," he whispered.

Brody was moved by the sudden reconciliation, but Sallah was obviously confused.

"Junior? You are Junior?"

Indy made a face. He was in no mood to talk about *that* topic. He stepped back and did his best to improvise a way of putting on his pants.

Henry answered Sallah's question. "That's his name. Henry Jones, Jr."

"I like Indiana," Indy said resolutely.

"We named the *dog* Indiana!" Henry countered. "We named *you* Henry, Jr."

Brody smiled, and Sallah laughed.

"The dog?" Sallah exclaimed.

Even Indy couldn't resist a grin. "I got a lot of fond memories about that dog."

Sallah laughed even louder and slapped Indy on the back, causing his pants to drop around his ankles.

CHAPTER TWENTY

◀◀ ▶▶

GRAIL TRAIL

The midafternoon sun was scorching the barren rocks around them. Elsa closed her eyes a moment, calming the anger she felt. She was doing her best to ignore the heat, but Donovan was another matter. She had dealt with her share of arrogant, overbearing men who preferred treating her like a piece of jewelry instead of a scientist, but Donovan was the worst. Even the Führer, for all his eccentricities, at least recognized her intellectual capabilities.

"It should be right here," Elsa said, pointing at the wall of rock in front of her.

"Nothing's there," Donovan replied in a flat, condescending tone.

"I've checked and rechecked the landmarks, Walter," she said evenly. "If the map is accurate, the hidden canyon is directly behind that wall. And that is where we'll find it."

Donovan shrugged. "We've already tried every possible route. There's no entrance. It's solid rock."

For someone who was as conniving as he was, Donovan wasn't much help when it came to practical matters. He would be better off allowing someone else to find the Grail Cup, and then stealing it, she thought.

"Then, I suppose we make our own entrance."

"How do you propose to do that?"

"I guess you've never worked with explosives."

He regarded her a moment with an icy stare that even the desert heat couldn't counteract. "I don't suppose that I have."

Not surprising. She turned and walked back to the supply

truck. She felt his eyes on the back of her head. Let him
worry, she thought. She would lead him to the Grail, then she
would watch, and at the right moment, she would act. The
Grail would be hers, or she would die. Period.

Indy, like his three companions, was wearing a hat draped
in white cloth and trying to get used to the way his camel
moved. It was nothing like riding a horse or even an elephant.
This was something completely unique—a steep dip, a rise,
another dip, another rise, but the camel's lope never felt quite
even. He couldn't grasp the rhythm and suspected you had to
be born into a nomadic desert life to ever feel comfortable on
one of these creatures.

The white cloth and his hat helped some against the relentless heat, but they didn't assuage his thirst. He thought of
water, bottles of it, rivers of it, cool and endless. He thought
of sliding into a pool, soaking his feet in cool, wet mud.

Sallah had recovered Indy's horse, and the four of them
had backtracked—two to a horse—to where they had last
seen Donovan's caravan. There had been no sign of either
Donovan or Elsa. But they had found tire tracks, several
abandoned camels, and even a couple of canteens of water.

Indy had urged his father and Brody to stay behind and
wait while he and Sallah pursued Donovan on horseback. But
neither would listen to him. Both insisted they were okay, and
could continue on. They could all go on the camels, Henry
had said.

They rested only a short time, attending to their cuts and
bruises and discomforts. Indy had found a pair of pants among
some of the supplies left behind, and they fashioned their
headwear. Finally, they climbed onto the camels, and set off
across the desert.

Without the map they would never be able to locate the
place where the Grail Cup was hidden, Indy thought. But the
route was clearly marked by the tracks left behind by the remaining vehicles of the caravan. Indy guessed that Donovan
and Elsa believed he and his group were dead, because other-
wise they wouldn't have been so careless about leaving a trail.
So let them believe it. It might prove to be his group's only
advantage.

A distant explosion resounded through the pass, snapping Indy to attention.

"What was that?" Brody asked.

"The secret canyon," Henry exclaimed. "They've found it."

Indy recalled the words from the Grail tablet. *Across the desert and through the mountain to the Canyon of the Crescent Moon, broad enough only for one man. To the Temple of the Sun, holy enough for all men.*

He urged his camel to pick up the pace. "Let's keep moving."

When they arrived at the site of the explosion, rocks were strewn about, and a gaping hole in the cliff led into a narrow canyon. Its walls were high and steep, the color of ocher.

Indy passed his canteen around. They were all weary, hot, and sore, but they knew they couldn't waste any time. Henry, who had taken off his jacket, led the way into the canyon. His shirt was open at the collar, and his hat was pulled low over his eyes. He didn't look like a medieval scholar now, Indy mused. If anything, his father looked like an aging adventurer who was secretly having the time of his life as he valiantly sought to fulfill his greatest desire.

As Henry entered the canyon, his camel stopped, snorted, and tried to back away. He cursed the beast, slapped it on the rear with his hand, and finally convinced it to move ahead.

They all experienced similar resistance from their camels as they followed single file behind Henry. Brody's animal was the most stubborn, and Indy finally was forced to dismount and pull it through. Once inside the canyon, the animals calmed down. It was the humans who felt wary, out of their element.

The farther they progressed, the narrower and steeper the walls became. The place was eerie, too still, too tight, too hot. The camels' hooves echoed, and the sound of them, Indy thought, had a strange quality, although he couldn't have said exactly what.

The air was more refined, as if they were at a higher elevation. Indy was light-headed and felt the dull throb of a headache. The light was different here, too, less harsh, gold against the stark canyon walls on either side of them.

He didn't like being here, he didn't like the feel of the place. None of them did—except for Henry. He was the optimist of the group, and why not: the project that had dominated his life was near fruition. The Grail wasn't in his hands yet, but it was close enough for him to imagine that it was. He actually seemed to be enjoying himself.

"Marcus," Henry said, "we're like the four heroes of the Grail legend. You're Percival, the holy innocent. Sallah is Bors, the ordinary man. My son is Galahad, the valiant knight. And his father . . . the old crusader, Lancelot, who was turned away because he was unworthy, as perhaps I am."

"I'm an old sot who'd rather be home safely with a nip of Scotch at hand," Brody replied. He was clinging to his saddle for support and glancing around, uncertainty etched in every line of his face. His fretting expression, Indy thought.

But Henry didn't seem to hear him. He nodded to himself, musing over his comparisons. Then he turned to Indy. "But remember, it was Galahad who succeeded where his father failed."

Terrific, Indy thought. It was just the sort of responsibility he didn't want. "I don't even know what the Grail looks like, Dad."

"Nobody does," Henry replied. "The one who is worthy will know the Grail."

Like King Arthur and Excalibur. As if this was all some sort of glorious quest, not a dangerous predicament. It annoyed him. In his father's mind, they had been elevated to the ranks of crusaders.

While Henry gazed ahead expectantly, Indy looked down at the dirt. They no longer needed the tracks of the vehicles, but the fact that they were there, inches inside either wall, kept him cognizant of the fact that they weren't alone.

"Look!" Sallah burst out, and pointed.

They stopped and stared. The narrow canyon led into a broad, open area like an arena, and carved into one of the rocks on the far side was a spectacular Greco-Roman facade. Wide steps led up to a landing with massive columns, and beyond them was the entrance to a darkened chamber. The Temple of the Sun, Indy thought.

"Let's go," Henry said eagerly.

The camels complained again, but the men spurred them on, and they grudgingly trotted ahead, crossing the open area and stopping in front of the temple steps. Indy stole a glance at his father: his expression was rapturous, struck with a childlike wonder. Even Indy was awed by the sight, but not as his father was. Henry's elation swept out of him in waves, like an odor. It was infectious.

"Monumental," Brody uttered.

"Built by the gods," Sallah mumbled.

Indy understood. In the presence of a structure of such grand scale, it was easy to think that it had been built for immortals twice their human size and strength.

For a long time none of them moved from the bottom of the steps. The temple had *that* sort of magic about it. But Indy finally broke the spell. He looked down at the ground again and saw the tracks crisscrossing behind them. So what had happened to the vehicles?

He squinted to the west, where the sun hovered low over the wall of the arena. Among the shadows he made out the shape of a troop carrier, a supply truck, an auto, and several horses.

He motioned toward the temple. "Come on. Let's take a look. But keep quiet."

He led the way, followed by Henry, Sallah, and Brody. Slowly they ascended the steps toward the dark entrance. As they reached the top, Indy glanced back, making sure the others were still behind him. Then he pressed on into the temple.

It took his eyes a moment to adjust to the darkness. But then he saw someone standing directly in front of him—a knight dressed in armor, a magnificent Herculean figure that was two, no three times, his size.

Indy stopped, stepped back, then smiled as he grasped the obvious. The knight was carved from an enormous block of stone.

The interior of the temple was ringed with exact copies of the stone sentinel, and beyond them was a ring of massive pillars. Indy relaxed and pointed at the knights. Then he heard something, a sound within the temple, and his senses instantly snapped to attention. His muscles tensed; he twitched nervously. In his fascination with the temple, he had momentarily forgotten that Donovan and Elsa were somewhere ahead of them.

He motioned for the others to follow and to remain as silent as possible. They slipped from one pillar to the next until they were close enough to see what was taking place in the center of the temple.

A soldier from the sultan's force, armed with a sword, cautiously climbed a set of stone stairs toward an arched opening in the back wall of the temple. Standing at the base of the steps, watching the soldier, were Donovan and Elsa. Behind them were several Nazis and more of the sultan's soldiers.

Elsa: Indy watched her. He noticed how she concentrated intensely on the soldier's progress.

She probably assumed Indy was dead. He was just another man from her past. Disposed of, forgotten. Despite everything she had said, it was obvious that her love affair was with the Grail, with its history and legends. Men were simply means of achieving her goal.

It didn't add up. There was something more, there had to be. It was something he wasn't seeing. Then he realized that perhaps it was simpler than it appeared. Maybe she believed the legends. Maybe she had convinced herself that the cup was actually a source of immortality.

And what about Donovan? He had discussed the myth with Indy. Did he actually believe it? He must. After all, he hardly needed to endanger his life to obtain another artifact. Sure, he was working with Elsa, but he wasn't about to let her claim the cup. Indy was sure of that.

He looked up at the soldier, who was nearing the top of the steps under the arch, and then saw something else. A body. A few steps away from the man was another of the sultan's soldiers, and near the sprawled corpse was something else. Indy leaned forward, trying to make it out.

Oh, God.

It was the soldier's head.

"Keep going," Donovan urged the soldier. "Keep going. You're almost there."

Elsa shook her head. "It's not possible."

The soldier stopped a step away from the body.

"Keep going," Donovan yelled.

The man took the next step under the arch, and it was his last. A loud whooshing sound like a sudden gust of wind swept through the temple, and suddenly the soldier's head was cleanly severed from his neck. It tumbled toward the steps, bounced down, and rolled toward Donovan and Elsa.

Donovan motioned to one of the other soldiers, who ran over and picked up the head. He turned and tossed it in the direction where Indy and the others were hiding. The head rolled within several feet of them. The mouth gaped open; an expression of horror was frozen on its features.

Indy looked away.

"The Breath of God," Henry said softly.

At first Indy wasn't sure what he meant. Then he remembered the three challenges from his father's Grail diary. The Breath of God . . . What where the other two? He couldn't think clearly now. He touched his pocket, where he kept the diary. It was still there. He would need it to reach the Grail. But right now he needed to find a way to get past Donovan and his entourage.

Then he heard Donovan order one of his Nazi guards to get another of the sultan's soldiers.

"Helmut, another volunteer."

The Nazi pointed to one of the soldiers, but the man shook his head and backed away. Two of the Nazis grabbed the soldier and dragged him forward.

"No-no-no!" he shouted, struggling to free himself.

They shoved him, and he stumbled up the first couple of steps. He turned; his eyes were globes of terror. The Nazi guard named Helmut pulled out his Luger and aimed it at the soldier.

Reluctantly he turned and started the deadly climb to the top.

Out of the corner of his eye, Indy saw Brody look away in disgust, unwilling to watch another decapitation. He didn't care to see the slaughter any more than Brody did. He felt like a spectator in a Roman coliseum, but he didn't know what else they could do. They needed a plan of attack, but . . .

Brody tapped him on the shoulder. "Uh, Indy."

The lines on Brody's face were so deep, they looked like shadows. Indy touched a finger to his lip, but then he saw what Brody had seen. A few feet away a Nazi soldier held his revolver on them.

"Raus! Raus!" he yelled, gesturing frantically with his gun, indicating that they should move.

Just then three more Nazis surrounded them, each with a rifle. Indy realized they had probably been hiding near the entrance and had been watching them since they walked into the temple. The Nazi with the pistol searched them for weapons and confiscated the guns Indy and Sallah were carrying.

They were pushed forward into full view of the others, their hands raised above their heads. The sultan's soldiers swung around and fixed their rifles on them. Indy saw Elsa spin on her heels, gaping at him. Her mouth seemed to quiver slightly. Donovan walked toward them, hiding his surprise behind a broad smile. He made it appear as if old friends had just arrived in town, guests for dinner, and he was the host.

"Ah, the Jones boys . . . and not a moment too soon. Welcome, welcome. We can use your expertise. I'm so happy you're still alive."

"You'll never get the Grail," Henry exploded. "It's beyond your understanding and capabilities."

"Don't be so sure about that, Dr. Jones." Donovan spoke between gritted teeth. "You're not the only expert on the Grail in the world."

He motioned the Nazi guards to take them to the steps. They were shoved forward and lined up opposite the sultan's soldiers. Targets in a shooting gallery, Indy thought.

Elsa stepped out from behind the soldiers and walked over to Indy. "I never expected to see you again."

"I'm like a bad penny. I keep showing up."

Donovan laid a hand on Elsa's shoulder. "Step back now, Dr. Schneider." His tone was disdainful, as if he questioned her loyalty. "Give Indiana some room."

Elsa ignored him a moment, holding her ground. She stared at Indy as if she didn't really believe she was standing in front of him.

Indy looked away. It was no time to renew old acquaintances, especially with her.

"Dr. Jones is going to recover the Grail for us," Donovan said.

Indy glanced in the direction of the decapitated bodies and laughed. The third soldier had stopped halfway up the steps and was slowly working his way down, acting as if no one saw him.

"You think it's funny. Here's your chance to go down in history if you are successful. What do you say, Indiana Jones?"

"Go down in history as what, Donovan, a Nazi stooge like you?"

Donovan regarded him for a moment, and Indy couldn't tell if he was angry or amused. Then Donovan smiled and shook his head, as though Indy were a child who had said something stupid. "The Nazis," he spat. "That's the limit of your vision?"

Indy didn't bother to answer him.

"The Nazis want to write themselves into the Grail legend and take on the world," Donovan continued. "They're welcome. Dr. Schneider and I want the Grail itself, the cup that gives everlasting life. Hitler can have the world, but he can't take it with him."

He moved closer to Indy, jutting out his square jaw. "I'm going to be drinking to my own health when he's gone the way of the dodo."

He pulled a pistol from his pocket and aimed it between Indy's eyes. He took a step backward. "The Grail is mine, and you're going to get it for me."

Indy grinned, feigning indifference. "Aren't you forgetting about Dr. Schneider?"

Donovan smiled. "She comes with the Grail. Too bad for you."

Indy's eyes strayed to Elsa, who was standing a few steps behind Donovan. Her face was a mask—lovely, soft, a riddle.

Donovan cocked the pistol. "Move."

Indy pointed at the gun. "Shooting me won't get you anywhere."

Donovan knew he was right. For a moment he didn't answer. Then his eyes slid to Henry and back again to Indy, and a slow smile spread across his face. "You know something, Dr. Jones? I totally agree with you. You're absolutely right."

He turned to Henry, aimed the gun at him.

"No!" Elsa and Indy yelled simultaneously.

But Donovan fired, hitting him in the stomach at point-blank range.

Henry's hands covered his stomach. He stumbled, and turned toward Indy.

"Dad!"

Elsa ran forward. Donovan caught her and shoved her back. "Stay out of this."

Henry collapsed in his son's arms. Brody and Sallah rushed over as Indy gently lowered him to the ground. Sallah cradled Henry's head, and Brody knelt down next to him.

Indy ripped open his father's shirt; the gaping wound nearly made him gag. Brody pushed a handkerchief into Indy's hand, and he pressed it against his father's abdomen. He held it there to slow the bleeding. Then he noticed the bullet had exited through his father's side, where there was more blood. He spoke softly to him, telling him it was going to be all right, really it was, and hoped to God his voice was convincing.

"Get up, Jones," Donovan snapped.

Indy whipped his head around, hate filling his eyes, and leapt to his feet as Brody cradled Henry. He was about to go for Donovan's throat, then hesitated when Donovan cocked his weapon.

"You can't save him if you're dead," Donovan said, training the gun on Indy's heart. "The healing power of the Grail is the only thing that can save your father now." He paused a moment. "Do you doubt me? It's time to ask yourself what to believe."

Henry groaned and coughed.

"Indy," Sallah called out. "He's not good."

He turned and knelt next to his father again. Brody whispered that Henry was badly injured. Indy nodded. He knew, he knew, he had eyes.

"The Grail is the only chance he's got," Donovan said,

smiling with certainty that Indy would accept the challenge, that Indy did not, in fact, even have a choice.

Indy looked up at Brody. "He's right. The Grail can save him, Indy. I believe it. You must, too."

Under other circumstances Indy might have laughed at the idea. But this was his father, and he was dying. He nodded to Brody, then reached in his pouch for the Grail diary. He was about to stand up, when Henry's hand fell on his wrist.

"Remember . . . the Breath of God."

"I will, Dad. And I'll get the Grail. For you."

CHAPTER TWENTY-ONE

◄◄ ►►

THE THREE CHALLENGES

Indy clutched the Grail diary and peered warily up the flight of steps. He could see an archway at the top and a dark passage. He drew in a deep breath and slowly climbed toward the two headless bodies.

Halfway up he stopped.

The silence was broken by the sound of cartridges slamming into the chambers of the sultan's soldiers' guns. The sound echoed in the temple. Donovan had told the soldiers to shoot him if he attempted to flee. They were definitely following his orders.

Indy opened the Grail diary and looked down at it. The light was dim and the writing a blur. But he had to find a way past the arch—the Breath of God. His father was lying on the ground, bleeding to death; he had to help him. He had to get the Grail Cup and bring it back as fast as he could.

Rationally he knew no ancient cup could heal a bullet wound, but that didn't matter. He had had enough strange experiences in his life to know that things that weren't supposed to happen sometimes did. Maybe the healing capacity of the Grail Cup could never be proven, could never be repeated in a scientific setting, but he was willing to try. All it had to do was work once, that was all. Just once.

He took two more steps. He could hear his father calling out to him. Indy turned and saw Henry's glazed eyes looking up at him. He listened; his father was muttering the phrase over and over.

"Only the penitent man will pass.

"Only the penitent man will pass.

"Only the penitent man will pass."

Indy repeated it to himself and carefully climbed the remainder of the steps. The corpses were a few feet in front of him. The top steps were soaked with blood.

He took another step toward the arch and then one more. He could see down the passageway beyond the arch. He stopped, sensing that he was only a pace away from being beheaded.

"Penitent . . . Only the penitent man will pass," he whispered. "Only the penitent man will pass. Only the penitent man will pass."

He spoke it like a mantra, a prayer, and each time he said it, he felt himself becoming more and more aware of his surroundings, aware that what he was seeking was not an ordinary artifact, aware that his father's quest was now his quest. He remembered his father's words as they passed through the canyon. It was Galahad who succeeded where his father failed.

He noticed a huge cobweb across the archway just ahead of him. Why hadn't he seen it before? Neither of the men had reached the cobweb. He knew that whatever it was—*The Breath of God*—lay between him and the cobweb.

"Only the penitent man will pass. Penitent . . . penitent. A penitent man."

He started to take a step forward but held his foot in midair, like an oversized bird at rest. Penitent. The penitent man is humble before God. The penitent man kneels before God. Kneel.

He set his foot down and fell to his knees. As he did so, he heard a loud whooshing overhead, and he instinctively tumbled forward. He lay there on his stomach a moment, then slowly rolled over. He peered up, and now he could see it above him—a razor-sharp triple pendulum, and it was still whirring just inches over him. The pendulum was attached to a pair of wooden wheels connected to the inside of the stone arch. It was probably activated by the slightest breath of air created by a person's movement, and stopped after it struck its target.

The pendulum had been there for centuries and still operated perfectly, as if under a spell. This part, at least, he could understand. He knew it would take millennia before anything disintegrated in this desert. He had seen bodies thousands of years old that had been discovered under the desert sands. The skin was still on the bones and the clothing intact, with the threads appearing as if they had only recently been woven.

Indy saw a rope hanging from one of the wheels and worked his way over to the side of the arch. He grabbed the rope and hooked the looped end over one of the spokes in the nearest wheel. Instantly the mechanism ground to a halt, and the blades jammed.

He was through; he had made it. He stood in the archway, the cobweb tangling in his clothing. He signaled to Brody and Sallah that he was okay. He saw Elsa smiling at him. She looked pleased. The longer he survived, the closer she was to the Grail.

"True love," he said softly, his voice riddled with irony.

His eyes met Donovan's for an instant. He rubbed his neck, and turned away.

Brody gently patted Henry's shoulder. "He did it, old boy. Indy made it."

Henry nodded his head, indicating that he understood, but Brody could see the effort it cost him for just this small movement. Then he murmured something under his breath.

Brody looked at Sallah, who still cradled Henry's head. "What did he say?"

Sallah shook his head, worried. "He's out of his mind with the pain and loss of blood."

Henry muttered again, and this time Brody understood a few of the words. "In the Latin alphabet it starts . . ."

"What?" He leaned closer and listened.

". . . with an *I*."

"In the Latin alphabet it starts with an *I*," Brody repeated. "Okay. But what . . ." He shook his head, confused, and conceded that Sallah was right. Henry was delirious.

He looked up toward the passageway, wishing Indy luck. Then he noticed Donovan, followed by Elsa, climbing the steps. "Those wretched schemers. Perfectly abhorrent," he muttered.

Henry suddenly rose up slightly and spoke in a raspy voice. "The Word of God . . . The Word of God . . ."

"No, Henry. Try not to talk," Brody said.

A spasm of pain shot through Henry's body, and Brody feared they were going to lose him.

"The name of God," Henry croaked. He relaxed a bit as the pain eased. "Jehovah," he muttered. "But in the Latin alphabet, Jehovah begins with an *I*."

His body was wracked by another jolt of pain. "Oh, dear," he gasped, sucking in his breath.

Sallah placed a hand on his shoulder and glanced up at the passageway. "It's okay, Henry."

Indy lit a match, held it up to the Grail diary, and translated the phrases from Latin. "The second challenge. The Word of God. Only in the footsteps of God will he proceed."

The match winked out.

Indy stood in the darkness and gazed ahead, wondering what the words meant. When he reached the challenge, he hoped he would recognize it in time to save his life. At least with the first one, with the pendulum, he had had the advantage of two failed attempts ahead of him. With this one he was truly in the dark.

"Only in the footsteps of God will he proceed," he said, memorizing the words. "The Word of God—the Word of God." What could it mean?

He lit another match and read the rest of the section. "Proceed in the footsteps of the word. In the name of God. Jehovah."

He heard a noise and looked back to see Donovan and Elsa. They stood just beyond the entrance to the passageway waiting for him to make his next move.

Parasites, Indy thought.

"Don't stop now, Dr. Jones," Donovan said, derisively. "You've just begun your journey."

Indy reminded himself that the only reason he was here was for his father. It had nothing to do with Donovan. Or with Elsa.

He turned and continued along the passageway until he came to a checkerboard of cobblestones. "Cobbles." He remembered the word from the diary; it was on the page with the diagrams. Pendulum. Cobbles. And something about a bridge.

He lit another match and turned the page of the diary. Now he realized the checkerboard diagram was the cobblestone. He held the match up to get a better look at the pattern of stones. As in the diagram, each one was marked with a letter. "The Word of God. Proceed in the footsteps of the Word of God. Jehovah."

He stepped tentatively on the *J*. Suddenly his foot plunged through a hole, and he almost lost his balance. He steadied himself, pulled his leg out. As he did, he felt something crawling on his ankle. He quickly shook his foot back, then brushed away a fist-sized, hairy black spider. It scrambled down the passage, a plump, hideous thing, and a moment later, Elsa shrieked.

She did better with the rats under the library.

He looked back at the diagram and shook his head in disgust as he realized his mistake. Okay. Wake up. Pay attention. We're not dealing with English. The Latin Jehovah begins with an *I*.

He lit another match and made a quick search of the cobblestones. Then, saying the letters aloud, he jumped across them from stone to stone. As he landed on the *O*, his foot slipped partially onto the stone with the letter *P*. Instantly it dropped down. He wobbled, regained his balance, and stepped across the last two letters. He had made it.

He looked back and saw Elsa and Donovan approaching the cobblestones. He wasn't going to give them any hints, but Elsa had already figured it out from what she had overheard him repeat from the Grail entries, and what she had seen him do on the cobbles.

She smiled at him and stepped ahead as if she were playing hopscotch. "*I-E-H-O-V-A*. Jehovah."

Indy scraped cobwebs from his hat, turned, and walked on. Behind him he heard Donovan yelling for Elsa to go on, to keep Indy in sight, and that he was right behind her.

Sallah knew Henry was slipping fast. He was no longer talking to himself or moving. His breathing was so shallow, it was nearly inaudible.

He felt for a pulse at the side of Henry's neck, then glanced up at Brody and shook his head. "I'm afraid that he's . . ."

"No. He can't die," Brody said. He glanced toward the steps. "I'm going for Indy. He's got to hurry. There's no time to waste."

Sallah watched him run up the steps, thinking that Brody was acting as delirious as Henry. "Father of Indy. Stay with us a little longer. Your son will come soon. Your son will come."

He muttered a prayer to himself as his eyes turned upward to the heavens.

As he finished, he heard a voice. It was Henry. He leaned over, pleased that God had answered his prayer so fast. "Father of Indy. What are you saying?"

"You must believe, boy. . . . You must believe. You have to believe. . . . Believe . . . Have to believe."

Indy stood at the edge of an abyss, holding on to the rock wall for support. The passage had abruptly ended. Across the gulf was a triangular-shaped opening, and on the rock facing above it was a carved lion's head.

"The Path of God."

He glanced up, saw a matching lion's head above him, then looked back at the diary. "Only in the leap from the lion's head will he prove his worth."

He looked down into the abyss, then across to the rock face. No, it was too far to leap. Nobody could make that jump.

Then he remembered the page with the diagrams and found it in the diary. The pendulum. The cobbles. The invisible bridge.

The third diagram was wedge-shaped, with a series of dotted lines leading across the top of the wedge. He studied it a moment, then slapped the diary shut.

Useless. It didn't make sense. He didn't believe in invisible bridges.

"Indy!"

He turned at the sound of Brody's voice coming from inside the passageway. "Marcus?" he yelled back.

"Indy, you've got to hurry."

He leaned his head back against the rock wall and closed his eyes. He could turn around now and go back and watch his father die. Or he could jump, and hope . . . even though there was no hope. He suddenly remembered himself as a child of ten with his father and wondered how the hell his life could be flashing before his eyes when he hadn't even jumped yet.

His father had given him a bow and arrow set for his tenth birthday and had put up a target in the backyard. "You stand behind this line, Junior, and practice, and when you get a bull's-eye come and get me. But don't cheat. Stay behind the line."

"Yes, sir." He was happy and excited and more than anything wanted to please his father. He practiced the rest of the afternoon, but didn't hit a single bull's-eye. Half of the time he missed the target completely and had to retrieve the arrows from the bushes at the far side of the yard.

The sun was low in the sky when his father came outside again. "Well, Junior?"

"I can't do it, Dad." His eyes were filled with tears. He was angry and frustrated. "I just can't hit the bull's-eye. I'm too far away."

"No you're not, Junior. You're not too far away. Your problem is, you don't believe. When you believe, you can do it, you will do it. *Believe, Junior. Believe*."

He had scoffed that believing wasn't going to make him any better. His father had pointed at him. "Don't grow up to be cynical, Junior. The cynic is a fearful person who accomplishes nothing."

He had lowered his bow and stared at the bull's-eye, saying over and over that he believed he could hit it. He raised the bow, but he felt his doubts returning. He lowered it again.

I believe. I believe. I believe I can hit it. I'll do it. I can hit the bull's-eye. I believe. I'll do it.

And he did.

Indy opened his eyes. The memory had been as clear as if he were still ten. He stared across the abyss again. When he grew up, he had relegated the experience to a coincidence. But now there was no time to question the power of faith. I've got to believe. That's the only way. I can make it. I believe it.

He stuffed the diary in his pouch and focused on the rock wall on the far side, saying over and over again that he believed. *If I don't believe, I won't jump. I'll jump when I believe.*

He brushed aside his doubts, concentrating, and repeating his belief until he felt the grooves of that faith etched inside him. His breathing was deep. It came faster and faster. *I can do it. Dad. I can do it. I'll make it.*

He crouched down on the edge of the abyss. With every bit of his strength, he pushed off and sprang like a lion.

It was a strong leap, the best he could have done. But, of course, it was far too short. The gap was too wide.

He was going to die. Yet, he knew he wouldn't. At that moment he landed and fell forward on his hands and knees.

He looked down and saw he was on a rock ledge a few feet below the passageway. But why hadn't he seen it? It was obviously there all the time.

He leaned back slightly, trying to look at the ledge from the perspective of the opposite wall. Then he saw there was something unusual about the rocks. It was ingenious. The ledge was colored to blend exactly with the rocks one hundred feet below. From the sight line on the opposite wall, it appeared there was no ledge. It was a perfect camouflage until he leaped.

He laughed aloud. He had believed, and he had found the impossible. *The Invisible Bridge.* If he hadn't believed he could survive, he would have never leaped and never found the bridge.

He stood, wobbled a moment, and looked back across the abyss. He saw Elsa and Donovan staring at him in astonishment. He chuckled, knowing that from their perspective, he looked as if he was standing in midair.

Gingerly he followed the ledge as it gradually rose, a gentle slope that ended beneath the lion's head. He was now just below the lip of the aperture in the rock wall.

Then he remembered something else. The lion was one of the symbols in the search for the Grail—the fifth level of awareness. It stood for leadership, conquest, and the attainment of high goals.

He had overcome the three challenges; a high goal had been achieved. Now he was ready to move on and find the Grail Cup. He had the feeling, though, that the toughest challenge of them all was still ahead.

CHAPTER TWENTY-TWO

◀◀ ▶▶

THE THIRD KNIGHT

Indy looked back once before pressing on and saw Elsa throwing pebbles and dirt out over the abyss and onto the invisible bridge.

Bright woman. Bright and dangerous.

The passageway narrowed and the ceiling lowered as he continued forward. He banged his head on the ceiling and scraped his shoulders on the walls. He was forced to crawl, but it didn't do much good: he still banged his head.

If this gets any tighter, I'll have to start believing I'm a rabbit, for Christ's sake.

Darkness wrapped around him like a thick overcoat. His fingers led the way, penetrating the darkness ahead. He worried that when he reached the end, it would be a rock wall. Then what? He hadn't overcome the challenges just to find out there was no Grail, only a dead end. This was no time for cosmic jokes. His father was dying.

He banged his forehead and, fearing the worst, extended his arm and patted the wall with his hand, defining the contours of the tunnel. He realized it was curving, not ending. He moved slowly ahead and noticed the tunnel was now dimly lit.

He crawled another ten feet. He could see a light ahead and moved faster. The light grew stronger, brighter. He squinted as brilliant sunshine beamed into the tunnel. Then, forcing his way through a narrow opening, he tumbled out of the tunnel. Sweet, fragrant air swirled around him. His eyes quickly adjusted to the daylight.

He stood, brushed the dirt off his shoulders, and stretched

his arms and legs. He was inside another temple, smaller than the other. His attention immediately focused on an altar in the center. It was draped in violet linen, and on it were dozens of chalices of various sizes. Some were gold, others were silver; some were festooned with precious jewels, others were less ornate. But all of them shone and glistened, and Indy was mesmerized by the spectacle.

He knew he had reached his destination.

He moved forward for a closer look, then saw another smaller altar off to one side—and something else. A figure in a tunic and a knit headdress knelt in front of the other altar with his back to him.

Indy walked closer. The man's thin, bony hands were folded, and his head bent in prayer. The skin on his fingers was paper-thin, translucent, and outlined the bones. He moved forward and saw a shaft of light striking the emblem of a cross that was stitched on the man's tunic.

Indy realized he was looking at the third Grail knight, the brother who had stayed behind to guard the cup.

He bent over and looked into the knight's face. His eyes were closed; his parched lips were slightly parted as if he were about to say something. The face had heavy, white eyebrows and a prominent nose. The body was dried and brittle by time and the desert, yet remarkably preserved, in far better condition than the gruesome remains of the knight's brother from the catacombs in Venice.

He leaned forward and frowned. For a moment, he thought he saw the knight blink. Then he smiled and shook his head. A candle was burning on the altar in front of the knight, and the flickering light was playing tricks with his eyes.

Indy raised his head. A candle. Who lit that?

He lifted his gaze and looked around the temple, wondering if he was being watched. "So who lit the candle, old fellow?"

The knight suddenly raised his head.

Indy drew back, astonished. "What the hell."

He watched in stunned disbelief as the knight rose slowly to his feet, then lifted an enormous sword with both hands. Before Indy even realized what had happened, the sword flashed in the air. The knight swung the weapon quickly, deftly, and the tip of it nicked the front of Indy's shirt and sliced the strap of his pouch, which slipped to the ground.

Indy leaped back as the knight hefted the sword again and took another swipe at him. This time the weight of the sword was too much, and the knight lost his balance. He stumbled back against the altar; the sword clattered as it struck the rock floor.

Indy moved over to him and helped him up. He was old but possessed an unmistakable vitality that made his eyes gleam. He opened his mouth, but no words came out. It was as if he were uncertain how to speak. Finally, he uttered a low groan.

"I knew ye would come," he said, looking Indy over, judging him against some image in his own mind. "But my strength has left me. I tire easily."

"Who are you?" Indy answered slowly.

"Ye know who I be. The last of three brothers who swore an oath to find and protect the Grail."

"That was more than eight hundred years ago."

"A long time to wait."

Indy smiled affably. The old guy was senile. "So when was the First Crusade?"

At first, Indy didn't think the old man heard him. Then he answered: "In the year of Our Lord 1095 at the Council of Clermont. Proclaimed by Pope Urban II."

"When did the Crusades end?"

The knight gave him a withering look that reminded Indy of his father. "They have not. The last crusader stands before ye eyes."

Indy nodded. He didn't have time to interrogate him, though. He needed to act. If this guy was the real thing, and still alive, then the Grail Cup could save his father.

He heard voices coming from the tunnel and started to turn, but the old knight tugged on the brim of his fedora. "Ye be strangely dressed . . . for a knight." He ran his fingers over Indy's bullwhip.

"Well, I'm not exactly . . . a knight."

"I think ye be one."

Indy shrugged.

"I was chosen as the bravest and the most worthy. The

honor of guarding the Grail was made mine until another
worthy knight arrived to challenge me in single combat." He
lifted the hilt of his sword. "I pass it to ye who vanquished
me."

"Look, let me explain. I need to borrow the Grail Cup from
you. You see, my father . . ."

"Hold it, Jones."

Indy whipped around to see Donovan squeezing through
the tunnel, aiming his pistol at him.

"Stay right there." Donovan glanced around, saw the altar
of chalices, and moved over to it. Elsa emerged from the
tunnel and quickly joined him.

Donovan glanced over at the knight, his gun still aimed at
Indy. "Okay, which one is it?"

The knight took a step forward and rose to his full height as
he stared at Donovan. "I no longer serve as guardian of the
Grail." He nodded toward Indy. "It is he who must answer the
challenge. I will neither help nor hinder."

Donovan grinned at Indy. "He's not stopping me."

"Then choose wisely," the knight advised. "For just as the
true Grail will bring ye life, the false Grail will take it away."

Indy smiled wryly at Donovan. "Take your pick, Donovan.
Good luck."

Elsa moved closer to the altar. "Do you see it?" Donovan
asked under his breath.

"Yes."

"Which is it?"

Elsa removed her hat and carefully picked up a shiny cup
encrusted with sparkling colored stones. Donovan instantly
grabbed it from her and held it up to the light. "Oh, yes. It's
more beautiful than I had ever imagined. And it's mine."

Indy expected Elsa to protest, but she remained silent. The
knight's face was implacable, revealing nothing.

Donovan looked up toward a font and carried the cup over
to it. Elsa followed him.

Indy knew that according to the legend, immortality was
achieved by drinking water from the cup.

Donovan admired the cup again. "This certainly is the cup
of a King of Kings. Now it's mine." He filled it with water
and held it high in one hand. He gazed triumphantly at Indy

and the knight. The gun was still in his other hand, but in his excitement, he no longer aimed it at Indy.

"Eternal life." He drank long and deeply. Donovan lowered the cup to his chest. His eyes were closed, and a beatific smile spread across his face.

Indy could have tackled him at that moment and wrestled the cup from him. But something inside him told him to wait and watch. He didn't have to wait long.

Suddenly Donovan's eyes opened wide. The hand that held the cup started to shake. He turned away and bent over the font. His face skewed in pain. His body shuddered. He dropped the gun.

With a great effort he pushed away from the font and stumbled toward the altar. He stopped several feet short of it, unable to take another step. "What . . . is . . . happening . . . to . . . me?" he gasped.

His features contorted into a grisly mask. His cheekbones projected. His skin shriveled and wrinkled. He looked frail and already ancient when he turned to Elsa, the cup still clutched in his hand. His eyes seemed to have sunk into his cheeks and lay there like old stones in dry sockets.

He then hurled himself toward her, hands digging into her shoulder. "What . . . is . . . happening?"

She screamed and tried to push him away from her as he kept repeating his question, his voice growing fainter by the second, his body aging rapidly now. His hair was growing long and gray and crisp. His face was sinking, his skin peeling away.

"No. No. No. No. No. No," he whispered. He shook his head and bits of skin flew away.

Elsa shrieked in terror.

Donovan's fingernails curled back on themselves. Milky cataracts coated his eyes. What remained of his skin turned brown and leathery and stretched across his face until it split and hung in flaps.

Then he crumpled to the ground, an ancient skeleton blackened with age.

Indy moved quickly to Elsa's side and pushed her away from the still-writhing remains. He kicked the pile of bones and cloth, and Donovan's skeletal arms fluttered, collapsed, and turned to dust.

Elsa clung to Indy, her face pressed against his shirt, sobbing as a cold wind swirled through the temple and gradually died away. Indy peered over Elsa's shoulder, looking at the pile of dust that had been Donovan. As she began to calm down, Indy let go of her and turned to the knight, an unspoken question on his face.

"He chose poorly," the old knight said, and shrugged as if Donovan's death was of no consequence to him. He had given him fair warning.

Indy glanced at Elsa and picked up the gun Donovan had dropped and tucked it in his belt. Then he hurried over to the altar. He was thinking of his father, of his father dying back there, of his father bleeding and in pain.

He stood in front of the chalices, took several deep breaths and let his eyes unfocus. A feeling of acute awareness overtook him. He felt light-headed. He closed his eyes a moment, concentrating, telling himself that he could do it, he could select the correct Grail, the one that would save his father.

He opened his eyes and cast a quick glance over the rows of glittering, bejeweled chalices. Then his eyes came to rest on one that was different. It was a simple cup, dull compared to the others. He didn't know why, but it seemed right. He picked it up and looked it over carefully. He didn't know what he expected to find. He knew there wouldn't be any stamp of authenticity.

"Is that it?" Elsa asked.

"I guess there's only one way to find out."

Indy moved quickly to the font, scooped up some of the water. He breathed deeply, took a quick drink from the cup, and waited an instant, wondering if something was going to happen, if he was looking at the last few seconds of his own life. He didn't feel any different, for better or worse.

Then suddenly his vision blurred. He felt dizzy; he blinked and squeezed his eyes shut. God, had he chosen wrong?

Oddly, he realized he could still see. But it was a different way of seeing. The cup in his hands was growing and transforming. It grew wings, a head, a beak. It was an eagle, spreading its massive wings and taking flight. It was the eagle of his vision quest and the eagle that signaled the sixth and last level of awareness in the Grail search.

"Indy?"

At the sound of Elsa's voice he blinked and shook his head. The cup was still in his hands. He glanced over at Elsa. From the questioning look on her face, he knew that she hadn't shared his experience. He looked over at the knight, who smiled knowingly.

"You've chosen wisely."

That was all the verification Indy needed. He didn't wait a second longer. He headed directly for the tunnel and crawled through it. He moved as rapidly as he could, while still carefully balancing the water-filled Grail Cup. He worried about banging the cup into the ceiling or the walls, and he worried about going so slowly that his father might die before he reached him. But as the tunnel expanded in size, he stood up and ran, at first at a low crouch, gradually rising up to his full height.

He slowed as he came to the ledge above the abyss. It was now speckled with dirt and clearly visible. He realized that it wasn't merely a protrusion, but actually was a bridge spanning the chasm between the two lion heads. Now it was easy. He walked quickly out onto the bridge, holding the Grail Cup in front of him.

He was hurrying, thinking about his father, and not paying enough attention. He was halfway across when his right foot slipped on the pebbles and dirt. His leg swung out, and he tottered back and forth, the Grail Cup wavering precariously over the abyss. Just as he almost regained his balance, his other foot slipped, and he fell unceremoniously onto his butt. Miraculously only a few drops had wet the sides of the Grail Cup. He carefully stood up and cautiously walked to the other side.

Brody stood at the top of the steps looking anxiously at Sallah and Henry and the dark passageway. There was still no sign of Indy, and he knew Henry wouldn't last much longer.

"Marcus!"

He looked up, peered down the passageway, and saw Indy moving quickly toward him, clutching the Grail Cup in his hands. His eyes widened, and his face lit up. He stepped back as Indy rushed past him and down the steps.

He moved forward and was about to follow Indy when he nearly collided with Elsa as she rushed out the passageway. By the time he reached the bottom of the steps, Indy was on his knees beside his father, and the sultan's soldiers had closed around him. Brody pushed his way through the soldiers as if they were of no consequence. They were without a leader now and simply watched out of curiosity.

Brody crouched down and helped Sallah lift Henry's head. Indy quickly put the cup to Henry's lips. Henry was too weak even to open his eyes. Indy poured, but the water just ran down the side of Henry's mouth.

"Come on, Dad. Drink. Please drink."

Brody looked anxiously at Indy and saw the worried look on his face. He had to do something. He leaned forward and helped him to open Henry's mouth. He felt Henry's throat move. He was drinking. He had swallowed some of the water. He was sure of it.

Indy then carefully removed the emergency dressing from Henry's wound and poured some of the water over it. Quickly he placed the cup to his father's lips again and poured more water down his throat.

They waited.

Indy was certain his father's breathing was growing stronger. He leaned over and listened to his heartbeat. It was steady and resolute. He could almost see and feel his father coming back to them.

Suddenly Henry's eyes fluttered open. They focused first on Sallah, then Brody, then his son. Finally, they settled on the Grail Cup.

Indy smiled, feeling a certainty in his heart that his father was out of danger. He probably would never be able to convince his skeptical colleagues that water from an ancient cup had healed his father, and there would be plenty of doubts and controversy about whether this was the real Grail Cup.

But so what? He knew. That's what mattered. He had seen and experienced the beauty and power of the Grail. In doing so, he had ascended in his own quest from cynicism to doubt to awakening. The quest was fulfilled, and with it the Last Crusade finally neared its end.

"Dad. You're going to be all right. I believe it. I know it."

CHAPTER TWENTY-THREE

◄◄ ►►

END OF THE QUEST

Henry's hands shook as he reached out for the Grail Cup, but now it was from excitement, not weakness. The color had returned to his face, and his eyes were wide open, clear, cognizant. His wound had been covered again, but it was no longer bleeding and didn't seem to be causing him any great discomfort. With Sallah's help, he had been able to rise up on his elbow.

As Indy proudly passed his father the Grail Cup, he heard a clatter behind him. He jerked his head around and saw the sultan's soldiers dropping their weapons and shrinking back. Their curiosity had turned to fear. They didn't want anything to do with guarding the wizards who had performed the miraculous healing, and suddenly all of them fled the temple.

All but a couple of the Nazi soldiers immediately gave chase, shouting and threatening to shoot the sultan's men. But they kept on running. Sallah swiftly made the most of it. As the two remaining Nazis called to their companions, he stealthily made his way toward the nearest rifle. He swept it up, spun around, and ordered the remaining Nazis to drop their weapons. *"Die Gewehr herunter,"* he repeated when they momentarily hesitated.

"Do as he says," Elsa snapped at them.

They hesitated but not for long. They set down their weapons and raised their hands.

Sallah, however, didn't realize that another Nazi had stayed behind and was standing a few feet behind Elsa. As the soldier reached for his pistol, Indy dove for his legs, tackling him. The Nazi twisted about and turned his gun on Indy. He was about to fire, when Elsa kicked the weapon from his hand.

Indy rose up on one knee, gazing at Elsa, amazed and baffled at what she had done. The Nazi took advantage of the moment and punched him. Indy grabbed his jaw, frowned, then collared the Nazi and landed a punch that was hard and direct. The soldier flopped to the ground and rolled over. Indy stood up and smiled at Elsa. He didn't know what to make of her. On one hand there was abundant evidence of her deceitfulness, yet she had just saved his life. Elsa's complacent look abruptly turned to horror. Her mouth dropped open, quivered a moment. "Watch out! Behind you!"

Indy turned just in time to block the arm of the same Nazi as he stabbed at him with a long, vicious-looking knife. Sallah ordered the soldier to drop it. The man looked up at the rifle barrel, his eyes flicked to Sallah's face, and he released the knife.

Indy grabbed it and spun the Nazi around. "Go join your buddies." He pushed him roughly toward the other two Nazis.

Indy looked over at his father and realized that when Sallah left him, he had remained sitting up, holding the Grail Cup to his stomach. Indy started to ask him how he felt, but Henry was gazing past him, eyes glazed, a rapturous expression on his face.

Now what?

Slowly Indy turned and saw the Grail knight standing on the steps.

"I know you," Henry called out to the knight. "Yes, I know you."

"Were we comrades in arms?"

"No, from the books. You're the third knight, the one who stayed behind. But I don't understand. You had the Grail Cup. Why are you so old?"

The knight descended the rest of the stairs. "Many times my spirit faltered, and I could not bear to drink from the cup, so I aged, a year for every day I did not drink. But now at last, I am released to death with honor, for this brave knight-errant cometh to take my place."

Indy looked from the knight to his father, uneasiness

churning a path through his gut. "Dad, there's a misunderstanding here. I didn't really. . ."

"He is not a knight-errant,," Henry scoffed. "He's just my errant son who has led an impure life. Unworthy of the honor you bestow."

Indy nodded. "Yes, an impure life."

"Totally unworthy. Son, do something worthy, and help your father stand up."

Henry set the Grail Cup down and wrapped an arm over Indy's shoulder.

"You sure you want to try this, Dad?"

"Of course. I'm feeling better by the moment."

Brody took the other side, and they gently lifted Henry to his feet. Indy hoped his father's recovery was not just a temporary one brought on by the sight of the Grail Cup and the belief that it could cure him. He wanted the cure to be real.

"There, see?" Henry cringed a moment, then courageously straightened up. "That wasn't so bad."

"Are you really cured, Dad?"

Henry frowned at his son as if he were still a child asking silly questions. He took his arms away from Indy and Brody. "How many times have I told you, Junior, that belief creates reality. I believe—I *knew*—the cup could heal me, and it has. It has."

After everything that had happened to him today, Indy didn't see any reason to doubt him. He thought back to what the old Indian had said to him after he had climbed down from the mesa and told him about the eagle. *Now you know that you have the power within you to attain all that you seek, no matter how difficult the challenge.*

Eagles and the Grail Cup; the knight and the Indian. It was all a jumble. But his father was alive, and they knew each other now as never before. He watched as the knight stepped closer and peered into Henry's face.

"Is it you then, brother? Are ye the knight who will relieve me?"

"Alas, no. I am but a scholar."

The knight gestured toward Brody. "Is it you, brother?"

"Me? I'm English."

The knight looked baffled and walked over to Sallah, who

had herded the Nazi guards away from the others and was still keeping an eye on them. He placed a hand on Sallah's shoulder, apparently confident that he'd found his replacement. "Ah, good Knight."

Sallah didn't understand. He looked at Indy.

"He said, 'Good knight.'"

Sallah nodded to the old man. "Yes. Good night. Sleep tight."

Indy bent down and picked up Henry's hat, tie, and watch. He froze as he saw Elsa out of the corner of his eye, inching closer to the Grail Cup. Suddenly she took two quick steps, grabbed the cup in both hands, and held it up. She gazed at it as if in a trance. Her eyes were fixed on it with such an intensity that Indy finally understood that nothing else truly mattered to her. Not him. Not the Führer. Not anyone. She was obsessed by the Grail.

Indy was distracted by the old knight, who stepped in front of him. "Why have these strange knights come," he muttered, "if not to challenge me?" He shook his head, bewildered, and walked away as Indy rose to his feet.

"For this, you fool," Elsa answered. She clutched the Grail Cup to her chest and bolted for the entrance of the temple.

Indy was about to give chase, when she stopped and turned. She was a few feet from the entrance of the temple, silhouetted in the late afternoon light. She must have realized, he thought, that she wouldn't go far in the desert on her own.

"We've got it. Come on. Let's go."

"No!" the knight yelled. "The Grail can never leave this place! Never!"

He looked over at Indy and Henry. "Remaining here is the price of immortality."

Henry glanced from the knight to Elsa. "Listen to him. He knows. The Grail will be nothing but an old cup if you take it from the temple."

"I don't believe him."

"You must not cross the seal," the knight warned, pointing past her.

Elsa turned and took several defiant steps toward the entrance.

"She will pay dearly," the knight said quietly.

"Wait," Indy shouted, running after her. The images of what happened to Donovan were still fresh in his mind. "Wait, Elsa. Don't move."

She neared a large metal seal on the floor but paid no attention to it. She was not only captivated but overwhelmed by the Grail Cup, and her eyes were glued to it.

"Elsa!" He reached her just in time and grabbed her arm.

She peered up at him with those incredibly blue eyes of hers, and he felt something shift and slide in his chest. "It's ours now, Indy," she said softly. "Ours. Don't you understand? Yours and mine. No one else matters. Donovan is dead; we'll keep it from the Führer."

He shook his head. "It's staying here."

With sudden and unexpected strength she pulled her arm free of his grasp. She cuddled the Grail, like a child with a stuffed animal, and stepped defiantly onto the seal. Then she backed across it out of the temple.

A moment or two passed, then a deep rumbling sound that was felt as much as heard erupted beneath the temple. The canyon walls started to shake. Dust flew as debris began to tumble from the shaking walls. Elsa spun around, terrified, and ran a few steps into the temple. Indy backed away from her as the floor shifted under his feet. He turned and saw one of the massive carved knights shuddering. The pillars rocked. He leapt aside as a stone cap shook loose and tumbled toward him, pulverizing at his feet.

Henry was holding his arms above his head, trying to protect himself from falling rocks. As the floor kept shaking, Brody lost his balance and fell to one knee. Sallah grabbed both men by the arms and jerked them away just as one of the pillars crashed where they had stood. The knight, meanwhile, fled up the steps toward the passageway and his inner sanctum.

Indy signaled the others to hurry toward the entrance. He turned and saw Elsa. She was looking up at one of the swaying columns of stone, her eyes wide with fear. The earth suddenly shifted again, and she lost her balance. She pitched forward, and the Grail Cup slipped from her hands.

As the cup rolled away from her, a jagged crack seared through the center of the seal and across the temple floor. Elsa struggled to her feet. Her legs straddled the gap, which was slowly widening.

The crack split apart the inner steps leading to the passage-way and knocked the knight from his feet. He fell back, rolling down the steps. Another crack ruptured the floor of the temple, perpendicular to the first one. Henry toppled like one of the pillars, and Brody wobbled like a drunk next to him. Sallah and Indy both froze, uncertain which way to turn. Behind them the knight crawled laboriously up the steps.

The Nazis made a run for the entrance and leapt across the crack that Elsa straddled. At the same instant, she pushed off with one foot, but as she did, the ground bulged on the side she had chosen. She desperately clawed and scratched, searching for a handhold.

The Nazis were in the same predicament. They had almost reached the top of the incline when they slid back and fell into the abyss. Their screams echoed long after they were smashed to their deaths below.

Elsa clung to a boulder protruding from the side of the crevice. Below her she could see the Grail Cup lying on a rock jutting over the edge of the crack. Instead of climbing up and away from the abyss, she lowered herself on one side of it and reached for the cup.

Indy realized the danger she was in and dashed over to her. He stretched out on his stomach and extended his arms, shouting to her to grab his hands. Their fingers brushed; then he inched forward and clasped both of her gloved hands. He pulled with every bit of strength he had, but it wasn't enough; he started to slide forward.

"Junior, Junior," Henry shouted.

"Indy," Sallah bellowed.

As Indy pulled, Elsa wrenched one of her hands free. She reached down toward the Grail Cup, which rocked back and forth, inches from the chasm. Her fingertips grazed the edge of it, but she couldn't quite grasp it.

"Elsa!" Indy yelled. With his free hand, he grabbed hold of a rock.

"I can reach it," she gasped. "I can."

Indy's hold on her was slipping. She stretched toward the cup and was about to grasp it when her glove slipped off her fingers. They each clung to the glove, their hands no longer touching. The glove stretched. It started to rip.

"Indy!" Alarm riddled her voice. "Don't let go. Please."

The glove ripped more.

"Elsa!"

He let go of the rock and lunged for her wrist, but it was too late. Her fingers slipped, and she fell backward into the chasm, her screams ringing out in the temple.

Indy slid forward, plowing his hands into the earth in a desperate attempt to stop himself from hurtling after her. He was about to slide into the blackness when hands squeezed around his ankles like a vise.

"Indy!" Sallah yelled. "I've got you. I'm going to pull you out."

"Wait." He reached out for the Grail Cup, but his fingers fell several inches short of it. "Lower me a little more."

"Don't be crazy, Indy," Sallah grunted, struggling to hold on to his friend. His feet were inching forward, and it wasn't because he was trying to lower Indy toward the chalice.

"A little more," Indy gasped.

"No, Indy. Please."

"Junior, get back up here," Henry barked from behind Sallah.

"I can get it. I can reach it."

"Indiana."

"Dad?" It was the first time his father had ever called him by name.

"Let it go," Henry said calmly.

Indy abandoned the Grail and clawed his way backward as Sallah pulled at his ankles. The dirt he loosened tumbled down onto the Grail Cup. He looked up once just in time to see the cup slide off its perch and into the abyss with Elsa.

Sallah gave one final yank, grunting loudly as he pulled Indy over the lip of the crevice. Indy sprawled on his stomach, staring into the black chasm that had swallowed Elsa and the cup. The horrified expression on her face as she slipped away had burned a path through his brain. If he had done what his father had, if he had told her just to forget the cup, he could have saved her.

Henry's hand was tight on his shoulder. His voice was urgent. "Come. Now. We've got to get out."

Indy nodded, picked up his hat, took one more glance over the side, and stood up.

Sallah guided them forward. "Where's Marcus?" Henry called out in alarm.

"I'm here," he said from somewhere nearby.

More and more debris was falling around them. Indy tried to clear his mind of guilt, of the nagging certainty that he could have saved Elsa if he had tried a little harder, if he had acted differently. After all, he owed her. She had saved him. And he had failed her.

But he knew she was partly responsible for her own death. She wasn't leaving without the Grail. There was nothing more to do but let go of his guilt and save his own life. Somehow, he knew, she would want it that way.

He followed after the others, then noticed that his father had stopped and was staring toward the steps. Indy followed his gaze and saw the Grail knight standing impassively at the top of the steps a few feet from the jagged crack. Rocks and dust were tumbling around him, but he seemed completely oblivious.

The knight raised his right hand, a farewell. It was as if he were saying the Last Crusade was finally over, and the Grail was safe. To Indy it made sense. He now realized the Holy Grail was more than an ancient and sacred cup. It was more than a means of attaining immortality, more than a way of miraculously healing.

He had sipped the ambrosial waters from the cup, and had understood. It was the essence of a higher awareness that was in him and in everyone who bothered to look for it. Now, he vowed, he would do the best he could with the understanding and knowledge he had gained.

Henry smiled back at the knight and nodded.

"Dad."

Indy pulled on his father's arm and hurried him away as massive rocks thundered down around them and pillars collapsed. The walls were crumbling, and jets of steam hissed up through the crevices. But Indy knew they would survive. They had made it this far—they would make the final steps.

A moment later they reached the top of the outer stairs. Indy took one more look inside the temple and thought he saw the Grail knight still standing at the top of the steps.

"Henry, Indy. Come on," Brody yelled from the saddle of a horse outside the temple. "I know the way. Grab a horse and follow me."

Brody spurred the horse, which bolted ahead, then circled and careened around them, nearly running over Sallah. He floundered in the saddle, but finally took control and galloped into the narrow canyon.

Henry shook his head and swung his leg over the back of a horse. "We better catch up with him. He got lost in his own museum."

"I know."

Henry gestured to Indy. "After you, Junior."

"Yes, sir," Indy said with a smile. It didn't matter any more what his father called him. The quest had been fulfilled.

For Henry, and especially for Indy.

He slapped his horse with the reins and galloped after Brody.

ABOUT THE AUTHOR

Rob MacGregor has written two other novels based on scripts, and also coauthored THE MAKING OF MIAMI VICE. He wrote much of this book in the Gran Sabana of Venezuela using a Tandy 1400 portable computer. He and his wife, Trish, live in South Florida.